DISTORTION

People are not always what they seem...

A T.C. Kelly Novel

DISTORTION

People are not always what they seem...

T.C. Kelly Novel

Published By: Sapphire Publishing

Copyright 2014 © Sapphire Publishing

All Kelly Book Publishing titles, imprints and distributed lines are available at special quantity discount for bulk purchases for sales promotions, premiums, fund raising, educational or institutional use.

FOR DISTRIBUTION INFO & BULK ORDERING

Contact: **Sapphire Publishing**
                    sapphirepublishing@gmail.com
                    757-589-6765

ISBN: 978-0692294468

Publication Date: September 2014

ACKNOWLEDGEMENTS

First and foremost all glory be unto Him for bestowing upon me such an awesome gift and giving me the perseverance to see it through. Without Him this book would not be possible. I would like to think all my family and friends that supported me through this grueling process. To my mother, thank you for helping me through the rough times without you I would not have accomplished my goals. To my Aunt Stella and Aunt Rickie, you two women mean the world to me and I love you with all my heart! Donald, Daryle, Sean and Tony even though you guys are my cousins you are more like brothers. Thanks for protecting me! A special thanks to three friends I've picked up along the way, Tekeisha 'Tuggles' Ballard, Michelle 'Byrdie' Johnson and Lakeisha Scott. You ladies have been my motivation and inspiration for completing this book without you I would not have done it. Thanks for all the love and feedback. I truly appreciate you! Black thanks for the love and the nagging, "when you gonna finish your book?" Streetz magazine family, Chris, Pharoh, Ak and J Bird thanks for giving me my first professional writing gig. You guys opened so many doors and I met so many people I wouldn't have otherwise. Thanks for believing in my abilities. Bestie Tyrone J. thanks for being there when I need an ear to talk to death. Austin & Eulandia you guys are two of my biggest fans and I love you for that. Austin thanks for always trying to get me in the door. I truly appreciate you. My friend Alona M. if I can do it you can to Boo! I love you like a sister! Niecy, Carla and Chantail thanks for being there for me and your loving words of advice. My very special cousin Shemeka, I am always there for you and you will be okay. Verolyn U. thanks for being a friend and I know you will reach all your goals! Monty O. wherever you are thanks for the ideas! I'm finally done-YAY! To all of my Bolling Brook family-no matter how far I go I always got your backs and love you forever! FM/Bloom I love you guys. Thanks for the wisdom, even though sometimes I strayed my own way I never forgot anything you told me. My RYLA family I've enjoyed the laughs, company, gossip and enduring hell for 8 hours everyday. Thanks to my buddies "scrumptious" Ray, Danny, Juan and Nestor. I couldn't have made it through the day without you guys, especially my IHD crew,

Sara

3

h, Sam, Ms. Adela (you're like a mom), Cerrita, Renita, Demario
a.k.a. super sperm, Mike, Gene, TT, LaJanese, Mr. Bamberg,
Tonya, Tiffany, Sheena, Rodney, Ms. Taylor, Jennifer J. Phyllis P,
Mieka and Big J . And I can't forget our fearless leader Tramaine
Alston. Sabrina J. no matter where I am I'll always be your DD-
just call me and I'll be there! Rodney B. stay clownin'& Marse W.
get it together! To the rest of my RYLA people – Let that
muthasucka burn!" To anybody I didn't mention
blame it on my head and not "my heart. Anybody in my life has a
special place in my heart and I sincerely thank you for all your support.
Without you I would not be where I am.

This book is dedicated to my father Donald M. Kelly R.I.P. I
love you and miss you!

CHAPTER I

"Hey girl, I ain't know you were working tonight," a tall, slim dark skinned chick dressed in a leopard onesie yelled to Nikki. Her soup coolers moved full blast while she smacked on a piece of chewing gum.

Nikki cracked a slight smirk flashing her pearly whites, "yeah, gotta make that money, rent is due." Nikki was well educated, but fell on hard times after her divorce. She was the kind of woman every man dreamed of, flawless coco brown skin except for a scar on the right side of her face, popping brown eyes, a banging shape and very assertive.

"Girl, you ain't gotta tell me. Ray Ray be trippin' if I don't have his rent money. It's bad enough he takin' almost all my paper." Joanne agreed.

Nikki shook her head. The cool breeze blew her jet-black hair into her mouth. She pulled the hair out of her mouth and smoothed her hair with her hand, "I don't know why you still fuckin' with that bum ass nigga. You can protect yo damn self out here and you can stay with me. I got your back."

6

"I know. I'ma leave him."

"Umm hmm." Nikki moaned and focused her attention on the silver Acura TL that pulled up to the curb. The dark tinted passenger's window of the Sedan slowly dropped down. Nikki approached the car with caution. She leaned over into the window and stared at the driver assessing her surroundings at the same time. A fat light skinned man with a mouth full of golds, a hand full of rings and a gold chain dangling from his neck occupied the driver seat.

"Hey baby," she started taking in the warmth of the car's heater. "What you looking for?" she continued staying alert and mindful of the situation.

"Why don't you get in and we can talk about that," he replied breathing heavily.

A bad feeling crept over Nikki's body when she opened the car door. The little voice in her head told her something wasn't right, but money was tight and she needed the loot. Nikki stepped into the car and the trick eyeballed her like a piece of meat. When she closed the door he placed the car in gear and placed his hand on her inner thigh.

Nikki looked at the man's face and gave him a fake smile. "So baby, what do you want to do?" she asked regrettably fearing his answer.

He laughed, "what do I want to do, huh? First, what's your name Ms. Lady?"

She hesitated, "why, you the police or something?" Nikki questioned jokingly.

"Nah baby, I just wanna know your name."

"It's Kendall." Nikki lied. She didn't like tricks to know anything about her, especially her government. It made it easier to separate business from pleasure and not get caught up in any feelings shit.

"Kendall, that's a nice name. So what's a pretty lady like yourself doin' out on these mean streets of the Cinci?" He asked.

Nikki was growing impatient. She didn't like for tricks to question her. She was a very private person and only shared her personal business with close friends and family.

Nikki took a deep breath, "I don't talk about that stuff. So, are we going to do this or what because I have other money I could be making?"

"I'm sorry Ms. Lady no harm intended. So where do you want to do this?"

Nikki pointed to a dark alley between two buildings. "Pull over there in that alley."

He maneuvered his car to fit in the narrow alley and turned the ignition off. "Now, how much to fuck you in the ass?"

Nikki frowned her face in disgust, "I don't do that. I'll do anything else but that."

"Aight, how much to fuck you from behind then?"

Nikki thought to herself that letting him get behind her was a bad idea, but she was already in his car and there was nothing she could do.

She sighed, "from the back is a hundred."

"That's cool," he agreed.

Nikki held her hand out waiting for him to pay her.

"I got you baby," he smiled in response to her. "I see you about your business. I respect that in a woman," he continued as he pulled a crisp hundred-dollar bill from his leather wallet. He snapped the crisp bill in Nikki's face, "here's your money right here baby girl."

She reached for the money.

The trick jerked the money back teasing her. He placed the money on the dash of the car. "You get this when I get that," he said with his eyes fixed on her vagina. She hesitantly climbed into the back seat and pulled down her underwear while he unzipped his pants and pulled his dick out. She positioned herself doggy style, all the while fearing what may happen. He opened his car door and walked around to the rear passenger side and got in the backseat with her.

"Can I get a little head before we start?" he whined.

"Head is an extra seventy-five." she replied.

"That's fine."

Nikki turned her body around and moved closer to his dick. His balls were musty and his pubic hairs were decorated with pieces of lent. Nikki didn't want to put her mouth on his dick. Just the thought made her gag. She reached over the seat and grabbed her purse and pulled out a cleansing wipe.

"Oh, you one of those sanitary bitches." he commented.

"I don't wanna get any diseases and shit."

"Baby girl you don't have to worry about that. I'm cleaner

8

than a whistle."

Nikki didn't comment and continued to wipe his dick and balls clean. She threw the wipe outside the window and pulled out a condom. She opened the condom and proceeded to place the condom on his stubby dick.

"Hold on," he interrupted. "I want to feel that shit. I can't feel it with a condom on."

Nikki looked up at him, "I'm sorry, but I don't go unprotected."

The trick rolled his eyes and let her put the condom on. She leaned down and put her lips on his dick. He grabbed the back of her head and forcefully pushed his dick down her throat causing her to gag. Nikki pushed away trying to release herself, but his strength overpowered her. It was that moment she knew he was going to rape her. Nikki's eyes started to water and she only hoped he wasn't going to kill her. The only thing she could think about was returning home to her son, Boston.

After five minutes of ramming his dick down her throat he forced Nikki to position herself doggy style again. She tried to imagine she was somewhere else. She closed her eyes and prayed as he shoved his dick into her ass.

"Yeah baby, tell me you love it," he demanded.

Nikki remained silent, but the more she remained quiet the harder he forced himself in her.

"Tell me you love it bitch!" he demanded once again.

Nikki's mouth was full of saliva, "I love it," she murmured

"Yeah bitch, daddy gonna give it to you." he continued.

He demoralized her until his salty sperm shot into her burning ass. Nikki heard a loud grunt and felt one final thrust into her ass. She prayed to God that he was finished. Her ass was on fire and she felt like she had been to hell and back. He pulled his dick out of her ass and grabbed her neck from behind. Nikki's life flashed in front of her eyes.

He flipped her over on her back and raped her again. He wrapped his chubby hands around her slim neck and rammed his dick in her tight vagina that rejected him with every push. It seemed like an eternity, but was only ten minutes. He grunted again, this time louder than before and pulled out his dick. Nikki lay limp while he ejaculated on her face. He took her by the neck one last time, "bitch, if you tell anybody about this I'll kill you. I'm not playing, Kendall." He released his hold leaving a red handprint on her neck.

She knew he was serious and was glad she gave him a fake name. He opened the rear driver's side door and pushed her out into the dark alley. He rummaged through her purse and grabbed the five hundred dollars tucked in a side pocket of her purse. He threw the purse out of the car and got out. He towered over her as she gathered her things that fell on the ground. He laughed and kicked her leg. Before getting into the car he looked at Nikki one last time and spit on her. He jumped in the car and sped out of the alley.

Nikki sat on the ground crying. She thought to herself she escaped death this time, but next time she may not be so lucky. She didn't want to end up dead like many friends before her, so tricking was no longer an option.

For the rest of the night she wandered the streets thinking about what happened. She wanted help getting off the streets, but didn't know where to turn. She dreamt of doing much more with her life, but her attempts to create a better life were a failure.

Nikki's ex-husband, an all-star top paid athlete was abusive and left her with mental, emotional and physical scars. She didn't know how to pull herself out of the deep ditch she dug for herself. She never acquired any type of job skills because her ex-husband refused to let her work. He didn't want her to attend school either, but Nikki enrolled in classes behind his back while he was out on the road. She was a top college grad and her resume read like a storybook.

- 3.7 G.P.A with a M.S. in Business Administration and a minor in International affairs
- Member of NAACP Jr. division
- Member of Alpha Kappa Alpha
- Volunteer at the local women's shelter

Her accomplishments were far and few in between, but the dissolution of her marriage left her homeless and broke. Nikki signed a pre-nup before she was married to prove she was marrying for love and not money. She thought that her marriage would last forever, especially after the birth of her son Boston-who was named after the team his father played for. With no money or family to turn to she was desperate and turned to the streets for help. Even though her life was grim now, she never gave up on her fairy tale ending.

CHAPTER II

Although Nikki was highly educated, she had no practical skills & tricking was all she knew. With no other cash flow, her options were limited. Weeks went by before she hit the streets again. She leaned against the brick wall of an abandoned building. A familiar face quickly approached her. It was her friend Christine. She and Christine worked the streets together for some years.

Christine, however, was no stranger to the streets. She started tricking when she was fifteen. Her family left her for self after they moved into a smaller apartment when she was fifteen. Her mother could not afford to feed everybody in the house, so she abandoned Christine because she was the oldest. Christine's mother was a crack head with six other children and none of them knew their fathers.

Christine was a dark brown chick with big round hazel eyes. Her high cheekbones and slender jaw line defined her face significantly. Her full lips were as thick as her hips that complimented her coke bottle figure perfectly. She was a stunningly beautiful woman that could pull any man, but all of her attempts at relationships failed and she always ended up back out the streets. Nikki wondered why she never tried to be more than what she was, but chalked it up to the same reasons she was on the streets—low self-esteem and no skills.

"Hey Nikki," she smiled. "I haven't seen you lately. What's been up?"

"Shit."

"Well girl, it's been some shit goin' on 'round here. You remember Joanne, that dark skinned chick with the freckles?"

Nikki thought hard trying to remember the girl Christine was describing. A visual picture of the girl Christine was referring to popped in her head. It was the girl she was talking to the night she was raped.

"Yeah, I know who you talking about. What happened?" Nikki questioned curiously.

"Um," Christine continued. "Some nigga did a job on her. Two of the other girls found her on the side of the CVS up the street. Word is the nigga raped her, burnt her with a cigarette or something and then slit her throat. They said she had burn marks all over her naked body."

Nikki was astonished. She wondered if it was the same guy that raped her. "What? Are you serious?" Nikki asked intrigued with what the answer was going to be.

"Hell yeah I'm serious! Nobody even saw what the guy looked like or nothing. So we watching each other back out here. These streets ain't safe no more."

Nikki nodded her head in agreement, "yeah, we got to girl. Damn, I can't believe that shit."

Christine rocked back and forth and nodded her headed in agreement with Nikki, " Umm hmm. That's what I said. Niggas be trippin over pussy."

"So how's it been tonight?" Nikki asked changing the subject.

Christine looked to her right then looked at Nikki, "to be honest with you e'rybody shook so nobody been makin' any real money. But, I'm like fuck that I need my dough. I just been real careful bout who I trick with."

Nikki didn't know what to think. She knew every trick was a potential threat. Nikki and Christine talked for an hour before a red and silver Navigator stopped in front of them. "Who the fuck is this?" Christine wondered aloud.

"Ladies, what's good?" A handsome man questioned.

Christine turned to Nikki, "damn girl, he fine as a muthafucka. Wonder what he doin' out here? You think he straight?"

"I don't know," Nikki was paranoid more than ever. Her trust

12

in the streets was gone. "I ain't never seen him before."

Nikki continued to lean against the wall, "so, what's a fine ass brotha like yourself doin' out her looking for some action? Don't you got a girl at home?" she spoke from a distance.

The man smiled and Nikki couldn't help but notice his white teeth. She was a sucker for a man with a nice smile and great teeth. "Well, I could ask you the same thing gorgeous. Actually, I'm looking for some ladies to come work for me."

Nikki and Christine became defensive. "What the fuck?" Christine started. "You a pimp? We don't fuck with no pimps, honey." she said alarmed by his statement.

"Oh nah," he quickly rebutted. "I'm trying to help y'all make some real money. Come with me and I'll explain everything."

Nikki spoke up, "we can't do that. You could be some type of serial killa or somethin'."

The man laughed once again. "C'mon baby. Do I look like a serial killa?"

Nikki shrugged her shoulders.

"Look, meet me at the Arts Pool Hall on Liberty Street at eleven o'clock. I'll explain then."

The two agreed and the man drove off. Nikki and Christine didn't know what the man was talking about but meeting at a pool hall couldn't be dangerous. It was nine thirty and the girls had an hour and a half to kill before going to the pool hall. They opted to go to a Waffle House around the corner the same one Nikki went to after she was raped.

When the ladies walked into the Waffle House all eyes were on them. Nikki was dressed in a short, tight, strapless red and black BeBe dress with a pair of strappy black 4" Guess stiletto heels with a small red Armani bag, one of the only items she seized from her wreck of a marriage. Christine was wearing a pair of dark denim skin-tight Seven jeans with a white off-the-shoulder blouse and a pair of white Payless pumps.

"Damn, we must look like Mary J. and Keyshia Cole up in this bitch." Christine joked observing all the attention they were getting.

Nikki couldn't do anything but laugh. One of the things she loved about Christine was her sense of humor. They sat at an empty table in a corner. Nikki fumbled through her purse and pulled out a

13

small tube of clear Mac lip glass and a compact mirror. She opened the mirror and applied the lip glass. She gave herself a kiss and refocused her attention on Christine. They began talking amongst themselves about the man in the Navigator.

Nikki started the conversation, "I wonder what he wants us to do. If he ain't no pimp, he gotta be a drug dealer."

"Your guess is as good as mine. He doin' something with that nice ass truck of his. I can tell you one thing, I'm damn sure not trickin' for no man."

"Well, he said he won't no pimp. We just got to keep our eyes and ears open when we meet him. You never know, this could be a set up."

"Girl, I know. After what happened to Joanne we got to be careful, but I do need some real money."

Nikki agreed wholeheartedly, "I know that's right."

A sloppy over weight waitress with a bad blonde weave approached the table in the corner with a pad and a pen in her hand. "Are you ladies ready to order?" she asked with a hint of frustration in her voice.

"Yeah, I know what I want," Christine began. "Let me have a buttermilk waffle, a scrambled egg with cheese and a side of grits."

The waitress scribbled quickly in her pad and repeated the order back to Christine who confirmed the order. The waitress turned to face Nikki who was still looking at the two-sided menu. "You ready to order ma'am?" the waitress barked impatiently.

Nikki sensed the frustration in the waitress's voice. "I think I'm ready. Give me the number two combo and can I have a Coke to drink please, light ice."

The waitress nodded and turned back to Christine. "What would you like to drink ma'am?"

Christine stared at the drinks on the menu before continuing, "hmm, I'll take a Sprite. Do you happen to have cherries?"

"Cherries," the waitress asked looking a bit confused by Christine's request. "No, we don't have any cherries."

"Okay," Christine said disappointingly. "Just the Sprite."

Moments later the waitress returned with the two drinks. Nikki and Christine chatted quietly, sipping on their drinks every now and then, while they waited for their food.

14

"So, where you been Ms. Nik? I haven't seen you in over a week."

Nikki had to think of a lie. She didn't want anybody on the streets to know she was raped. In a way she was ashamed even though she knew many of the other girls faced the same situation.

"I've been taking care of some personal issues and spending some time with my son. He's had a hard year."

"How is Mr. B? I haven't seen him in a while." Christine reminisced.

"He's well." Before Nikki could complete her sentence her cell phone rang. The sounds of Chrisette Michele's, "Epiphany," sounded throughout the packed restaurant. She glanced at her caller ID. It was her cousin Charmaine. "Hey girl, wasup?"

Charmaine's voice was frantic on the other end of the phone. "Lashonna is in the hospital. I think she owed some dealers some money and they tried to kill her."

"Calm down. Is she okay?"

Charmaine take a deep breath before continuing, "she's in critical condition right now. They threw gasoline on her and set her on fire. Luckily, somebody drove by and saw what was happening so they scared off whoever it was. She's burned pretty badly."

Nikki shook her head, "oh my God! It's always something with that girl. She needs to get herself together before she ends up dead. I'll call you later to make sure she's fine."

Christine stared out the window and watched the cars drive up and down the street. She didn't want to be nosey, but she couldn't help but ease drop on Nikki's conversation. Nikki closed her cell phone and let out a sigh.

"Is everything okay?" Christine asked hoping to get information out of her.

"Yeah. My family is so dramafied. My cousin is always getting herself into some shit. I don't even feel sorry for her anymore."

"I know what you mean. I think everybody has people like that in their family."

Seconds later the waitress walked over with two plates of food. She dropped the plates of food on the table almost spilling them.

"Is there anything else I can get for you ladies?" the waitress asked frustratingly.

15

Christine frowned her face, "yeah, your manager you rude—"

"Chris," Nikki shouted. She stared at Christine and lipped the word, "behave." She turned to the waitress, "no ma'am we're fine." The waitress walked away and mumbled under her breath.

Nikki bowed her head silently to say her prayers while Christine begin to eat her food. "You pray like that all the time?" Christine inquired.

Nikki looked at her like she was crazy. "What you mean? Yes, I do. I give thanks to Him for everything. Don't you?"

"No," Christine responded quickly. "In all honesty, I don't believe in God. I stopped believing after He let me be raped by my father and my two uncles. Then He let me have my uncle's baby and now I'm in this fucked up ass situation. Where was your God then?"

Nikki didn't know what to say. She knew that everything in life happened for a reason and only you had control over what happened with the rest of your life, but she couldn't very well tell Christine that.

"I'm sorry to hear that," she responded and changed the conversation to the man in the Navigator. "So, you ready to go meet this joker and see what he talking bout."

Christine scarfed down the rest of her buttermilk waffle before answering Nikki's question. "I guess."

They sat at the table for another fifteen minutes finishing their food. Christine let out a belch. "Um, that was good. Excuse me."

Nikki laughed and gulped down the rest of her Coke. She leaned back in the small booth rubbing her belly. "I'm full. I don't even feel like moving."

"Who you telling?" Christine giggled.

"What time is it?"

"10:30." Christine stated peering at her worn down silver watch.

"Damn, we better call a cab." Nikki pulled out her cell and dialed the number to the cab company. They sat at the diner table for ten minutes before the cab showed up. They walked out the restaurant the same way they entered it, with all eyes on them. Christine slid in the cab first and Nikki followed.

"Where to ladies?" the balding white cab driver asked.

"Arts Pool Hall." Christine answered.

16

"That's on Liberty Street, correct?"

"Uh huh." she responded.

On the way to the pool hall the cab driver bobbed his head along to the tunes of an old Kenny Rogers song. He pretended not to listen to the conversation between Nikki and Christine.

"Nik, can I ask you a question?"

"Oh Lord, here we go. What is it Chris?" Nikki whined.

Christine fumbled through her purse for a minute, "you ever been with another chick?"

Nikki was caught off guard, "what kinda question is that? Have you?"

"Just answer the damn question chick."

Nikki was silent. "To answer your question," she paused. "Once. My ex wanted to have a threesome, so for his birthday I hired a girl."

"Okay, so you do have a little freaky deaky in you. I knew it! Did you like it?"

Nikki rolled her eyes and sighed. "Girl, it wasn't even like that. I was trying to save my marriage by pleasing him by any means necessary. And no I didn't like it."

"Shit, that's because the right woman ain't turn you out yet." Christine mumbled under her breath.

"What you say Chris?"

"Nothing. I was just saying women must not turn you on."

"Hell no! Strictly dickly boo boo, strictly dickly."

Christine smiled and kept her wandering thoughts to herself.

"Oh look, there's the pool hall." Nikki yelled changing the subject.

The pool hall's parking lot was filled with cars. Nikki spotted the red and silver Navigator from earlier. "There's his car." She looked at the meter in the cab and pulled a twenty-dollar bill out of her Armani bag. She handed the money over the front seat to the cab driver and slid out of the back seat of the cab with Christine.

Two men lingered outside the hall littering the parking lot with Newport cigarette butts. One of them was of average height and resembled Red Fox; the other was an older bald man with noticeably missing front teeth and the remaining teeth were covered with a cottage cheese looking substance. They were enjoying a conversation about

17

who was more fuckable, Megan Goode or Sanaa Latham. The closer Nikki and Christine moved towards the door of the pool hall the more the men's attention turned to them.

"Oh God," Christine whispered to Nikki. "They 'bout to try and holla." she commented trying to turn her head in the opposite direction. By the time they reached the door the two men were breathing down their necks.

The older of the men grabbed Nikki's arm as she walked by, "why the rush, Red?" Nikki yanked her arm away as she fought off the smell of cheap Vodka that was fuming from his breathe.

"Well, fuck you bitch!" the man yelled angrily, upset over the blatant rejection.

Nikki and Christine turned around abruptly. Christine was a hood chick that didn't tolerate disrespect from anybody, especially men. She had a quick temper and didn't back down from anybody.

"Wait a minute! Did that musty, no tooth muthafucka just call you a bitch? Ah, fuck that shit I'm 'bout to chin check this nigga right now!"

Nikki stepped in front of Christine and put her arms around her. "Not tonight girl. We gotta find dude and see what the fuck he talking bout."

Christine backed down hesitantly. "You know I don't play that shit girl. These muthafuckas take our beauty for weakness."

"I know, I know, but we got business to handle, Boo."

They walked through the crowed pool hall for five minutes before they spotted the man playing a game of pool with an equally handsome man. They stood a few feet in front of the pool table until their presence was acknowledged.

"Hey, I see you two made it. Have a seat at the bar and order some drinks. This game will be over shortly." he assured them.

They made their way back through the sea of people and found two empty seats at the bar. A young female bartender filled glasses with Hennessey and exchanged money over the counter. Two other male bartenders were busy flirting with a group of females and supplying them with Jager bombs and Blue Motorcycles. It took about five minutes before one of the bartenders noticed Nikki and Christine.

"What would you two lovely ladies like to order?" the suave bartender asked.

18

"I'll have a Sex on the Beach." Nikki ordered.

"And I'll have a Singapore Sling." Christine added.

The two women observed their surroundings while they waited for their drinks. Nikki noticed a familiar woman sitting at the other end of the bar. "Hey Chris, do you know that chick right there with the blue and black hair. She looks very familiar."

Christine stretched out her neck and squinted her eyes to see the woman Nikki was speaking of. "I don't think so. Never seen her."

The bartender placed the drinks in front of Nikki and Christine. Christine swirled her drink around with a straw before taking a sip. She noticed Nikki still staring at the woman at the end of the bar.

"Why you still staring at her?" Christine inquired.

Nikki continued staring, "I swear I know her. It's going to wreck my brain all night trying to figure out where I know her from." Nikki turned towards Christine with a confused look on her face.

"Anyway, I'll figure it out later." Nikki examined her drink before taking a sip. She looked in the direction of the pool tables and saw two balls left on the table. "Well, they're almost finished their game. It's only two balls left on the table."

Christine picked up her glass and took a sip. She turned to face Nikki, "damn girl, you got some good eyes. I can barely see the table from here."

Nikki laughed and continued to watch the pool game until the only ball left on the table was the cue ball. The man at the pool table looked up and flashed his pearly whites at Nikki. He threw up his index finger telling her to give him a minute. She looked at Christine who was watching the CNN channel on a small T.V. screen in the corner of the bar. She nudged Christine with her arm.

"I didn't know you watched the news like that. You don't strike me as the type of person interested in world affairs." Nikki stated referring to Christine's ghetto attitude and mannerisms.

Christine swung her legs around, "what you trying to say heifer? A chick from the hood can't be interested in shit other than what goes on in the streets." she came back jokingly.

Nikki chuckled and channeled her attention to the man walking towards her. He approached the bar and ordered a straight shot of gin. "Hi again ladies." he started. "Let's go have a seat over here in this corner." he told them pointing to an empty table in the corner of the

19

hall. He picked up his gin and followed behind them. They sat down at the table with their drinks, the ladies anxious to find out what kind of work he had lined up for them.

"So, what's up?" Nikki asked eagerly.

He grinned, "I see you want to get right down to business. What's your name sweetheart?"

"I'm Nikki and this is my girl Christine," Nikki answered anxious to find out more information.

"Nice to meet you ladies. Let me introduce myself, my name is Fatz and I'm about my paper. Know, what I mean," Nikki and Christine nodded their heads. "I need a couple of chicks to work in my shop. Let me ask you ladies a question."

Nikki and Christine looked at each other. Christine shrugged her shoulders, "okay what is it?"

"Do either of you smoke?"

Nikki was confused, "smoke? What you mean? Like cigarettes?"

"I'm sorry, let me be a little more clear. Do either of you mess with coke, eight balls anything like that?"

Christine became defensive, "what the fuck kind of question is that? Do we look like crack heads to you nigga?"

"I apologize ladies. I didn't mean to offend you at all. I just needed to know. I need to be able to trust you. I can trust females more than I can trust my own niggas. And judging by your reaction, I don't have anything to worry about. You would be chopping, weighing and bagging my coke, occasionally mixing. I just needed to make sure you don't get down like that."

"What else?" Christine asked, a slight attitude still lingering in her voice.

"Nothing," Fatz responded. "Oh, there is one more thing. All the chicks in my shop work naked."

"Naked?" Nikki belted with confusion in her voice.

"Yes, naked. I need to make sure nobody is stealing from me. You dig?"

"Shit, I ain't got a problem with that." Christine squealed. "So how much we talkin'?"

Fatz laughed at Christine's delight. "I'll pay you a stack a day. Cool?" He waited for the women's approval.

"Hell yeah!" Christine yelped once again. She looked at her friend across the table. "Nik, you down?"

Nikki sat silently contemplating her decision. The voice in her head told her something wasn't quite right with the situation, but her pockets said something else. "Alright, I'll do it." Nikki sat back in her chair and finished off her drink. Christine and Fatz continued talking while Nikki listened intently to every word.

"You kinda quiet Ms. Nikki. You got some questions for me?"

Nikki stared in the direction of the familiar young lady at the bar. "No, just thinking about something else."

"Well, in that case, meet me tomorrow. Here's the address and my cell." Fatz jotted down the address on a napkin and smiled at Nikki as he wrote down his cell. "Call me with any questions, alright. I'll see you ladies manana."

Christine frowned her face, "man who?"

Fatz and Nikki laughed. "Tomorrow girl, tomorrow." Nikki replied.

CHAPTER III

Nikki walked briskly towards the windowless brick building yards in front of her. She really didn't know what to expect when she got inside. She pictured hundreds of naked women sweating their asses off in a hot ass warehouse inhaling cocaine fumes. Her thoughts were interrupted when her cell phone vibrated in the pocket of her denim shorts. She pulled out the cell phone and glanced at the number flashing across the caller ID. She was hesitant to answer it because she didn't recognize the number. She pressed the send key on the phone, "hello," she said fumbling the phone in her hand.

"Is this Nikki?" a male voice questioned.

Nikki didn't recognize the voice so she acted like she was somebody else, the same way she did when bill collectors called her phone. "No, this is not Nikki. May I ask who's calling?"

The male paused for a brief moment. "Uh, tell her Fatz called."

Nikki changed her tone quickly and resumed speaking as her normal self. "Hey Fatz. It's me."

"Nikki?"

"Yeah, I screen calls when I don't recognize the number."

Fatz laughed, "Oh, okay. I was checking to see if you were still interested in my offer."

22

"Definitely. I'm right here. You did say the brick building with no windows right?"

"Yea. The one with the for lease sign on it. Is your girl with you?"

"No, but I'll call her."

"Do that. A couple of the girls didn't show so I'm short today. You ladies will be right on time."

Nikki looked down at her $1500 Movado watch, another possession she siphoned out of her marriage. It was 11:13 in the morning. Nikki was use to working nights, so getting up that morning was a challenge.

"Alright, I'll call her."

"Cool, cool. I'll see you in a minute. Make sure you get your girl, I need her ass."

She hung up the phone and stopped walking. She scrolled through the contacts in her cell phone looking for Christine's number. J. Holiday's, "With You," played while she waited for Christine to answer her phone.

"What's good Nikki?" Christine shouted.

"I was about to ask you the same thing. You still coming? He said he need you."

"Yeah girl, I just had to drop Kev off at my momma house. I'll be there in about ten minutes. It's on Clay Street, right?"

"Yea. Alright girl. I'll see you then."

Nikki hung her cell up and continued walking to the building. The closer she got the more clearly she could see Fatz standing in front of the building.

Fatz smiled as Nikki approached him. "Hey Nikki, what's good?"

"Nothing. Ready to make this dough. My girl will be here in ten minutes."

Fatz continued smiling while he stared at Nikki. "Cool, cool. She got the address, right?"

"Yeah."

"You ready to go inside?"

"I guess." Nikki followed Fatz into the building. The smell of ether almost knocked Nikki on her ass. She stumbled and grabbed onto to Fatz to keep from falling. Fatz turned around and held Nikki's

23

balance. "You okay?"

"Whew, I just got dizzy all of a sudden. What's that smell? Smells like paint thinner."

"Sorry 'bout that, I should of warned you about the smell. You'll get use to it real quick."

"What is it?" Nikki asked again, sensing that he avoided her question.

Fatz laughed, "you're going to learn a lot here. I'll explain what we do when your girl gets here."

One minute later Nikki's phone rang, "speaking of the devil."

"You talkin' 'bout me?" Christine said in a playful, phony New York accent.

"I sure am hooker," Nikki joked. "Where you at?"

"I'm walking up now. Can you meet me at the door?"

"Yeah, I'm right here. Be prepared when you walk in. The smell will 'bout kill you."

Christine giggled, "Okay."

Nikki and Fatz walked to the door to let Christine in. She was dressed in white Capri's, a black shirt with a big pair of red lips painted on it, and wedged red and black shoes. Fatz poked his head out the door and made sure nobody else was around. "Damn, what you doin' in here?" Christine barked in a loud ghetto voice holding her hand up to her noise and frowning her face.

Fatz was irritated by Christine's loud voice. "Yo, keep it down. Can't be all that loud talkin' and shit. Like I was telling your girl before you got here I will explain everything to you. Follow me to my office."

Christine mimicked Fatz behind his back. Nikki gave her a slight shove and they followed him to his office. While walking to his office Nikki and Christine observed six naked women with doctor's masks and gloves standing in front of a table with scales covered in cocaine. When they passed the table the women paused for a minute and their eyes followed Nikki and Christine down the hall until they were out of sight. Fatz looked back at them and pointed to a curtain, "behind there is where you'll leave your clothes and stuff when you're about to work."

Nikki and Christine glimpsed at the curtain and kept walking. They reached a wooden door with a hole in it where the doorknob

24

should have been. Fatz opened the door and took a seat in front of a metal desk. He directed the ladies to sit on a black futon and asked Christine to close the door.

"Okay, we got some rules to discuss before I start explaining anything to you," he said calmly, his eyes switching quickly between Nikki and Christine. The girls listened attentively as he spoke. "First, no ghetto shit!" he demanded staring directly at Christine. Christine rolled her eyes. Fatz continued to run down the list of rules. "No loud talking, no fussing with other ladies, no discussing what goes on in here outside of here and no clothes while working."

"Seems easy enough." Nikki stated.

"I can handle that as long as your bitches don't fuck with me." Christine screeched in a high pitch voice.

"That's that ghetto shit right there. Listen, my girls are cool. You need to make sure you keep it that way. Just do your time, make your money and bounce. That's it. Cool?"

Christine sucked her teeth and rolled her eyes once again. "Yeah, yeah whateva. I'm cool."

"Good, so we have an agreement. Now let me explain what we do in here. You saw those ladies we passed; they weigh and bag my coke. The smell you smelled was ether. We use it to cut the cocaine. It recovers the freebase in the cocaine. This makes my shit stronger and keeps 'em coming back. Your job is simple; you weigh the shit and bag it, that's it. We bag four sizes that you'll need to remember: .3 gram which is a "deck," 1 gram which is a "fifty rock," 1/8 of ounce which is an "eight ball" and one ounce. After you weigh the shit, put it in one of these bags." Fatz held up three different sizes of zip lock bags. "You'll need to wear this mask so you don't inhale the fumes." He turned to Nikki, "you saw what happened earlier." She nodded her head remembering how she almost fell because of the smell. "I want you to wear them also because I don't want anybody sniffing shit on the sneak," he said turning his attention to Christine. "This shit can kill you; it's way more potent than regular blow. Now that you know what to do grab some plastic gloves, a mask, take off your clothes and I'll introduce you to the girls."

Nikki and Christine exited the office. "I can't believe I'm doing this shit." Nikki whispered to Christine.

"Why the fuck not? You sleep with niggas for money

25

everyday. We making twice the money and we don't have to fuck anybody. Shit, I'll do this for as long as he wants me to."

"Iono. It just seems weird to me, but like you said I ain't got to fuck nobody."

They walked behind the blue curtain and saw ten cardboard boxes labeled with names against the wall. Christine began to unzip her Capri pants. Nikki looked around the small space that looked like it used to be some kind of storage room. "What's wrong?" Christine questioned her while stepping out of her pants.

"Nothing," Nikki sighed. "So, I guess we put our clothes in one of those empty boxes."

Christine shrugged her shoulders. Nikki looked at Christine who was leaning against a shelf in her lace pink matching bra and underwear. Nikki slowly pulled down her denim shorts exposing her blue and white underwear.

"Saturday?" Christine laughed. "Why you got on Saturday underwear and it's Friday. You a day early, ain't you?" Christine joked unclasping her bra.

"Yeah, yeah. Whateva heffa. Who sees my under anyway?"

"Uh, everybody, hooker."

"Oh, yeah." Nikki chuckled and pulled her yellow Abercrombie & Fitch tank top over her long wavy hair.

Christine was finished undressing and stood in the middle of the floor waiting for Nikki. "C'mon Ms. Nikki we don't have all day," she pushed.

"I know chick, I'm coming," she replied pulling down her underwear. "I didn't know you had a tramp stamp," she said referring to the crown on top of a bee's head sketched on Christine's lower back.

"Yo momma's a tramp," Christine twisted her body as best she could to look at the tattoo on her back. Girl, I've had this thing for almost two years now. Where you been?"

"Sorry, I'm not accustomed to seeing you naked."

"As many times as I have worn short shirts and low waist pants. You mean to tell me you ain't never seen this thing."

Nikki shook her head and looked at her naked body in the full-length mirror hanging on the wall above the cardboard boxes. She combed her fingers through her hair and rubbed her belly. "Okay, I'm ready." she told Christine in a low voice. They walked down the hall to

26

the open area where Fatz was talking to the ladies. The ladies were all lined up around a wooden rectangle table with a black top that reminded Nikki of a high school science table. On the table were eight measuring scales and small pales with measuring cups within reach.

Fatz held out his arm as Nikki got closer. He placed his arm around Nikki's shoulder. "Ladies, I'd like you to meet the newest members to our family, Nikki and Christine. I told them what to do and you ladies show them how to do it, alright. I need to make some phone calls so you ladies get acquainted." Fatz slapped Nikki and Christine on the ass as he walked away.

A couple of the girls looked at Nikki and Christine like they were not welcome. "So, where'd he find you two?" one of the females asked.

"We met him on the other end of The Rhine. He told us he needed some girls. So, here we are." Nikki stated.

"Um, really," the girl said sarcastically.

"Don't pay Angel any mind," another girl interjected. "My name is Sam. I don't know why they get defensive when somebody new comes through."

"That's okay. I understand. We're invading their territory." Nikki added.

"I don't," Christine snarled. "Fatz came to us, we didn't go to him. I'm just trying to make my money not friends."

Nikki sighed and rolled her eyes. She knew Christine was not one to bite her tongue and didn't want her to start any mess with any of Fatz's girls. "Chris!" Nikki shouted to signal her to shut up. Christine looked at her and frowned her face.

Sam continued to introduce Nikki and Christine to the rest of the ladies at the table. All the ladies fit the typical description of a stripper; fat asses, small to medium titties, long weaves and average faces except for Angel. Angel resembled Vivica Fox, but had a very nasty attitude that made her ugly. Nikki and Christine placed the surgical mask on their faces and slid their fingers into the plastic gloves. They stood around Sam as she began to show them how to chop, weigh and bag the coke.

"This is what you do," Sam began to explain. "Each of us has a one gallon bucket. This bucket has 128 ounces of "freebase" coke. Did he tell you what "freebase" coke was?"

27

Nikki and Christine nodded. "Briefly." Nikki confirmed.

"Well, pretty much this shit is potent as hell. If you have any ideas, don't! That's all I'm gonna say. I done seen a lot a come, done seen a lot a go," she joked lightly quoting DMX. Anyway, they "freebase" it upstairs somewhere. So you take one of the measuring cups, scoop some coke, pour it on the table, take a metal nail file and chop it into five or six lines, put one line back in the measuring cup and weigh it on the scale," she explained while showing them step by step. Do the decks first then the fifty rocks and a few eight balls. We don't fuck with the ounces really unless he tells us to specifically. You got it?"

"Simple enough." Christine belted sarcastically.

"I got it." Nikki walked around to the other side of the table and stood in front of a pail of coke. Christine stood next to her in front of a separate pail. They began scooping, chopping, weighing and bagging the freebase cocaine like they were instructed. A few hours later Fatz returned to check on the ladies.

"Ladies, how is everything going?"

Nikki stopped what she was doing and looked over at Fatz. He could tell she was smiling because it showed in her eyes. "We're fine. How long you want us to stay."

Fatz lifted his wrist and looked at the time on his $15,000 Rolex. "You got here at eleven thirty and its quarter 'til four now, you can go put your clothes on and meet me in my office."

Sam turned in Nikki and Christine's direction, "see you chicks later."

Nikki and Christine waved their hands bye. Fatz followed down behind them staring at Nikki's ass the whole time. Angel watched Fatz as he hurried behind the two ladies, "I see he got him some new pussy to chase after," she remarked with a jealous undertone.

Sam stared at Angel before speaking, "shut the fuck up. You mad cause he ain't chasin' yo pussy anymore."

Angel rolled her eyes, "what the fuck ever. If I wanted his ass I could have him. Compared to my nigga, he broke anyway. But, those little bitches think they can walk up in here and take over shit. It ain't goin' down like that."

"Angel, what are you talking about? They jus tryin' to make some money like yo ass. You always gotta start some shit. You a hating' ass bitch. Plus, if yo nigga got more bread than Fatz why you so worried about who he tryin' to fuck?"

"Fuck you!" Angel barked back at Sam. "I ain't got no reason to hate."

Sam flicked Angel off and continued what she was doing. Meanwhile, Nikki and Christine started to put their clothes back on.

"Girl, this is the easiest job I've ever had." Christine giggled.

Nikki pulled her shirt over her head, "yeah, it is, but I don't think them chicks liked us."

"Fuck dem bitches Nik. They ain't gotta like us. Long as they don't start no shit, we good."

They finished putting their clothes on and walked to Fatz's office. He was on his cell phone and signaled for the ladies to have a seat. "Alright Mannie, I'll see you next week. Make sure you have some of those bad ass Columbian bitches waiting for me," he joked and hung up his cell phone. He turned his attention back to Nikki and Christine. "So ladies, how did the first day go for you?"

"It was ok," Nikki started. "But, I don't think your girl Angel liked us too much."

Fatz sat on the edge of the metal desk with his arms folded on his leg. "Pssh, don't worry 'bout that broad. She always got a bunch of drama goin' on. Other than that, was every thing good?"

Both girls nodded in agreement.

Fatz stood up. "Aight, I guess I'll see you ladies tomorrow?" he said waiting for a response.

Christine looked at Nikki and nudged her with her elbow. Nikki stared at Fatz and thought to herself what a fine ass nigga he was. He had caramel brown skin and a Caesar haircut with deep waves. His eyes were light brown with a hint of gray, his lips were full like LL Cool J and he boar the body of The Rock. All she wanted to do was fuck him until they were both raw. Fatz waived his hands in front of her face to snap her out of her daydream.

"Hello, earth to Nikki." he laughed.

"I'm sorry," she apologized. "I was in deep thought."

Christine grinned, "I bet!"

"So, you down?" Fatz asked, patiently waiting for her response.

"Yea, I'm down. We'll be back tomorrow."

29

"Aight, let me walk you ladies to the door."

They exited the small room and headed down the narrow hallway. As they walked pass the table Christine and Angel gave each other hard looks. Both of them had the same attitude and neither was backing down. When they reached the exit Christine exited first because she knew Fatz wanted to have a few last words with Nikki.

As Nikki proceeded to walk out the door Fatz grabbed her arm. An instant smile spread across her face, but she tried her hardest to hold in her smile. She did not want him to know she was feeling him, but she could not contain herself.

"What?" she questioned playfully as she turned to face him.

"So, uh, do you have a man?" he inquired.

"Not really. Why?"

"I wanna take you out. I don't usually mix business with pleasure, but damn you sexy as hell." he commented while trying to get a look at her ass.

"That can be arranged. You got the number, use it." Nikki pulled her arm away and joined Christine who was waiting a few feet away. Fatz stood at the door and watched Nikki walk away until her silhouette disappeared.

"Um hmm, what was that all about?" Christine asked as if she didn't already know.

Nikki started smiling again, "nothin'. He just wanted to know if I had a man."

"Um hmm. I know you Nik. You wanna fuck him! Just be careful. I don't trust those bitches. I don't wanna have to go back to my Vaseline and sneaker days, but I will beat a bitch ass."

"I know, I know. He just so damn sexy it don't make no sense. And I bet he workin' wit a lil' sumin' sumin' too." Nikki thought aloud.

Christine knew what she was saying was going in one ear and out the other. "I'm sure he is, but just watch ya back and don't get caught up in that nigga. I don't trust his ass either. Yeah, he cakin' and kickin' out dough, but shit those niggas come a dime a dozen. Plus, I know they type. Don't forget who you fuckin' wit. I'm the number one stunna."

Nikki couldn't do anything, but laugh, "you a stupid ass chick, but I hear what you sayin' and I appreciate you having my back. I know you my girl." Nikki wrapped her arm around Christine's neck and they continued to walk towards the bus stop.

CHAPTER IV

"Damn, you and Fatz goin' out again. Y'all been seeing each other damn near everyday for about six months. Dat shit must be good!" Chris yelled from the living room of Nikki's quaint two-bedroom apartment.

Nikki stood in front of the mirror applying the final touches of her make-up. The silver and plum eye shadow she applied immaculately made her brown oval eyes dazzle. "Hmm, well, what can I say," she started to reply as she traced her pink-tinted glossy lips with a light brown lip pencil. "The brotha got it goin' on. He's sexy, got paper and he knows how to put it down. He have a sista screamin'!" she shouted with enthusiasm before kissing herself in the mirror and giving herself one last look.

"Ow, Ow! Mamacita. Show me what you workin' with!" Chris smiled as Nikki did her catwalk across the living room floor.

"How do I look? Should I wear the black and red Gucci pumps or the green and red striped Guess sandals?" Nikki waited patiently as Chris looked her up and down. Nikki had on a multi-colored, silk short-sleeved shirt that hung off her shoulder and a pair of dark denim skinny jeans with her matching Gucci purse. Fashion was always one of Nikki's strong suits and it wasn't hard for her to put together the perfect outfit that complimented her size C breasts and

apple

31

bottom ass.

"The Gucci pumps. You look fine, girl. Why you so nervous? You act like you ain't never fucked him. Hell, you gave it up the first night." Chris said sarcastically as she leaned over to pick up a glass of Mountain Dew off the tan Berber carpet.

Nikki sucked her teeth, "whateva chick. You fuck niggas after knowing them five minutes. If I'm not mistaken' you are a trick like me, right? Anyway, are you and Bo going to be okay?"

"Yes ma'am. I am a grown ass woman. Plus he's knocked out and he's grown anyway. I don't know why you want me here."

"I told you ever since those dude's broke in and attacked him, I don't like him to be here alone at night for real. At least not until I get

an alarm or move. I know he's 18-years old, but he's my only baby."

Aaliyah's, "Rock the Boat," filled the small room. Nikki sprinted to the kitchen to grab her purse that was sitting on the marble counter, A smile crept over her face, "hello, are you outside?"

Yeah, bring yo fine ass down here." Fatz's deep voice echoed loudly through the phone jokingly. Nikki slung her cell phone into her purse and ran into her bedroom. On her nightstand was a small .22 Caliber pistol she carried with her at all times after she was raped. She tucked the pistol in a side pocket of her black Gucci purse and slipped her French manicured feet into her size 6 peep toe pumps.

"Alright Chris, I'm gone."

By the time Chris peeked her head around the kitchen wall to say bye Nikki was gone. She finished preparing her burger, walked into the living room and plopped down on the couch in front of the television. She curled up into a ball and finished watching her favorite movie, The Five Heartbeats. She felt her cell phone vibrate beside her. She looked down at the screen before answering it.

"Hey boy, what's up?" she said in a surprising tone.

"C baby, what's the deal? I haven't talked to you in a minute. What you been up to?"

"Nothing much. Same shit, different day. Just tryin' to make that money. What about you?"

"I hear that. So, when am I going to see you again? We need to catch up. I miss you."

"You miss me, huh. Or do you miss this good pussy?"

32

The man laughed at Chris' response. "Girl, you funny, but, uh, yeah, you right. Where you at now?"

"You mean, where I stay now?"

"Naw. I mean where are you right now. You know a nigga tryin' to get his rocks off."

Chris paused for a moment. She was caught off guard by her friend's question. "Oh, I'm at my girl's crib."

"Who? Nikki, that chick you always be with."

Chris was silent for a few seconds. "How'd you know I was at Nikki's house?"

"I didn't but I know y'all use to hang tight."

"Yeah, I'm at Nikki's crib. If you want you can come throught for a minute. She won't be back for a couple hours. She out wit her boo thang."

"Ok, cool. I'll swing through in about an hour. Make sure yo sexy ass ready for whateva. You know how I do."

Chris laughed, "If I remember correctly yeah I know. Well, she lives two blocks from the Rhine. Just call me when you get close."

"Alright. Like I said, give me about an hour and I'll be on my way. I have some business to handle first."

"Okay. See you then." Chris hung up the phone and continued watching the movie. Forty-five minutes later she heard a knock at the door. She was surprised to hear a knock so soon; her friend was never on time. She muted the television, quietly placed her plate of food on the floor and tiptoed over to the door to look through the peephole. At first glance she didn't see anyone, but a second later she found herself lying on the floor. Two masked men dressed in all black forced themselves through the wooden door.

"Bitch, turn over. Don't look at me!" the first man demanded forcefully.

Chris started crying uncontrollably and began to plead for her life, "please, don't kill! Please. My Godson is sleep in the other room, don't hurt him!"

"Shut the fuck up bitch!" the man continued to demand while pointing the barrel of his gun to the back of her head. "Yo, go get that nigga and bring him in here."

"Who are you looking for? You have the wrong person?" Chris cried as tears streamed down her face.

33

The man seemed to grow annoyed with Chris and her talking. "Bitch, I'm not going to tell you again. Shut the fuck up! The next time you say something, I swear to God, I'ma pull this trigger," he belted as he rocked back and forth. He kept the gun cocked sideways and moved in sync with his motions.

Chris placed her head on the floor and closed her eyes to pray. She did not believe in God, but she figured this was the time to start. She promised herself if she made it through this event alive she would start going to church.

The second gunman reentered the room and pushed Bo on the floor. He sat on the couch staring at Chris and Bo. He dangled his gun between his legs slightly angled at Chris. "So, tell me everything you know about Fatz's and his business," he sniffed.

She started to turn her head slowly. The man standing over her cocked his gun, "don't fucking move! Just answer the muthafuckin' question."

"I don't know anything. I just met him a few months ago."

The gunman on the couch sighed loudly. "I'm only goin' to ask you one more time," he stood up and walked over stopping in front of her. "Now, what the fuck do you know about Fatz? I know you been workin' over on Clay Street. And I know yo girl been fuckin' wit him and she wit him now. So, again, what do you know about him?"

"All I know is where his shop is. Please, don't kill me! That's all I know!" she stated crying hysterically.

The man stooped down in front of her, his gold money chain grazing the tip of her nose. He was so close she could smell the God-awful scent of his breath. Every breath reeked of onions, vodka and halitosis. "Alright, this is what we're gonna do. You and him are going to sit on the couch. You are going to call yo girl and tell her she needs to come home. If you say anything out the way, he's dead!" the man calmly explained while looking at Bo who scowled his face at the men.

Chris reluctantly picked up her cell phone and dialed Nikki's number, "it went to her voicemail."

"Dial the fucking number again then. You gon' keep dialing til' she pick it up," he demanded.

She dialed the number three more times before Nikki picked up. "Hey girl, is everything okay?" Nikki questioned.

Chris sniffled softly before answering, "you need to come

34

back home."

Nikki's mood quickly shifted from happy to panicked. She turned the radio down so she could hear Chris better, "what's wrong? What happened?"

Fatz looked over at Nikki with a worried expression on his face. "Is everything okay?" he asked pulling the car over to the side of the road.

Chris was silent. "Chris, Chris. Hello, are you there?" Nikki looked at her cell phone. The phone disconnected. She looked at Fatz with a look of confusion and worry. "We need to go back to the house. I don't know what's goin' on, but I'm worried." Nikki stared at Fatz. Even though they hadn't known each other long, they were close. Fatz knew how much Nikki's son meant to her and if anything happened to either one of them he would lose his mind.

The car squealed as he cut across the two-lane highway to head back to Nikki's house. He thought of the right words to say to Nikki, but he couldn't think of anything that would comfort her so he remained silent. Neither, Nikki or Fatz knew what to think because they just left the house forty-five minutes before. Nikki rocked her legs and fidgeted in the small bucket seat, anxious to get home.

They pulled into the apartment complex and Nikki barely let the car stop before she jumped out and ran to the hallway of her building. She ran up the twenty stairs leading to her apartment. She frantically tried to open the lock that sometimes stuck because it was rusted. She opened the door and saw Chris and Bo sitting on the couch. Chris had a look of terror on her face and Nikki could tell she had been crying. She ran over to the couch, hugged Bo, ran her hand down the side of his face and looked him in his eyes. "Oh my God baby, are you alright?" He nodded his head as his eyes shifted to the right to signal that somebody else was in the apartment, but Nikki did not realize what he was doing.

Nikki turned around stunned when a man came up behind her. "Where's Fatz? I know he with you bitch." The baritone voice barked.

She immediately focused her attention on Chris who was silently crying. "I don't know. He dropped me off." Outside Nikki could hear Fatz opening the hallway door and she knew he was about to walk into some trouble. She wanted to call out to warn him, but she feared for their lives. Fatz knocked on the door a couple of times before

35

opening it.

Fatz saw Nikki, Chris and Bo seated on the couch. "Nikki, what the hell is going on?"

Nikki stood up. "Fatz." Before she could finish warning him the man walked up behind him.

"What's up fat boy? It's been a long time." Fatz facial expression changed to disappointment. He thought Nikki set him up and she knew that is what he was thinking. The second man emerged from out of the bedroom. Fatz did not have time to draw his gun to get any shots off. "Maurice 'Fatz' Johnson you knew I was goin' to find yo ass, right." the second man continued. "Seems you have some unfinished business. You have two choices, the money or the package. Matter of fact make that one choice, give me both."

Fatz knew he was caught in a no win situation because either way the only people leaving out of the situation alive were the two men. "I don't have it." Fatz had the money and told Nikki where it was in case of an emergency. It was something about her that made him trust her. Now, he doubted his trust in her.

The man standing in front of Fatz lowered his head briefly. "Boy, you got about sixty seconds to hand over that shit or I'ma start knocking niggas off in here. Starting wit yo girl." the man said slyly looking over at Nikki.

Fatz stood there silently. He knew the man wasn't playing. In exactly sixty seconds he was going to start buckin' shots. Fatz tried to stall for time. He didn't want innocent people to get hurt even though he still had doubts about Nikki. "Aight, I got yo money in my money clip." Fatz went to reach in his belt when the man stopped him.

"Wait a minute." He signaled for the man standing behind Fatz to reach into his belt. Fatz knew he needed to think and act quickly. When the man went to reach into his belt Fatz grabbed his gun and shot the first man in his shoulder. A scuffle broke out. Nikki grabbed Bo's arm and ran into the bedroom. Christine followed suit. The three of them huddled together in a closet. A few minutes went by before either one of them spoke.

"Do you hear anything?" Nikki asked.

Christine shook her head. Nikki slid the closet door open slowly, peaking her head out. Just as she was about to step out the closet she heard the front door slam. She jumped back in the closet and

36

waited a few more minutes.

"I think they're gone." Chris whispered.

"Okay, Bo you wait in here. Me and Chris will be back in a minute." Nikki reassured.

Bo pulled his mother back, "you ain't goin' out there. I'm the man of the house and I'll make sure it's okay."

Nikki smiled. It made her proud that she raised such a bold young man even though she was over protective. She kissed Bo on the forehead and waited for him to say it was safe to come out. Bo quietly opened the door and peeked his head into the hallway. "Ma, Chris they gone!"

Nikki opened the bedroom door and crept into the hallway. Christine followed closely behind her and held onto her shirt. Nikki peered around the corner and saw Fatz on the floor, "Oh my God!"

Fatz was lying on the ground gasping for air. The two men were gone, but their faces remained sketched in Nikki's head. In the midst of the commotion Fatz pulled off both of their masks and Nikki looked both of them dead in the eyes. She knew if she saw them again she would remember them.

Chris ran to the window to see where the men went. "Are they gone?" Nikki belted.

Chris continued to peep through the blinds. "I don't know. I don't see them."

"Call an ambulance now!" Nikki demanded of Chris. Nikki held Fatz's hand and tried to keep him calm. "You'll be okay baby. Just relax. I can't lose you now!" Tears flowed down her cheeks. Even though Fatz was close to dying he heard everything Nikki was saying. It was at that point he realized that she didn't set him up. Nikki ran to the closet in the hallway and grabbed a towel. She knew she had to apply pressure to the open wound. With the amount of blood Fatz lost, Nikki knew he probably would not live much longer.

The ambulance arrived twenty minutes later. The paramedics worked diligently to save Fatz's life, but were unsuccessful. Fatz was pronounced dead at the scene.

The police questioned the ladies for hours asking them the same questions in different ways. Nikki gave the police a detailed description of the gunmen. The police suggested that Nikki and Christine find somewhere else to stay because it was a possibility the men would return since Nikki could positively identify them. The two men were part of a notorious gang in the area known for wiping out witnesses and potential threats.

Nikki sat on the couch and drowned out all of the noise around her. Fatz's body was gone and the police started to clear out. Nikki snapped back to reality when she felt a hand on her shoulder.

"Are you okay ma?" Bo asked.

Nikki looked up at her son and smiled. "I'm fine, honey." She thought to herself, how much of a good man her son was growing to be and she refused to let him end up like Fatz or the two thugs that killed him.

Boston was 18 years of age and a handsome young man. She kept her occupation a secret from him because she did not want him to be teased or judged by any of his friends. She lied to him and told him that she worked as a night janitor.

Nikki gave her son a hug. "Bo bear, I love you so much. You know that, don't you?" Bo nodded his head in confirmation. She rubbed his leg, "Baby, I know you love it here, but we can't stay here. We gotta go."

Bo looked at his mother. He saw the fear and desperation in her eyes. "But why ma? You can't let them punk ass niggas scare you. I got yo back and from now on I'll make sure I pack heat."

Nikki looked up at her son, "I know you got my back baby, but it's for our protection. I don't want you getting involved with this. I can't bear to think what I would do if anything happened to you."

"But-"

She took a deep breath and cut him off in mid sentence, "We're leaving Boston and that's it, it's not up for discussion! We can't stay here any longer." Nikki glimpsed over at Chris. She was still looking out the window. "Chris, they're gone. Come here, we need to talk."

Chris eyed the outside surroundings one last time before letting go of the blinds. "I can't believe this shit. I mean, what the fuck just happened?"

"I'm asking myself the same question. Look, we need to get out of here like now. I'm going to have one of the cops escort us to Fatz's house. He has some money and a car there."

"Okay, but where are we going to go?" Chris inquired. "I'm

38

sure those dudes got peoples all over Ohio. Ain't nowhere safe." she wailed.

"I had an aunt that used to live in VA. Me and my sister stayed with her after our parents died. It was a nice place. Nobody would think to look for us there."

Chris kept quiet for a moment. "Sounds good, but what if somebody's watchin' us?" she worried.

"It doesn't fucking matter at this point. You wanna stay here and risk your life." Chris shook her head no. Bo sat on the couch observing the last few cops come in and out of the apartment. The cops were collecting the last bit of forensic evidence.

A male officer approached Nikki and Chris. "Are you ladies ready to go?"

The two women looked at each other. "Yeah, just let me grab a couple of things and we can go." Nikki stated. "Boston go get some of your things. You can only take stuff you really need. Leave everything else here." she directed him.

She walked into her bedroom and grabbed an armful of clothes out of her closet, dumped two drawers of underwear into a large rolling suitcase and grabbed a bag of shoes. "Bo bear, you got your stuff together?" she yelled.

"Yes, I'm ready." he replied.

Nikki met Bo in the living and signaled to the officer that they were ready to go. The officer looked at Chris awkwardly. "Ma'am, are you ready?"

"Yeah, I'm ready. Why?" she inquired in an unpleasant tone.

"I'm sorry ma'am, I didn't mean to offend you, but you don't have any bags."

"Don't worry about me. Just take us where we need to go," she stated in a nasty tone.

The officer brushed off the comment and proceeded to walk out the door. Another female officer followed behind them to ensure their security. On the drive to Fatz's house there was dead silence. All they could think about was getting out of Ohio. It was filled with bad memories for Chris and Nikki. When they arrived at Fatz's house the female officer got out and escorted Nikki into the house. "Ma'am you have five minutes to get whatever belongings you need to get."

"Okay." she replied. She ran upstairs to a spare bedroom Fatz

39

had setup as a computer room. She opened the hard drive of the computer and removed a plastic bag full of money. She ran into Fatz's bedroom and opened a shoebox hidden in the closet behind some books. Inside the box was a pair of old Timberland boots. Inside the boots was a package. She threw the money and package in her purse and covered it with a scarf. She ran downstairs where the cop was waiting. "I'm ready," she told the officer.

The officer scanned the premises to make sure nobody was around. She escorted Nikki back to the car and did one last security check. "Excuse me," Nikki interrupted. "I have the keys to a car that's parked in the garage. Is it okay for me to drive."

The officers looked at each other and shrugged. "I guess it would be okay. We just have to follow you across state lines to make sure you're okay. We have to make sure nobody is following you."

"Well, that's fine with me."

The female officer let Chris and Bo out of the car and escorted them to the garage. The male officer shined a bright light on the garage door while the other officer walked inside to do another security check. Nikki walked in and opened the car door. She backed out of the garage to allow Chris and Bo to get in the car. The cop car backed out of the driveway and Nikki pulled in front of them.

"How long before we get to VA, ma?" Bo asked curiously.

"I don't know, probably fifteen hours."

"God damn!" Bo accidentally slipped.

Nikki adjusted the rearview mirror. "You better watch your damn mouth, boy. I let it slide at the house, don't let it happen again."

Christine chuckled at Nikki's attempt to be stern.

"What you laughin' at? That shit isn't funny. He ain't too big to be put across my knee." Nikki sternly said still looking in the rearview at the sour faces Bo was making.

Chris interjected, "I agree with Bo. It is a long ass drive though. But, At least in fifteen hours we will be starting a new life. Hopefully, this will be a better one."

"Amen to that!" Nikki smiled.

CHAPTER V

Three years passed since the move to VA and the money Nikki took from Fatz's house was running low. She desperately wanted to start her own business, but she foolishly spent the money she took. Even though money was low she refused to go back to tricking.

She kept her hopes up about the business loan she applied for. If all went well she would be able to start her record label she dreamt of. She waited anxiously in the busy lobby of Bank of America to meet with the loan officer.

"Ms. Rodriguez," a young black female dressed in a tweed paisley suit called. "The loan officer is ready to see you. Go down the hall and it's the third door on the left."

Nikki could barely stand. Her knees buckled with anticipation. Her mind was cluttered with a million thoughts. She knocked on the door tagged, Ms. T. Finch.

"Come in." A husky voice replied to the soft knock. A middle-aged white woman sat stiffly behind a large desk riffling through a stack of papers. "Ms. Nicole Rodriguez, correct?" she belted never looking up.

Nikki was so nervous she could barely speak. "Yes, that's correct."

"I'm sorry Ms. Rodriguez, but we're unable to approve your loan request. I wish we could help. Good luck."

41

The loan officer handed a set of papers over the desk to Nikki. Nikki's perfectly poised body slumped down into the cushioned chair. She fought back her tears as she gave the loan officer a fake smile.

"I don't understand, why not," she pleaded to the loan officer.

The loan officer set the stack of papers down. She opened the desk drawer and pulled out the file labeled Rodriguez, N. "Well, let's see Ms. Rodriguez. You have no credit, no assets and your business plan lacks sufficient material. When you can provide some sort of collateral, then maybe you'll be able to qualify for a small business loan, but nowhere near the amount you're asking for. Do you have any other questions?"

"I do have collateral, my car. It's paid for and has to be worth something." Nikki whined.

The loan officer sighed, "I'm sorry. I really wish there was something I could do, but the application has already been denied. But, like I said, you could reapply when you have substantial collateral and an ironclad business plan. Have a nice day." The loan officer went back to shuffling through the stack of papers on her desk. Nikki stood up and walked out of the office with her head hold low. After the disappointing meeting Nikki felt all her means of securing the money were exhausted.

She sat in her car wondering what she could do. In a flash it hit her: Maleek. Maleek was her son's best friend and liked to splurge on materialistic things. Nikki knew that he would help her if she played him right. Besides, she and Maleek messed around before and she knew he would have her back.

Maleek was a kingpin in the drug business and washed his money by investing in numerous small businesses. She knew Maleek had the money because the business he was in had a quick return. Maleek could move ten keys in one day, no problem. So the money would be no issue, and she had no issue with doing whatever it took to get the money.

Nikki opened her purse and anxiously looked for her cell phone. She scrolled through her contact list until she reached 'L,' which was Maleek's nickname.

A smooth and mellow voice answered, "what's good Nik? Everything okay?"

"Hey L, everything's good. Are you busy? I want to come over," she didn't want to make her intentions known for fear that

Maleek may say no off the bat.

Maleek was silent. He was always attracted to Nikki and knew if the timing was right he could get that again.

"Yea, you can come ova. I was just finishin' some biz. Mo and MJ just left." Maleek said with a certain confidence in his voice that made him more attractive than he already was. Maleek was 6'3", had the body of a model and the face of a chocolate angel. His two dimples were enough to make any woman cream in her panties when he smiled. His chocolate skin was smooth and his razor line stayed sharp. When he smiled his bright white teeth were blinding.

Nikki could sense that Maleek felt something was going to happen which is exactly what she wanted.

"Good, I'll be there in ten minutes." She began to plot on how she was going to get Maleek to give her the money. She always kept an over-night bag in her car with lingerie and a change of clothes. Immediately, she put her plan into action. She knew it was hard for a man to resist her.

Nikki pulled over on the side of the road so she could change into something more seductive. No matter what she wore she was sexy, but she wanted to drive Maleek over the edge. She put on a light pink, low cut V-neck shirt that was too small for her. Through her shirt you could see her Very Sexy Victoria Secret lace bra. Her cleavage was spilling out of her shirt and the pair of low-ride, skin-tight jeans she slipped into accentuated her full ass. She knew what to wear to entice a man, after all, enticing played a big part in her former career choice.

Nikki sprayed her body with her Sweet Pea body spray from her Bath & Body Works collection before knocking on the door. She tossed the spray into her pink and white Gucci hobo bag. She observed her surroundings to make sure no cars were coming up the winding road. Before Nikki could knock on the door again Maleek opened it with a grin on his face.

"Damn Nik, you sexy as hell girl. You keep comin' around here like that and I'ma have to tear that ass up?" Maleek joked.

Nikki just smiled. Those were her intentions and he probably knew it too. "Hey L, I just wanted to see how you were doin', that's all," she responded pushing the door open.

He slapped her on the ass as she walked through the door. They sat down on an oversized couch close to the door. Nikki rubbed

43

her sweaty palms on her jeans. Moments of awkward silence filled the air.

"Nervous, Nik?" Maleek continued to joke rubbing his hands on her leg. "What's good? It's been a while," Maleek said with a playa's swag as he glimpsed at Nikki, staring at her breasts.

Nikki held her head down finding it hard to look into Maleek's sparkling brown eyes.

"I'm cool," she started. "It has been a while, I just wanted to see you and catch up on old times."

Nikki lifted her head and felt the chemistry between them. At that precise moment Maleek leaned over and began to kiss her without warning.

She fell back onto the couch finding it hard to fight the temptation of kissing Maleek. His big, soft, juicy lips barely touched hers making the sensation greater.

He slid his oversized hands under Nikki's shirt, unhooking her bra and slightly brushing her stiff nipples.

Nikki found it hard to contain herself. It had been a while since she felt the gentle caressing of a man. It made her feel desirable and wanted, even though Maleek's wife was now one of her closest friends and he was her son's best friend.

Maleek continued to slowly move his hands over the most delicate parts of Nikki's body, stopping every time he felt her body tense up. He knew when he hit a sensitive spot. He slipped off Nikki's shirt and kissed her softly on the neck. He looked into her eyes and pressed his lips against hers. Maleek's large hands slid inside her pink lace Victoria Secret underwear.

Nikki didn't put up any fight. She wanted him bad, just as bad as he wanted her. She didn't care about morals or friendship at that time. She lost focus of her primary goal as Maleek's warm tongue and soft lips kissed forbidden places. Her back arched in pleasure with every lick and suck. She could feel herself losing control and he could too.

She let out a loud and fierce moan as she began to reach her peak. The sound of a woman climaxing made Maleek want her even more. He found it sexy and gratifying. He eased his 10" dick into her inviting pussy. He groaned as its warmth and tightness welcomed him. Maleek could feel her vagina throbbing like a heartbeat. If it was one

44

thing he could do, aside from hustling, it was satisfy a woman.

Every stroke gave her intense pleasure and he knew this because of the expressions on Nikki's face. He thrust even harder giving Nikki more satisfaction and making her squeal even louder. He cracked a slight smile as Nikki continuously bit on her lower lip in pleasure. Her eyes rolled to the back of her head in excitement.

He turned Nikki over on her stomach and entered her from the rear. He rubbed her round ass and kissed her softly on her lower back. Maleek fantasized about this moment ever since the last time the two fooled around a year earlier. Her independence and ambition turned him on. She was nothing like the other gold-diggin' chicken heads he was accustomed to. She was a real woman that could hold her own.

Maleek couldn't hold out any longer. His thrusts got harder and deeper and Nikki's moans grew louder. He grabbed her long black hair and closed his eyes. "Ah, shit! Nik, baby you feel so good! Damn!" He blurted, which was highly unusual because Maleek did not show any emotion while he fucked. He thought it was a sign of weakness and if a woman knew she had you she could get over, but he couldn't help himself.

He laid his heavy body on top of Nikki's basking in the after glow. She didn't mind the weight because he had put it on her and she needed that.

Maleek stared at her running his finger along the crevice in her back, "so is this what you came ova here fo'?"

Nikki turned around and looked at him. She couldn't form her lips to say the words, *I need some money.*

"I wanted to see you. You know I've had a thing for you, but out of respect for Bo and Monique I couldn't go there. Bo's grown now and as for Mo, what she doesn't know won't hurt her. So here I am." she giggled.

In her mind she knew she was lying. Yes, she did desperately need a good nut and she forgot what a real dick felt like, but her true intentions were to secure the money she needed. She did not count on getting caught up in head-over-hills, mind-blowing sex.

Nikki sat up on the sofa and began to put on her clothes still planning in her mind how to get the money from Maleek. At the same time she continued with the charade she started.

"So, now what?" she questioned, looking over her shoulder at

45

Maleek.

Maleek was a little puzzled. "What you mean? It is what it is. Nothing more, nothing less. You're my boy's mom and my wife's friend. Yea, that shit was it, but we both know Bo and Mo can't find out 'bout this shit. I can't risk my family for no side pussy."

Nikki felt a little used, even though she was using him. She did not expect such a cold answer, but it was the truth. Besides, she knew the real reason she was there.

"Well, you're right. Can I use your bathroom to freshen myself up before I leave?" Nikki asked with a nonchalant attitude.

Maleek pointed upstairs. Nikki knew almost every inch of his house because she visited times before. She grabbed her bag and sprinted upstairs.

Nikki went in the bathroom and locked the door. She sat her purse on a decorative stand beside the toilet. She glanced in the mirror combing through her hair with her fingers. After Nikki used the toilet she tried to flush it, but the water in the toilet bowl continued to run.

She lifted the lid off the toilet to flush it manually. Her eyes widened at what she saw. Her prayers were answered. She grabbed her bag before flushing it, pulled the chain to allow the toilet to flush, and placed the lid back on. She washed her hands and quickly made her way back downstairs. Maleek was in the kitchen in his tank top and boxers cooking.

"You gone, Nik?" Maleek yelled from the kitchen.

"Yeah, I gotta meet Nae. Look, L, I don't know what we just did, but keep this between us, okay," she shouted back.

"That's cool. I didn't mean to be so blunt, but I can't get down wit you like dat. Just know you the shit! And that's word." Maleek didn't want to hurt Nikki's feelings, but he meant every word he said to her.

Nikki smiled, "thanks, L." and walked out the door. She threw her bag in the back seat of the car and stared at the front door of the house waiting for Maleek to emerge with a look of anger on his face. She took a deep breath, *Nikki calm down,* she whispered under her breath before putting the key in the ignition. The tires squealed when she sped off. She couldn't believe what she had done, but she couldn't look back.

46

CHAPTER VI

Nikki looked at Bo with excitement in her eyes about to put on the act of her life, "guess what, Bo Bear?"

"What?" he anticipated.

"I got it!"

"You got it?" he questioned happily.

Nikki nodded her head.

Bo embraced his mother and hugged her as tight as he could. "Mom, that is great! I'm so happy for you. You deserve it. You've worked so hard to get that loan."

"Oh my God Bo, it's really happening. I'm going to start my own label. I gotta call Chris to let her know." Nikki ran upstairs to her room and closed her door. She felt like from the moment she walked in the door that Bo could see right through her. She lay across her bed and closed her eyes. Her guilty conscious nagged at her. She replayed the images of her and Maleek in her head over and over. She drifted to sleep and was awakened by the blare of her cell phone playing Mary J's, "No More Drama." She pulled her right hand out of her panties and thought to herself she must have been having a damn good dream because her panties were wet and her fingers were sticky.

"Hello," she answered in a groggy voice holding her phone with her left hand.

"So, how'd it go heffa?" Christine inquired.

"Oh yeah, I meant to call you."

Christine was getting excited, "okay, and—and, what happened?"

"I GOT IT!" Nikki screamed into the phone.

Christine started screaming too. "I am so proud of you! I knew you were gon' get that shit! I told you."

"Girl, I was so scared. That loan officer was evil as hell, but they were impressed with my business plan."

"So, now what? What do you do from here?" Christine wanted to hear more about Nikki's plan. She was happy to see her friend rebuild her life for the better. She saw how unhappy Nikki was not being able to splurge like she use to when Fatz was alive and when she still had his money. She knew Nikki missed being spoiled.

"Well," Nikki started as she got up and walked towards the bathroom, "I have to start putting together my team, find a building, buy equipment. Oh my goodness Chris, there's so much I need to do. I don't even know where to start."

"If you need me to do anything, I mean anything, just let me know. You know I got yo back girl." Christine assured.

Nikki washed her hands and looked in the bathroom mirror picking at her pearly white teeth, "I will girl. You know that. Aye Chris, let me call you back."

"Alright. I'll talk to you later." Christine replied hanging up the phone.

Nikki laid the phone on the bathroom sink and continued to pick at her teeth. She opened the large cabinet in front of her and took out a vitamin bottle. She popped two pills in her mouth and swallowed quickly then washed them down with a small cup of water.

She grabbed her cell phone, walked back into her bedroom and sat on her king size bed. Her slender fingers dialed an Ohio number. The phone rang four times before a husky, male voice answered, "speak ya piece."

Nikki laughed, "I see some things neva change."

"Who dis?" the male grunted.

"Yo favorite bitch, but I'm sure you've replaced me by now." she played.

The male on the other end was not in the mood to play, "I ain't got time for this playin' shit. Who the fuck is dis?"

Nikki stopped playing around, "It's me Class, Nikki."

The man thought for a second, "Nikki? Nikki? Nikki, who?"

"I can't believe you don't remember me E-Class," she said in

48

an insulted tone.

"Only one bitch ever called me E-Class and I ain't heard from her in years. I know dis ain't her," he laughed.

Nikki smiled, "oh. So, now you remember me chump. Took you long enough."

"Damn, baby. What the fuck you been up to? I ain't heard from you since you dipped out without telling anybody. Where you at now?"

Nikki hadn't spoke to anybody in Ohio since she left for VA. For the safety of her family she cutoff her ties with anybody in Cincinnati. "Yeah, Class. It's been a while. I been chillin'. I'm in VA and I need yo help with something."

Class was willing to do anything for Nikki. He tried to get at her, but he wasn't her type. That didn't matter to him. He was still down to do whatever she needed. By trade he was a bouncer, but his off-the-clock job involved a lot of broken legs, arms, necks and other body parts. "Anything for you baby. What is it?"

"I'm trying to start a label and I don't mean no bullshit type stuff. This is the real," she began.

"I'm listening."

"I got some shit I need you to flip like ASAP and I need you to get me in touch wit yo people up top. This is on some major level shit." Nikki kicked into hustler mode. Fatz taught her how to hustle and check niggas.

Class couldn't believe his ears. She was speaking his language. Nikki was a classy lady, even though she was a former hoe. "Shit girl. I ain't figure you for the hustlin' type. I mean, I know you were a hustler, but I ain't neva seen you like this."

Nikki knew that was a good thing. Nobody ever thought she could get her hands dirty and that was working in her favor. "I know and I want to keep it that way. I'll hit you off with some major change. You know I got you Boo."

He trusted Nikki and knew that her word was bond. "So, when you want this done? You plan on comin' down here soon?"

"Yeah. I'll be there on Saturday. Make sure you ain't got nothing to do that day. I want to be the center of attention." she joked.

"No doubt. Always. I'll see you then baby. Nice to hear from you."

49

Nikki hung up the phone and lay back across her bed. Her mind raced as she thought about building her business, a life long dream. Nikki knew she was going to be successful. Her business education was about to pay off. Her only problem was returning to Cincinnati.

She hadn't stepped foot in Cincinnati since she had left years before. She didn't want anybody to know she was coming back for fear that the men who killed Fatz would still have a hit out on her. Nikki pushed those thoughts to the back of her mind and focused on her main goals. She needed to flip her money and invest it as soon as possible and Nikki knew she had the right person to do it. The other obstacle was telling Bo she was returning to Cincinnati. She knew Bo would object instantly, so she opted to lie about where she was going.

"Bo," she called from her bedroom. When he didn't answer she screamed his name louder. "Bo Bear!" The walls in her house were thick and she liked that, but when she was in lazy mode she wished they weren't. After calling Bo a second time she pushed herself up from her bed and walked over to her door. She stuck her head into the hallway calling him again, "Boston!"

"Huh," he screamed back.

"C'mere."

Bo stopped what he was doing and ran upstairs to see what his mother wanted, "yeah."

Her lie was straight in her head. She knew Bo would be okay with her leaving as long as she was leaving for business purposes and as long as she was not going anywhere near Ohio. "Baby, I just got off the phone with one of my business associates and I need to go to New York for a few days. I'm leaving on Saturday."

Bo was not the least bit worried, "cool. I see you're makin' moves already. I'm proud of you." He leaned in and kissed his mother on the cheek.

Nikki wasn't expecting that kind of reaction, but Bo was older now and he didn't need her as much as he use to. "Alright. Just make sure you look out for J'nae."

"J'nae?" he questioned curiously.

"Yes, J'nae, your cousin. Did you forget she was coming?"

Bo frowned his face and mumbled, "shit."

Nikki heard him and corrected his language, "excuse me,

50

Boston Rodriguez. Do you have a problem?"

"Nah, ma. But you know Nae a lil' wild and I don't want to have to fu—."

Nikki gave Bo a hard look before he finished the words coming out of his mouth.

"I mean, mess anybody up behind her," he finished.

"Well, you know she's going through a hard time right now. So, just make sure she's okay while I'm gone. I'll only be gone until Tuesday. I'll make sure to check up on y'all while I'm gone." Nikki gave Bo a hug and closed her room door.

Nikki only had a couple of days to make sure everything was in order before she left for Cincinnati. She pulled her laptop off her dresser and started looking for flights and hotels. She booked a round trip flight first class and a hotel room at the Hyatt Regency. Now, that she was making big moves she needed to portray this image in every aspect of her life. Nikki enjoyed the finer things in life and whenever possible she treated herself.

Since Nikki suffered from a small case of OCD, she liked to make sure all of her clothes were packed and ready to go well in advance. She kept her luggage in a closet in her basement. Instead of yelling for Bo to retrieve her luggage she called his cell.

"Why are you calling me?" he answered in a somewhat irritated voice like most children when their parents are nagging the hell out of them.

"I didn't feel like screaming at the top of my lungs for you to take forever to see what I wanted. Anyway, can you go down to the basement and bring me my luggage. Thanks, Bo Bear."

Bo took a deep breath before answering, "okay, but do you need it now?"

"Yes. You know how I am. I need to pack my stuff, so I'm not rushing on Saturday morning." Nikki snapped.

Bo hung up the phone and slammed it on the counter. "Damn, she gets on my nerves. I ain't her damn slave," he remarked to himself. He made his way down into the basement that was converted into a den. He opened the closet door where his mother kept her luggage and pulled it from a top self. A manila envelope fell on the floor.

He picked up the envelope and looked upstairs to make sure his mother was nowhere around before he opened it. He pulled out two

51

certificates of death, one with the name Maurice F. Johnson and the other one James R. Rodriguez, his father. Bo knew that his parents were divorced, but he never knew his father had passed away and his mother never mentioned it, which didn't bother Bo since he didn't really know his father and he definitely didn't know Maurice Johnson. But, he was curious about why his mother had the death certificate.

He was about to slide the death certificates back into the envelope when he saw something fall to the floor. It was a small gold key with the numbers 1681 embedded on it. Bo had enough sense to know that the key fit either a small lock or a lockbox of some kind. He put the key and certificates back in the envelope and placed it back on the shelf from where it had fallen. He made his way back up the stairs with the luggage. Nikki was busy folding her clothes when Bo knocked on the door.

"Mom, here's your luggage," he interrupted. "Anything else, your majesty?" he joked.

"No, you're free to go." she smiled.

Once Bo closed her door she snatched two large brown packages out of her oversized tote. She wrapped both packages with saran wrap and placed each package inside a sweater before placing it in the bottom of her large, brown/apple-green American Flyer bag. She piled the rest of her clothes on top of the sweaters and zipped the bag. She dragged the luggage down the spiral staircase and placed it beside the front door. Her bags were packed and she was ready for her trip to Cincinnati.

CHAPTER VII

Maleek's heart pounded a thousand times a minute as he stared down the barrel of the black nine-millimeter. "What the fuck? I told Jungle I would have his money next week."

The tall, slender dark skinned Jamaican man cocked his gun. The veins in his head popped and the wrinkles in his face rippled when he frowned his face. "Dat not good enough, mudafucka!" the man barked with a heavy Jamaican accent. "Jungle need his money now. I give you five secons bumba clot," the man started to count emphasizing each number, "*ONE, CHOO, TREE…*"

"HOLD THE FUCK UP!" Maleek shouted. He stretched out his arm to signal stop with is hand. "Wait, wait, wait! I got 10Gs in my pocket. Lemme give that to you as a down payment."

The Jamaican reached in his pocket and pulled out a compact cellular phone, keeping an eye on Maleek. "Aye bossman, bumba clot only got 10Gs. Wha you won me to do?" Maleek could hear Jungle's voice through the phone. He hung up the phone and stared at Maleek. "Gimme da money!"

Maleek hesitated, "so we cool?" he questioned nervously.

The Jamaican walked up to Maleek and placed the barrel of the gun to the temple of his forehead.

"Gimme the mudafuckin' money!"

Maleek pulled out a wad of cash that was neatly stuffed in a silver money clip. He handed the money to the impatient Jamaican.

The Jamaican snatched the wad of cash and shuffled through it like a deck of cards with his left hand and kept the gun pressed against the temple of Maleek's forehead with his right.

"Yo, can I go now? Are we cool?" Maleek whimpered. He knew

the Jamaicans had a reputation of violence and that his situation could go quickly from bad to worse.

The man lowered the gun and signaled for Maleek to leave. Maleek stood motionless for a moment before he decided to walk away. He was so much in a hurry that he broke his cardinal rule: never turn your back. Maleek felt a sting in the back of his leg and then in his right leg. A second later he was lying on the ground and his pant legs were soaked in blood. The stings were bullets.

"Turn ova!" the Jamaican shouted. "Turn ova!" he shouted again kicking the bottom of Maleek's left leg. "Now, stand up!" he demanded.

Maleek slowly stood up. The agonizing pain was written on his face.

"Dat way." The Jamaican pointed his gun towards a dark room in the corner of the warehouse.

Maleek slowly limped across the cold cement floor. His mind wondered when he realized his chances of survival were decreasing by the minute. He fell to the ground because his legs gave way.

"Getup, you pussy!" the Jamaican demanded. Maleek lay motionless. "Get da fuck up, mudafuckin' bumba clout!"

Maleek pushed himself up and staggered into the dark room. He didn't know what to expect, but knew it wasn't good. The room was colder than the rest of the warehouse and smelled of urine and ammonia. The darkness blinded him instantly. Maleek stood helplessly as the steel door behind slammed close. He was alone. He wasn't a weak man, but the fear of dying began to break him down. He now faced the same fate he ordered on many others and it didn't feel good to be on the receiving end.

He forced himself to move slowly about the cold room, although he was in pain. He knew he needed to familiarize himself with the room if he were going to survive. He fumbled around in dark feeling on the cement walls. A stifling pain shot through his body when he bumped into a table and fell forward. He pushed himself up from the table. His hands were wet from some kind of liquid that covered the table, but he didn't want to think about what he touched.

Maleek made his way around the table and continued to move along the wall in search of a light switch. He maintained his balance as his head began to spin and he started to feel dizzy. He stumbled a few

54

feet and held his head, a few seconds later he was on the ground.

Maleek awoke to find his hands, knees and feet tied to a metal chair. A bright light swung from the ceiling in the middle of the room. Maleek's eyes scanned the room. He spotted the table that he bumped into earlier. The substance on his hands was blood. Someone tried to wash blood off the table by dumping a bucket of water over it but it didn't clean the table. Bright red spots still adorned the table. Spray paint colored cement walls with gang graffiti.

Outside Maleek could hear men with thick Jamaican accents. He recognized the voices of two of the men. One was the voice of Jungle, the Jamaican kingpin that raised him on the streets. The other was the voice of the man that disabled him. The steel door flew open and five men with an assortment of guns stormed in the room. Behind them, a stout dark-skinned man with a slight limp walked in. His face was marked with scars that the purest coco butter could not heal. The name Jungle fit him perfectly, a rough black man covered with war wounds. He looked like he lived in the jungle. He sported a black leather Kangol to cover the balding tangled dreads that were matted to his head. He stood in front of Maleek and let out a low grunt.

"Maleek, ya know ya like a son to me, no. So ya know me don't play wit my money. I wou' kill me own mama if she cross me. So why you not have me money? Wha you tryin choo make Jungle look like a punk bitch?" he paused for a second to give Maleek time to reply. When he didn't reply Jungle pulled out a silver magnum and struck Maleek across the face, "answer me."

Maleek lifted his head. He tried to remain conscious as blood dripped from his face. "Nigga, I got yo money. I'll have it to you by tomorrow. You know me Jungle. I wouldn't steal from you."

Jungle laughed. The other men laughed on cue. "Do you hear dis?" Jungle asked looking around the room at the other men. The men nodded their heads. "Dis mudafucka won Jungle to wait fo his money." He walked up to Maleek and lifted his chin with the barrel of the gun. "Listen. I give choo seventy choo hours to get me money because ya like a son to me. If you don't have me money, I will cut off all your fingers and dip your dick in battery acid."

Before Jungle walked away he struck Maleek once more with his gun. He wanted to leave him with a brutal reminder to have his money. He leaned over and whispered in Maleek's ear, "choo know it's not personal, only business." Jungle exited the room, but the five men remained behind. Maleek's body was weak and his mental was fragile.

The men began to speak amongst each other, but Maleek could not understand what they were saying. A tall man dressed in all black with an overly large silver chain dangling from his neck untied Maleek. He could barely make out the faces of the men because his eyes were beginning to swell shut and blood clouded his eyes. Maleek was instructed to strip naked and lay on the wet table face down. He felt powerless while he was being strapped down to the wooden table. Maleek used all his inner strength to prepare himself for what was about to happen.

"You such a pretty boy now, aye." One of the men commented to Maleek. "Wha da pretty boys like?" Maleek tried to concentrate on other things. He blocked out the laughter and movement around him. Maleek cringed when he felt the head of one of the men's dick rub against his leg.

"AAAAAAAAWWWWWWWWWW!" Maleek let out a blood-curdling scream. He fought back his tears. He never experienced so much pain in his life. He clinched his fist as another dick was rammed into his ass over and over. He gritted his teeth to endure the continuous pain.

They laughed at his humiliation. "Ain't dis wha da pretty boys like." The man gave a few more thrusts. He shook his dick and sprinkled semen on Maleek's back. As soon as he was off another was on. Maleek was violated for over an hour as the five men took turns shoving their dicks into his ass. When they were done they left him lying on the table.

"Remember pretty boy, Jungle won his money. Nex time it will be painful." the Jamaican reminded.

Maleek listened attentively as the footsteps and voices outside the door faded away. Still strapped to the table he tried to figure out how to free himself. He wiggled his hands and slipped one of his wrists through the belted strap. He ignored all his pain and twisted his body free dislocating his wrist in the process. Maleek could barely stand let alone walk, but he knew if he wanted to live he needed to put the pain behind him and get the hell out of the warehouse.

He put on his clothes and made his way to the metal door. He listened to make sure everybody was gone. His vision was so poor that

56

even if somebody were still in the warehouse he would not have seen them. But, Maleek knew if Jungle wanted him dead he would be dead and he would not have made it out of the room alive. He smiled as he walked out the entrance of the warehouse and saw his car. Once in the car he took a deep breath and fumbled through some items in his glove box.

"Hey, it's me. I need you to come get me! I'm at the steel warehouse on 13. Hurry the fuck up!" Maleek belted with urgency into his cellular phone.

He closed his eyes and drifted in and out of consciousness. He woke up screaming because visions repeatedly played in his head. Maleek couldn't tell what was reality or a dream. He jumped when he heard a tap on his car window. He stared at the woman on the other side.

"Maleek, Maleek! Open the door baby!" she screamed.

Maleek was dazed and confused. He reluctantly unlocked the car door.

"Oh my God! Baby, what---what in the hell happened to you? We gotta get you to the hospital!"

Maleek was nonresponsive for a moment. "Chris, what took you so long?" he questioned sluggishly.

"No baby, it's me, Mo. Oh my God, c'mon we gotta get you in the car." she screeched. Tears formed in her eyes. She stroked Maleek's face and body tenderly with her tiny fingers. She gently guided Maleek to her cherry red Porsche Boxster that was parked a few feet away from his car. She adjusted the seat so that his legs were completely stretched out.

"Don't worry baby, its going to be okay," she assured him while she buckled his seatbelt. "Just relax we'll be at the hospital in a few minutes." Monique ran around the front of the car. She moved her short legs as fast as she could. She jumped in the car and sped away. Her tires kicked up gravel and dust from the dirt parking lot. Monique pulled out her cell phone and accessed her speed dial.

"Nikki, oh my God something has happened to L. Meet me at the hospital!" she sputtered in a panicked voice. Monique was pushing her Boxster to the limit swerving all over the dark road lined with trees. She tried to keep check on Maleek and maintain control of the car while speeding down the road and holding her phone. Monique's face was dotted with black lines because her mascara started to run.

"I don't know what the fuck happened! He called me and told me to pick him up!" she screamed inaudibly into the phone. On the other end, Nikki tried to calm her down because she was hysterical. A series of quick, loud horn blasts startled Monique. She was so hysterical she did not realize she swerved into oncoming traffic. Her cell phone dropped to the floor and she cut her wheel to avoid hitting a F-150 head on. Her small Roadster swiped the metal railing that kept her from going into a ditch.

"Shit!" she yelled glancing over at Maleek to make sure he was okay. "L, baby are you okay? L." she called to him gently shaking him. Maleek let out a low groan. "I'm sorry baby, just hang in there a few more minutes. Monique regained control of her car just in time to take the exit to the hospital. She heard a distant voice and remembered she dropped her cell phone while she was talking to Nikki.

"Nik, Nik—I'm here! Yeah, we're okay. I'm taking the exit now. I'll be at the hospital in a couple of minutes. Meet me in the lobby. Okay, bye." Monique tossed the phone in her monogram Coach purse and took the exit at the fastest speed possible. She ran through two read lights and a stop sign before pulling the car up to the emergency room entrance. "Somebody help me! I need help!"

An ambulance driver walking to his truck saw Monique trying to pull Maleek out of the car. He ran over to Monique to assist her. He signaled a hospital worker to help. "We need a stretcher! Now!" he yelled to the worker. Two men wearing ambulance shirts rushed out of the hospital pushing a stretcher. "We need to get him to the OR stat!" one of the men commanded. The men placed Maleek on the stretcher and rushed him into the ER. Monique rushed in behind them, forgetting her car was blocking the ambulance entrance.

"Excuse me, ma'am," a deep voice muttered to Monique.

She turned around flustered, her eyes red from crying.

"Ma'am is that your car?"

Monique nodded her head.

"You're blocking the ambulance entrance. I need you to move your car," the security guard explained.

Without saying a word Monique ran to the car and pulled her car into a visitor's parking space. When she stepped out of the car she heard a familiar voice.

"Mo, Mo." Nikki ran up to her and embraced her. "Mo do you know what happened?"

Monique broke down crying. "No. They just took him to the operating room."

"Alright. Let's go inside in case the doctor comes out. He's going to be okay Mo. Where's MJ?"

Monique sniffled, "he's with my mom."

"Okay, that's good. You need to be strong right now. I know it's hard, but be strong. L needs you right now, okay." she said caringly.

Monique and Nikki were both restless as they waited in the crowded waiting room.

"What's taking them so long? Shouldn't somebody have come out here by now, damn!" Monique belted.

Nikki remained silent. Before Monique could continue her rant a doctor's physique appeared in the doorway.

"Mrs. Johnson?" the doctor called looking down at his clipboard.

Both Nikki and Monique hurried over to the doctor.

"Hello, I'm Dr. Holloman."

Monique didn't give the doctor a chance to speak. "Is Maleek okay? Can I see him now?"

Dr. Holloman looked at the ladies and took a breath. "I'm not going to lie to you Mrs. Johnson, your husband was in extremely bad shape. Frankly, I'm surprised that he is still alive."

Monique covered her mouth in awe. "Oh my God," she mumbled under her breath. Nikki listened intensely while the doctor continued.

"He's recovering in ICU right now. He's in critical condition, but we're expecting for him to stabilize over the next few days. He lost a lot of blood and we had to give him a blood transfusion. Mrs. Johnson, may I ask what happened to your husband?" he questioned curiously.

"No, I don't. Why?" she responded inquisitively.

The doctor glanced at Nikki and refocused his attention on Monique silently questioning if it were okay to speak in front of her.

Monique paused, "doctor, what is it?"

"I think it's best that we speak alone in my office." he

59

suggested.

She looked at Nikki with a confused look. She signaled for Monique to go with the doctor.

"I'll be right here when you get back." Nikki reassured.

Monique followed the doctor down the hall to his office. Nikki remained in the waiting room. The doctor explained to Monique the extent of Maleek's injuries. Monique was in shock. She stared out the big bay window of the doctor's office. She saw Nikki running through the parking lot. Nikki surveyed the parking lot around her in paranoia. She jumped in her silver 2006 Audi A6 and sped off. She almost hit two pedestrians walking behind her car.

Monique didn't understand why her friend would leave when she needed her support the most, but she couldn't think about that because Maleek needed her attention more than ever. The doctor made it extremely clear that to get through the type of trauma Maleek experienced he would need Monique to provide unconditional love, support, and a listening ear if Maleek ever wanted to talk about what happened. The doctor also recommended professional counseling, but Monique knew the type of man Maleek was. He would want revenge not counseling.

Nikki sat on the edge of her couch. She moved her legs nervously and puffed on a cigarette. Her cell phone vibrated and moved across the table. Monique called her three times, but Nikki didn't want to talk. She was feeling a certain way about what happened to Maleek. She couldn't shake the feeling that everything was her fault.

She jumped when she heard the front door close. She almost burnt herself on the leg because she tried to put the cigarette out before Bo or J'nae saw her. Nikki didn't smoke and if anybody saw her with a cigarette they would know something was up.

"Hey auntie, what ya doin'?"

"Oh, hey baby. I'm not doin' nothin'. How was your day?"

J'nae paused, "is something burning in here? I smell smoke."

Nikki looked around the room. She hoped J'nae would not figure out she was smoking. She pushed the small square ashtray under the couch with her foot before J'nae could see it. "I don't smell anything, but go get the Febreze and spray in here."

"Alright, but my day was okay," she yelled from the kitchen. "So, what you doin' home? I thought you would be out getting everything straight with the label."

"Not today. I needed a break. Everything has been so hectic, I just needed time to myself." Nikki hollered as she peered out the window. She glanced at the table and saw the light on her cell phone flashing. She walked away from her phone and ran upstairs to her room. She sprawled across the bed. *Was it her fault Maleek was in the hospital?* She wondered. She rolled over on her stomach and closed her eyes. *No. It couldn't be because of me.* She spoke aloud.

"Auntie, Mo's on the phone. She said she need to talk to you NOW!" J'nae yelled through the door.

Shit! Nikki muttered under her breath. "Okay, I'm coming." Nikki pushed herself off the bed and walked across the room to open the door. She grabbed the phone out of J'nae's hand and closed the door. "Hello," her voice quivered.

"Nikki, where'd you go? I saw you running to your car. Are you ok?"

"I'm alright girl. I forgot I had an important meeting. Sorry, I left you. I know you needed somebody there with you. How's Maleek?" Nikki could here the somberness in Monique's voice.

Monique sniffled, "he's in bad shape Nik. He was tortured in ways you wouldn't believe!" Monique broke down in tears over the phone. Nikki couldn't believe what she just heard.

"Oh my God Mo! Who I mean why would they do that to him? Damn!"

"I don't know! He's fucked over so many people it's no tellin' who did this." Mo cried uncontrollably.

"Do you need me to come back?"

"No, I know you have so much goin' on in your life right now. I just needed somebody to talk to. I'm goin' to be here for a while, but I'll call you later."

Nikki was happy Monique didn't want her to come back to the hospital. A little piece of her felt guilty. In the back of her mind she couldn't shake the thought that this was her fault. Meanwhile, she had other things to deal with in her life like her record label, so she pushed

61

all her thoughts about Maleek to the back of her mind and focused on building her label.

CHAPTER VIII

Two Years Later...

The silky tan sheets entangled Nikki's body like a spider web. Her nipples hardened as her fingertips outlined the brown rings around them. She smiled at the memories from the night before. She slowly opened her eyes and gazed out the window watching the raindrops hit the windowsill,

"Hey, what are you doing in there? I'm ready for another round!" Nikki sat up and positioned herself upright against the fluffed pillows. She leaned over the king size bed and glimpsed at the time on the round-faced clock. It was 5:16 a.m., time for her to get ready for work.

She finally accomplished her goal. Her label was one of the most successful labels on the east coast. Two years of grinding paid off. She was the youngest CEO to run her own major recording label, Kaew Records, 43 years old and in her prime. She worked like a slave day and night securing deals, artists, writing contracts and making sure everybody else was doing their job. Hundreds of thousands of dollars were funneled through her company on a daily basis. Making sure employees weren't skimming from the top was a job that was hectic and demanding at all times.

She worked in a male dominated industry and nobody was to be trusted. Her employees plotted on her daily. The industry was treacherous. She was one of the only females in the office, and one of the only minorities besides the typical gangsta rappers that popped in every now and then to drop off a CD filled with colorful lyrics about fucking bitches and killing niggas.

Nikki built her label from the ground up with the help of a few friends and business partners. She secured investors, offered them a major return on their money and in return they continued to back her business. She was back at the top of her game.

Nikki began to grow impatient because her lover was taking forever to come out of the bathroom. She called out again with a hint of frustration in her voice.

"Sweetie, are you okay?"

No answer came from the bathroom that was just steps away. She swung her smooth legs over the edge of the bed her newly manicured toes barely touched the floor. She grabbed her favorite blue satin embroidered robe from the wicker chair next to the bed. She slipped her feet into her bedroom slippers and slung the flowing robe over her naked body, tying a perfect bow in the front.

"Baby, are you okay?" She called in an inquisitive voice. "Hey, baby?" Still, no answer. She pushed the bathroom door open with hesitation. Nikki's worst fears played in her head. She flashed back to a traumatic moment in her childhood.

"Mommy, where are you? Mommy!!" A young Nikki pushed the door to her mother's bedroom open. Tears streamed down her face when she saw the body of her mother on the floor.

Nikki ran over to her mother's body that was covered in blood and kneeled down beside her.

She walked toward the bathroom because she heard the shower running. She opened the door and saw blood on the mirror and shower curtain.

"Daddy," she called with fear in her voice. "Daddy, are you in there?"

She pulled the shower curtain back and saw her father sitting in the bathtub with water running down his face hiding his tears.

"I'm sorry baby girl, I love you!" Her father cried out to her.

Nikki was confused. "Daddy what's wrong? What happened to mommy?"

Her father picked up a black revolver that was lying on the side of the stainless still bathtub.

"Daddy, NO!" she screamed.

A deafening gunshot pierced the silent house. In an instant Nikki lost the only two people that meant the world to her, her mother and father.

63

Nikki was only eight-years-old and her older sister was nine. She fell to her knees and cried until she fainted.

Nikki snapped back to reality and pushed the door open. She could see one side of the vanity mirror was cracked. When she entered the bathroom she knew something wasn't right. The bathroom was a mess. The towel rack was broken, liquid soap and blood covered the floor, and bloody handprints splattered the wall. Her lover was nowhere to be found. *What the hell happened?*

Her first thoughts were her son and niece, Boston and J'nae. She ran through the bathroom door leading into the narrow hallway that led to J'nae's, room. She frantically entered the room and pulled the blanket down on the bed. J'nae was gone.

"Bo, Bo," she screamed as she ran across the hall to awaken him. "Bobo, Bobo. Wake up!"

Bo was 23-years old now and could double for a young version of the actor, Boris Kudjoe.

He rubbed his eyes and rolled over on his back. He slowly opened his eyes enough to make out the tall silhouette of his mother.

"I'm up!" he grunted.

"Where's your cousin Nae?" she asked worriedly.

Bo looked at the clock. It was 5:25 a.m. too early for him to think clearly. He sighed and placed his right arm over his face before he answered his mother's question.

"Iono. She prolly downstairs." He grunted with a country swagger before he rolled over on his side and pulled the red covers over his head.

Nikki ran over to the side of her son's bed and pulled the cover from over his head. "Bo, listen to me! Something has happened. Call the police now!"

Before he could say anything he saw his mother's flowing robe vanish into the hall and heard her panicky voice screaming his cousin's name.

Nikki walked down the narrow hallway until she reached the spiral staircase. She leaned over the rail and called out her niece's name. "J'nae. J'nae Mashelle." When she didn't get a response she started walking down the staircase.

Where in the hell is she? She thought to herself. J'nae constantly snuck out the house to meet her boyfriend, Peps, who Nikki

64

disapproved of. She was only 15-years old and her boyfriend was 26-years old. Too old Nikki thought. Nikki promised her sister she would take care of J'Nae after she died of cancer two years before.

Before she reached the bottom of the stairs she slipped and fell in a puddle. She looked down and saw bright red blood covering her robe. Nikki frowned her face and whispered in a low voice, "*what the fuck?*" She saw the body of her niece lying limp halfway between the stairs and the stair rail.

Nikki's muscular arms lifted her body off the tile floor. Nikki's perfectly made up face was now blemished by runny mascara. She covered her mouth and stretched out her arms to touch J'nae's head. "My baby, my baby oh God, NO!" she cried. J'nae was like a daughter to Nikki. They were already close, but when she came to live with Nikki their bond became tighter. Nikki cradled J'nae in her arms rocking back and forth. In a low voice she called out, "Bo. Bo." She moved her lips, but nothing came out.

Before she could call any louder she felt an overwhelming pressure on the back of her head. She turned to see what struck her. This time she was hit in the face repeatedly with a steel baseball bat until her face was covered in blood. Nikki's face was barely noticeable. On the fourth blow her body fell. Nikki's body fell over the stairs directly below J'nae. Her battered, bruised and bloody body lye naked and exposed at the bottom of the stairs.

Meanwhile, Bo was oblivious to what happened. He was still in his bed half sleep. He fumbled around in the dark, reaching for his phone on the nightstand beside his bed. It was early in the morning and Bo was still trying to wake himself. The night before he and Maleek got fucked up and he was still hung over.

Bo struggled to dial the tiny numbers on his cell phone. His head throbbed continuously and his vision was blurry. His fingers felt crippled as he dialed 911.

"Emergency 911, what's your emergency?"

"Yeah, I need an ambulance to my house. It's an emergency, please send somebody to 6657 Main St."

"Are you calling from 757-555-8767?" the operator inquired.

Bo was slow to respond. "I'm sorry, yeah, yeah. That's my numba."

"Okay sir, I still need to know your emergency."

65

"I'm not sure. My mother ran in my room all worked up and said something happened, but than she ran out the room."

"Where's your mother now?"

"I don't know. Hold on one moment." Bo ran into the hallway with the phone held to his ear. "Ma, ma, Where you at?" Bo pushed the door to her bathroom. "Oh my God! Please send somebody asap. My mother has been attacked!"

"Calm down sir. Somebody is on the way. They should be there in a few minutes." The operator disconnected the call.

Bo ran back in his room his extra large fish covered boxer shorts hanging halfway off his butt. He grabbed his navy blue jogging pants off the bed and jumped into them with both legs. He peeped out the window and squinted his eyes trying to make out the dark figure running from the front yard. He walked closer to the window to make sure his eyes were not playing tricks on him. He spread the cream colored blinds apart with his fingers. The figure disappeared like a ghost in thin air.

"Ma, Ma," he screamed at the top of his lungs walking into a jog down the hallway. His eyes searched for any sign of movement.

"Mama, J! Where y'all at?"

He ran down the hall and peered over the staircase. The house was dark except for a stream of light from the bathroom that lit the hall. Bo ran to the bathroom and stuck his head in. "Oh my God!" he yelled in horror. His eyes gazed over in disbelief. Blood discolored the lilac wallpaper and the tile floor. The dolphin covered shower curtain hung half way off of the rail.

He ran down the stairs and stopped midway when he saw two bodies lying on the staircase. He tried to yell for help, but no sound came out his mouth. Bo's long legs skipped stairs as he moved towards the bodies of his cousin and mother. He fell against the brown wallpaper and covered his face. He fell to his knees and pulled the bloody head of his cousin into his chest.

She was a popular girl with her whole life ahead of her. She was an only child and very close to Bo and his mom. J'nae spent the earlier part of her childhood living with her father, but later moved to Ohio to live with her sick mother. She moved in with Nikki and Bo after the death of her mother. She didn't have any enemies that Bo knew of and everybody loved her like their own family.

66

He stroked Nae's long black hair that was tangled and matted with blood and hair grease. "J, wake up baby! C'mon get up!" he cried as he stood and walked down two more stairs and cried out to his mother. "Mama, mama!"

He ran his fingers across the make-up covered scar on his mother's face. The scar was a constant reminder of the hell his father put his mother through. Bo could never forget that night his father sliced his mother's face. He was young, but the images of that night were so vivid he could never forget. Bo wrapped his strong arms around his mother's body and closed her robe.

"Who did this to you, mama? Tell me, who did this to you?" he whispered in her ear. Bo nervously jumped to his feet when he heard a loud knock at the door. His long legs took two leaps and he was at the door. He pointed two EMTs, dressed in matching navy blue outfits, to his mother and J'nae that lay on the stairs.

"They're over there! I couldn't find a pulse and I don't think they're breathing! Please, hurry!" Bo started to panic. His body began to shake uncontrollably.

Not even one minute after the EMTs arrived an army of cops swarmed the oversized front yard of the two-story brick home. Bo knew he was about to be thoroughly interrogated. He also knew it wasn't going to look good for him.

A chiseled cop with blue eyes and blond hair noticed Bo's reaction and approached him. "Sir, are you okay?"

Bo was speechless for a moment. "No. I don't know who could of done this. Is my mom and cousin going to be okay?"

"Well, I can't answer that sir. But, we're going to need to ask you some questions." The officer was suspicious of Bo and kept his eye on him.

It was 5:45 a.m. and the sun was rising in the rural area of Suffolk County, VA. The neighbors gathered in the empty streets like fascinated children and whispered amongst themselves while they watched the cops scurry in and out of the lavish home.

Some of the neighbors speculated about possible motives and others dreamt up wild scenarios about the morning's events. A couple of elderly women with rollers in their hair and mismatched Rocawear jogging suits discussed rumors of embezzlement, prostitution rings, and drugs.

67

Bo watched three cops contain the congregating crowd outside his home. A middle aged, female detective approached him. She was no ordinary detective. She had a coke bottle figure and the face of a model. The woman approached Bo with a sense of urgency in her approach. As she came closer Bo realized he and the woman were already well acquainted. "Izz, what the fuck are you doing here?" Bo questioned in a high-pitched voice.

The detective standing in front of him was one of his friends. Her name was Isabella Cruz and the relationship her and Bo shared was one of sex, sex and more sex. Bo met Isabella at a bar a few months earlier and the two hit it off instantly. She was extremely attractive and the center of attention no matter where she went. Aside from her attractiveness she was one of the toughest homicide detectives in her office. She never divulged her line of work for many different reasons, one being intimidation.

Bo had not talked to her in a few weeks and the very sight of her brought back fond memories of night long sex-a-thons. Isabella grabbed Bo by the arm and pulled him to the side. "Bo, what the hell happened here?"

He looked around to make sure nobody was listening before he continued. "I don't fucking know. What the fuck? You never told me you were a fuckin' cop. I can't believe this shit!"

She took a deep breath, "look, that's not what you need to be thinking about right now. Shit Bo, I know these cops and they don't play. They're out for blood. Just be cool and go along with what I say." Isabella's distinctive Puerto Rican accent became more noticable, "I'm sorry, sir are you okay?" She widened her eyes to signal Bo to go along with her charade.

"No, I'm not. My mom and cousin…" Bo paused while he swallowed his saliva, fighting back his tears. "I saw somebody running from the yard so I got up and went to find my mom and my cousin. When I walked pass the bathroom it was blood everywhere and the mirror was broken. Then I found my mom and cousin on the stairs. They were just laying there…"

Isabella continued with her questioning, "did you hear anything before or after your mom came in the room?"

"No, I didn't hear anything at all. I was out of it. I went out last night and I was drunk, so I had a major hang over. I think I blacked

68

out for a minute."

"What time did you get home?"

Bo hesitated before answering the question, "I think it was like 3:15. I remember because when I got in bed I looked at the clock beside my bed. I can't remember anything after that."

Isabella hands were moving fast as she scribbled in her notepad key points from the conversation. She looked up at Bo with worry in her eyes. "Shit, this doesn't look good Bo. Who were you with?"

"My boy Maleek and some other guys."

"Well," Isabella continued, "I know this isn't the best time, but we're going to need you to come down to the station for further questioning."

Bo looked confused. "Why? I need to go to the hospital with my mom and cousin. Can this wait?"

Bo knew that when the cops got you down to the station it was down hill from there. He had been in trouble before and this wasn't a good sign. Bo knew he was a suspect. He peered into Isabella's dazzling green eyes begging for some sort of help. "Is it really necessary?"

Isabella's eyes stared back. Bo felt like she could see right through to his soul. She leaned in towards him so that only he could hear her. "Bo, I have to take you down for questioning. I promise I'll look out for you. I'll handle as much of this as I can myself. Just be straight forward and honest with me."

Bo sucked his teeth and let out a sigh. "Aight, I trust you man, but just make sure *YOU* handle this. I can't afford to do any more time." Bo was for the most part a straightforward guy, but got in some trouble the year before. He was arrested for driving under the influence, possession of cocaine and reckless endangerment. He did six months in jail and paid a hefty fine of $15,000 for damaging a city lamppost that he slammed into while he was intoxicated.

Isabella continued to play the part and finished with her typical cop spiel. "I'm really sorry. I know this is difficult Mr. Rodriguez, but I have to ask you to come with me, since you're the only witness to the crime. You can go directly to the hospital after we are finished." Isabella led Bo to the police car. Her busty chest brushed against his arm when she opened the back door and assisted him into

69

the car.

The paramedics left for the hospital and the crowd outside in the streets began to dwindle. The only thing remaining was the yellow crime scene tape around the house and a few cop cars. Bo's eyes surveyed the area around the home. He saw a couple of cops taking the last pictures of the scene and collecting evidence. *What now?* He thought to himself.

CHAPTER IX

"Damn, how much longer is this shit goin' to take?" Bo was irritated and ready to go. It was almost an hour and a half since the police brought him in for questioning. The interrogation room was extremely cold and Bo fidgeted trying to make himself comfortable in the small, wobbly wooden chair.

"I can't believe this b.s. Y'all got me in here on some made up shit and you should be out there looking for my mom and cousin's attacker."

The two detectives in the room refused to entertain Bo's comments. "It'll just be one more moment. We just want to clear up a some things," one of the detectives responded. The detective was short and stout. The sleeves of his white shirt were rolled up to his elbows and his black pants touched the ground when he walked. The other detective was slightly taller with a slimmer build. He seemed to be the more coordinated of the two in dress and stance.

"Mr. Rodriguez," the stout detective belted. "You were the only one in the home that wasn't attacked. Yet you said you didn't hear anything. That sounds a little odd. Maybe this was a drug deal gone wrong. We know all about your priors." The officer took a quick look at his partner as to say, *we got this muthafucka now.*

Bo stared at the detective with anger in his eyes. "What? I told y'all muthafu--," he put his head down and took a deep breath. He was very temperamental and his attitude wasn't helping the situation. "Look, I told Officer Cruz everything I know. Now, I know my rights.

I'm not under arrest so you need to let me go before I sue you doughnut eating bastards for false arrest."

The detectives looked at each other and knew he was right, but they knew it was more to the story, but they didn't have enough evidence to hold him. The detectives signaled for Bo to leave. Bo gritted on the detectives and mumbled, *fuck y'all,* under his breath before leaving the small, musty interrogation room.

His long fingers pressed the elevator button impatiently. He turned to his left and saw Isabella walking towards him. The elevator door opened, but Bo waited for her to come within speaking distance. "Hi, Officer Cruz, right?" Bo pretended like they didn't know each other.

"That's correct. Are you on your way to the hospital now?" she played along. They didn't want anybody to figure out their history. Isabella would be pulled off the case and an investigation launched immediately into her actions.

"Yes, I am. My boy is waiting for me in the lobby. Are you going down?"

"I am actually." Isabella's curvaceous body bumped the already lit elevator button in a flirtatious attempt to hold Bo's attention. The chemistry between the two was undeniable. When the doors opened Isabella stepped on the elevator and smiled at the young lady with flowing blond hair that was standing in the corner of the elevator. Bo followed suit and gave a 'what's up' head nod to the same woman.

The ride from the 3rd floor to the lobby seemed like an eternity. Bo was speechless. He felt like a love struck kid. The elevator doors opened and Isabella's stunning eyes locked with Bo's saying, "follow me." The lobby was a sea of confusion and Isabella's perfectly fit Arden B jeans made it hard for Bo to concentrate. His eyes scanned the lobby, but like a ghost she was gone.

"Ay, B!" a familiar voice yelled from across the room. "B ova here."

Bo turned around and saw the worried face of his best friend, Maleek Johnson. Maleek was thirteen years older than Bo and a few years younger than Nikki. They were introduced to each other by a mutual friend and hit it off right away even though there was a noticeable age difference. Maleek kept Bo out of trouble; something nobody ever did for him. Maleek lived a tough life and experienced

71

more than Bo ever would, so he felt it was his duty to guide Bo.

Maleek was raised by the streets and gained street creds by fuckin' niggas up and runnin' one of the tightest drug ops in the area. Maleek was a good dude, but something about him wasn't quite right, but that didn't bother Bo. Whenever he needed anything Maleek was there, no questions asked.

Maleek was frantic, "yo man, what the fuck happened? Is moms okay? What about Nae?" Maleek's deep voice remained smooth even through his worry. His muscular body parted the sea of confusion like Moses did the Red Sea. His flawless dark chocolate face wrinkled in disgust from the horrific news. Not only was Bo a friend, but more like family.

Bo could tell by the desperation in Maleek's eyes that he searched for an answer. Bo did not want to upset him anymore so he gave an assurance that they were alright. "Calm down, I'm sure they're fine. Just get me to the hospital and I'll explain everything I know in the car."

The two walked outside to see a rainbow stretched across the sky. The sun was beginning to peek through the clouds. The rainbow was the only beautiful thing in Bo's day. They ran across the street to the public parking garage and walked up two flights of stars. Maleek pressed the alarm button to deactivate the alarm on his car before unlocking it. Two packages were in the seat with a detailed invoice attached. "Just put that stuff in the back. I was on my way to do a drop when you called." Maleek told Bo.

"Man, I'm sorry. It's been a crazy morning. I don't know what the fuck is goin' on. Mom woke me up talkin' 'bout call the police and next thing I know, I find them laid out on the stairs." Bo exhaled a deep breath. "Blood was everywhere, man. I saw somebody run out the yard and then I found mom and J on the stairs. I broke down. I swear they're my life." His eyes began to swell with tears.

Maleek was at a loss for words. "It's okay man. We goin' to find the niggas that did this shit and handle our business. First we gotta make sure moms and Nae okay." Maleek made a sharp turn into the hospital's parking lot. He pulled into a space a few hundred feet from the hospital entrance.

"Yo, B. You know where dey at?" Maleek questioned as if Bo had already been to the hospital.

72

Bo didn't respond. He blocked out everything around him. His focus was on his mom and cousin.

An elderly woman dressed in a pink and white candy stripper outfit was seated behind the information desk. She occupied herself by rearranging papers and folders on the counter.

"Excuse me." Bo interrupted politely. The woman behind the counter stopped shuffling papers and looked up at Bo and Maleek like they were disturbing her.

"Yes, may I help you gentleman?"

They could tell the woman was irritated, but it was not the time or the place to give her a piece of their minds.

"Yeah, we're looking for my mother, Nikki Rodriguez and my cousin J'nae Strong. They came in about two hours ago. They were bought to the ER by ambulance."

"Let me check to see if we have any newly admitted patients."

A pair of eyeglasses dangled around the woman's neck like a necklace. She placed the eyeglasses on the bridge of her nose before she slowly typed information into a computer, occasionally peering over the eyeglasses. She spoke in a sluggish manner when addressing the men.

"What are the last names of the patients?"

Bo and Maleek were getting more irritated by the woman's slow speech manner. "Strong and Rodriguez. Now, can you please tell me where the hell they are?"

The candy stripper's cloudy eyes rolled to the back of her head. She waited a minute before pointing the two towards the ER, her voice dragging, "go down this hall make a right, at the second set of elevators turn left and go straight back. The ER should be able to give you more information."

Before she finished her sentence Bo and Maleek were half way down the hall. The ER was like a ghost town. A pretty black woman with short colorful hair sat in a chair restless. Bo always wondered why people were in the ER, especially younger woman. It made him think they had infections or STDs something embarrassing that they did not want anybody else to know about. Bo made a mental note not to talk to her if he ever saw her on the streets and approached the lady behind the desk in the ER. "Yeah, I'm looking for my mom and cousin they were admitted about two hours ago."

73

The middle aged white lady dressed in a red and blue-stripped shirt looked up at the two men. In her mind they were two black thugs out of the hood. "Yyyyees. Two wommmen were admitted a littttlllle while ago. Thhhey went to suuurrggery. Theyyy should bbbeee in ICU by nnnow. Go up to the 3rd floor," she stuttered.

Bo and Maleek smirked at each other. As soon as they were out of sight they burst out laughing, anything to lighten the mood.

"B, that bitch sounded like Elmer Fudd." Maleek laughed.

Bo followed suit, "Ba-de-ba-de-ba-de, that's all folks!"

Maleek pressed the elevator button impatiently. He looked at the time on his $25,000 Citizens watch. It was 8:23 a.m.

Bo and Maleek's mood changed from light-hearted to serious when they reached the 3rd the floor. Maleek approached the receptionist seated at the information desk.

"Ms., where is Ms. Strong and Ms. Rodriguez?" he asked sternly. Maleek was the type of nigga that demanded respect. He had an air of authority about him.

The young lady that looked to be no older than 18 years old smiled at him and looked down at the piece of paper in front of her.

"Well, first I need to know, who you are?" she flirted.

Maleek smiled back. "I'm her son Maleek and this is my brother Bo."

"In that case, room 311," she replied grinning from ear to ear.

Bo walked to the room. When he entered the room a woman dressed in a yellow halter sundress was holding his mother's hand.

"A.C." Bo was shocked. He hadn't seen her in over a year. Christine turned around startled.

"Hey, Bo." Her eyes were blood shot red. She held out her arms and hugged Bo tightly. She gave him a kiss on the cheek and released her toned arms from his tiny waist.

Bo continued to speak in a shaky voice, "how did you know? Where have you been?" His heart was full of questions.

"I got a strange phone call from somebody calling from a private number telling me Nik was in the hospital. Then they hung up."

Bo's eyes watered. He moved closer to the bedside of his mother. Her head was wrapped in white bandages that were soaked with her blood. He softly touched the side of her face with his hand. He turned his head towards the door as Maleek entered.

74

"Yo man, uhhh, I just talked to the doctor and Nae still in the operating room. She got it bad and they don't know if she gone make it." Maleek looked at Christine in confusion, trying to make out her face and name.

"Leek, you remember Christine, my mom's best friend. My surrogate aunt."

Maleek eyes grew big, "oh yeah, I remember you now. I thought you looked familiar. How you been?"

Christine gave Maleek a quick smile. "I've been better. In times like this you can only call on the Lord."

Bo looked at his mother in silence and then lifted his head towards the ceiling, saying a silent prayer. Maleek walked over to the bed and rested his hand on Bo's shoulder slightly touching Christine's hand.

"Man what am I gonna do?" Bo was lost and didn't know which way to turn. His only family now was Maleek and Christine and he didn't know how long she would be around. He lost touch with most of his family long before they moved from Cincinnati to Suffolk County.

Maleek didn't know what to say. "I'm here for ya homie. Anything you need, I got you. If you don't wanna stay at your crib you can crash at my place, Monique won't mind."

The room fell silent except for the occasional beep from the monitor attached to Nikki.

"Excuse me," a deep voice bellowed. "Are you family of the patient?"

The three turned towards the door. A doctor in a white coat with grey hair and black-framed glasses stood in the doorway.

"Hi, docta. I'm Bo her son and this is my aunt and my brother. How is she? How's my cousin. I want to see her. Where is she?"

The doctor knew family members always asked a million questions he could not answer. He paused before he began to speak, "well, first off I'm Dr. Green. Your mother is in critical condition. We have to monitor her at all times. The blows she suffered to the head damaged the frontal lobes in her brain. We won't know the severity of the damage for sure until we get the test results back. As for the young lady that came in with her,"

Bo interrupted the doctor. "Yes, my cousin, J'nae. How is

75

she?"

The doctor continued, "she is in a deep coma. We don't know if she is going to make it. I wish I had better news for all of you. I'm sorry." The doctor turned to exit the room but Bo stopped him.

"Wait, where is she? Can I see her?"

The doctor was hesitant. "Yes, but only one visitor at a time and you can not stay more than 30 minutes at a time due to her condition. We are still heavily monitoring her every five to ten minutes. If her condition improves in the next day or two we will move her to a different room. For now she is on the 5th floor, room 524."

As soon as the doctor left Bo began to break down. He blamed himself for not hearing anything in the house. He blamed himself for staying out the night before and partying. He could not bare the thought of losing his mother or his cousin. Christine and Maleek hung their heads down in silence as they all prayed for Nikki and J'nae's recovery.

The long silence in the room turned awkward. Christine and Maleek tried hard not to look at each other, but it was hard for them not to. Maleek was a fine ass brother whose sex appeal bounced off of him immediately and caught the attention of any woman within an inch of him. He was the type of man a woman could smell minutes before he entered the room. It wasn't an overpowering Old Spice smell, but a damn that brother smell good, I want to fuck, Aphrodisiac type of smell. And Christine was intrigued, even with her best friend lying battered and bruised in a hospital bed.

Maleek couldn't stop staring at her either, but it wasn't a strong sexual attraction. Christine was pretty, but he had other things on his mind. Bo noticed the two playing peek-a-boo, but he thought nothing of it. He was use to females literally throwing themselves on Maleek and just figured Christine was about to become another M-groupie.

Bo kissed his mother on the forehead and squeezed her hand. "C'mon ma, fight! I need you, Nae needs you!" A tear fell from Bo's eye and wet Nikki's cheek. He embraced his mother and silently cried to himself.

Maleek's cell phone vibrated in his pocket. He glanced at the number and walked away from Bo. "Yo, it's done," Maleek barked.

"So, you got my shit, right?" the unknown voice responded.

"I'll let you know by tomorrow. I'll be in Cali in three days,

76

then we done." Maleek shot back.

"Look bitch, don't play games! I want my money and my shit. Two days, muthafucka, two days."

The phone call disconnected.

Bo sat on a bench outside the hospital staring at a little girl in a pink and white ruffled dress. He reminisced about when he and J'nae were young children playing together in the park. His last words to her were harsh. He called her a stupid ass ho and said he hoped she caught AIDs from the trifflin' ass niggas she was fuckin' wit. He wished he could relive the entire day over and change everything that happened. He placed his head in the palm of his hands and leaned forward rocking back and forth. The scorching sun set his back on fire, but no pain could be worse than what he was feeling at that moment.

A gentle hand touched his shoulder. "Are you okay Bo Bear?" A soft voice murmured in his ear.

Bo lifted his head. His eyes were blood shot red like he smoked some killa Ganja.

"Hey AC," he said addressing his Aunt Christine. "I'm cool. Just so much goin' on right now, I can't think clearly. Who would want to hurt my mom and Nae?"

He started to cry again. Christine pulled Bo's head toward her body resting it right below her navel. Bo felt like a little kid again. Whenever he didn't feel well or had a problem Christine would comfort him in the same way. She always smelled of a pleasant scent that reminded him of Honey Dew and she still smelled the same. Christine lowered her head and placed her forehead on Bo's wavy hair. "Your mother is like a sister to me. I don't know who or where that phone call came from, but in a way I thank God or else I wouldn't have known what happened."

Maleek walked back over to the bench where Bo was sitting. "Y'all aight?"

Bo and Christine turned towards Maleek. They both gave him a quick head nod. Bo stood up releasing Christine hands from his head.

He looked at Christine with a puzzled look. Many questions popped in his head.

He glanced at Maleek, "yo man, let's go. I gotta clear my head."

Bo and Maleek walked away leaving Christine standing in the same spot. She watched from afar as Bo and Maleek disappeared into the pool of cars in the hospital parking lot.

Once in the car Maleek began to ask questions, "how is Nae doin'? Is she goin' to be aight? Was she woke? Talk to me man, tell me somethin'."

Bo didn't say anything. He stared out the window at the shabby houses they passed along Main St. His mind wandered while his spirit dwindled. He was not in the mood to answer any questions. All he knew was that he was the only suspect and his mother and cousin were in critical condition.

Bo turned up the radio to let Maleek know he didn't feel like talking. His lean body sunk low in the seat. His eyes became heavy and he slowly drifted to sleep. The morning's events drained him and his hangover was still not completely gone. Bo's head pounded. He felt like a Mac truck had hit him. No matter how hard he tried he couldn't relax.

The images of Nikki and J'nae played over and over in Bo;s head. Maleek couldn't help but to notice his friend's fidgeting. He knew how worried Bo was about his mother and cousin and he wanted to help him relax any way he could.

Maleek felt partially responsible for the position Bo was in. After all, it was his suggestion that all of them go out to the bar. He told Bo he wanted to celebrate life because it was too short. Bo didn't like getting fucked up because he had gotten into trouble before and he wanted to stay clean. Bo had some issues that he kept secret and he wanted them to stay that way, but that night Bo agreed with Maleek, like was too short!

CHAPTER X

Maleek's phone vibrated in his pocket again. He pulled the phone out and adjusted the volume on the radio. He was hesitant about answering the call because it was from a private number. He changed his number twice that year because crazy ass chicks would call and either hang up or start some shit and Maleek wasn't in the mood for games.

"Who the fuck is this?" he answered frustratingly.

"Hey bey it's me." It was a familiar voice, one Maleek didn't mind hearing. A smile stretched across his face when he heard her voice.

"What's up baby?" Maleek glimpsed at Bo to make sure he was sleep. "Ya know I haven't forgotten 'bout you. I can't wait to see you later. You gone let me tap that ass real good. I gotta make up for loss time. We handled the bu'ness now it's time for the pleasure." Maleek had a sexy phone voice and body for that matter that could make any woman cream in her Vickie's panties.

The female chuckled in delight, "umm, of course, but you got to do that trick you do too and don't act like you don't know what I'm talkin' 'bout, punk."

"I got you, but look I'ma hit you back. Gimme an hour or so. Make sure you wearin' sumum sexy for daddy, aight, one." Maleek ended the call and placed his phone in the cup holder. He glimpsed over at Bo again who was fast asleep.

He crossed over two lanes and hugged the curve of the exit. He swung the car into the small parking lot of "Majic City." It was 5:30 in the evening and the parking lot was overflowing with oversized SUVs and compact luxury cars. "Majic City" was infamous for the strippers with the biggest asses, best dances and other services Maleek

benefite

79

d from on a regular.

He pulled the car around to the back employee entrance of the club. Maleek was VIP and carried privileges other patrons didn't because of the amount of money he spent in the club. Not to mention the investment he made into the club. He had access to free drinks, dances and whatever and whoever he liked 24/7.

"Bo, Bo. Wake up man," he gave Bo a slight nudge to wake him up.

Bo sat up in his seat. He frowned his face, than glanced out the tinted window. "Majic City man, really. You gotta be fuckin' kiddin' me. I just wanna go home man. I need to clear my head and I don't feel like bein' bothered wit no fishy pussy ass bitches." he grunted.

"I'm tryin' to get yo mind off shit. You don't need to be in the house by yoself. Plus you stayin' wit me and Mo and I damn show don't feel like goin' home to her naggin' ass yet," Maleek opened his door and gave Bo one last look, "you comin?"

Bo let out a breath of aggravation. "Shit!" He mumbled to himself before stepping out of the car. Bo had more serious things to worry about and didn't understand why Maleek wasn't as worried as him. Seeing naked women wasn't going to make him feel any better. They walked through the steel back door that led to a small kitchen.

Maleek was pleasantly greeted when he entered the club. "Maleek, my man. What's up witcha?" A tall light skinned man grinned with a giant smile that showed his yellow, jagged teeth.

"Chillin', Chillin'. Aye, where Stacey? She workin' tonight right?"

Maleek peered through a glass window on a door leading into the main lobby and dance area. The lobby was packed with screaming men and a few dykes that were throwing money to three naked women on stage popping their pussies. One of the women was lying on her back letting a drunk dyke lick her twat. He glanced over his shoulder awaiting an answer from the balding man.

"Yea. Her fine ass should be in the back," he replied.

Maleek gave Bo a head nod to signal him to follow. They walked through a narrow hallway leading to a brown wooden door. Maleek tapped on the door twice before he peeped his head in.

"Stace, you back here girl?"

A brown complexion female that stood 5'2 with a body Halle

80

Berry would kill for walked around the corner. Ironically, Stacey resembled a more youthful Stacey Dash.

The see-through short grey robe she was wearing hardly came past her waist and showed the matching pair of thong underwear that accentuated her round basketball ass. Maleek could see her hardened dark brown nipples through the robe.

"Oh my God," she ran to Maleek with open arms and embraced him like she hadn't seen him in years not paying attention to Bo.

"Baby, where have you been? I haven't head from you in weeks!"

Maleek was flattered by Stacey's reaction. She could pull any nigga she wanted, but she was in love with him. He gently pushed her back drawing attention to Bo. Stacey was not at all shy about showing her body to strangers. After all it was her job.

"Baby, this is my boy Bo. He's had a very rough day. He needs to get his mind off some things. Can you take care of him while I handle some business up front?" Maleek looked at Bo and grinned. Bo didn't know what Maleek was up to.

Stacey turned to Bo and studied him. "Sure L, anything for you plus he's a cutie. I'll take real good care of him." Stacey remarked coyly. Maleek headed back down the hall, "not too good, I hope," he yelled jokingly.

Stacey took Bo by the hand and walked him through a beaded curtain to a secluded room. He took note of his surroundings remembering every detail. In the room was a small bed with two shelves above the bed aligned with various oils and lotions. In the corner was a lamp in the shape of a naked woman.

Stacey smiled at Bo, "don't be scared baby, I promise to make you forget all about your problems, at least for the next hour." She pushed Bo on to the bed and climbed on top of him, her reddish black hair hanging over her shoulder. She pressed her firm D breasts against his rippling six-pack. Bo started to squirm, uneasy with what was going on. He was not comfortable with tricks, no matter how pretty they were.

He laid on the bed and relaxed. She pulled down his jogging pants and pulled his dick through the hole in his boxer shorts. His body jerked when he felt a warm wet feeling against his dick. Bo tilted his

81

head to inspect what was happening. He dropped his head and closed his eyes as Stacey's mouth moved up and down his thick nine and a half inch dick. He placed his left hand on the back of her head to guide her motions.

Bo blocked out the external sounds coming from the front of the bar and focused on the slurping and moaning sounds Stacey was making. He was trying hard to contain himself.

"Is it good baby?" Stacey asked tilting her head up to peep at Bo.

He didn't answer. He did not want her to think she had control even though the truth was she did. His anticipation continued to grow with every slurp and burp. Bo was at his peak when a slamming door interrupted them.

"Yo, we gotta roll, now!" Maleek's silhouette outlined the beaded curtain. His muscular shadow overpowered Bo and Stacey.

They jumped up stunned at the brazen interruption. Bo pulled his jogging pants up quickly leaving a small wet spot in the front of his crotch.

"Damn Leek, can't a brotha get his nut off," he grunted showing a hint of annoyance.

"Another time B, we gotta get the hell outta here, now!"
Maleek turned and sprinted out the back room.

Bo looked at Stacey and smiled, "I'll catch up with you later." He turned and exited the room. Bo heard a lot of commotion coming from the front of the club as he walked down the hallway.
"Bo bring yo ass!" Maleek yelled from the back door of the club.

Bo hurried to the back door. In the corner of his eye he could see two men coming through the kitchen with guns. Bo opened the car door and Maleek pulled off with Bo's feet dragging on the gravel. He turned to Maleek in confusion and disbelief, "man, what the fuck?"

Maleek turned his head towards Bo with rage in his eyes. Bo saw the same look in his eyes only one other time. Maleek had the same look in his eye when he discovered someone stole his stash and half a million in cash. The stolen stash belonged to Jungle, the notorious Kingpin and Maleek faced the consequences like a man. Since than he was never the same. He never spoke a word of what happened, but he vowed to kill the muthafucka that set him up.

Bo glanced at Maleek and kept quiet.

82

Maleek was driving crazy and swerving all over the road. "Dem niggas ripped me off, so I got dem niggas back!" Maleek grunted. Maleek pulled a wad of cash out of his pocket, all hundred-dollar bills.

Bo's eyes grew big. "Shit Leek! What the hell did you do? You robbed dem niggas?"

"Hell yea! Dem stick up kids got stuck! What goes around comes around my nig."

Bo's cell phone rang. He flipped it open to screen the call before he answered. "757-934-4000." He mumbled to himself. "Hello," he raised his voice in frustration.

A soft voice responded to Bo's irritation, "Hello, this is Nurse Jones from Obici Hospital. May I speak with Boston Rodriguez?"

Bo's attitude instantly went from frustrated to worried. "Hi, nurse. I'm sorry you caught me off guard. Do you have any news for me?"

"Well, the doctor would like to see you. I know you left a few hours ago, but we need you to come back in as soon as possible. There have been some developments in your mother's health."

Bo looked at Maleek out the corner of his eyes. "Yes, I'll be there as soon as I can. Thank you nurse, goodbye." Bo hung up the cell phone and looked at Maleek with a little fear. Maleek was doing 110 down a dark narrow road.

"What up homie? What dey say?" Maleek questioned never once taking his eyes off the road.

"Uh, they want me to come back up to the hospital. I told 'em I'd be there as soon as I could."

"Cool, Cool. I need to drop dis money and package off at the crib and pick sumum up. Then I'll drop you off." Maleek continued driving erratically until he reached his mini mansion hidden in a cut down a long driveway. "Wait here," Maleek cautioned, "I'll be right back."

83

CHAPTER XI

Bo approached the nurse's station nervously not knowing what news he was going to receive. "Hi, I'm looking for Dr. Green. His nurse called and said they had news about my mother and cousin, Nikki Rodriguez and J'nae Strong."

An elderly woman dressed in a pink and white candy stripper suit stared at Bo. "My goodness young man, has anybody ever told you that you look like that actor…um what's his name, I can't think of his name…"

Bo looked at the woman with aggravation, "yea, yea Boris Kudjoe. Now can you tell me where I find the doctor?"

"Oh yes, I'm sorry. I'll page him for you."

Bo waited patiently at the nurse's station for the doctor. Three minutes passed and it seemed like an eternity. "Nurse, can you page the doctor again?"

"I'm sorry, but he is on his rounds. He will be with you as soon as he can."

Bo rolled his eyes, "well is it okay if I go to my mother's room. He can meet me in there."

The nurse glanced at a chart on the desk, "Mr. Rodriguez, I think you should wait here. It'll just be a couple more minutes."

Bo looked at the time. It was quarter after eight in the evening. He sighed loudly so the nurses at the station would be aware of his growing impatience. He reached into his pocket and pulled out his cell phone. The screen read private number; he ignored the call and focused his attention on the doctor walking towards him.

"Hey Dr. Green," Bo called as the doctor approached. The doctor peered over his thin-framed Polo glasses. "Dr. Green, Nurse Jones

84

called and told me you had some news about my mom and cousin."

The doctor placed his clipboard by his side and removed his glasses.

"Yes, Mr…"

"Rodriguez," the two said simultaneously.

The doctor continued speaking, "please, step into my office," He guided Bo into a large office. The room was uninviting and smelled of Bengay. Bo took a seat on a small couch in front of a large window with a panoramic view of the parking lot.

"It seems that over the course of the past two hours there have been some complications with your mother. Out of nowhere her vitals started to fail without warning and we weren't able to save her. I'm sorry Mr. Rodriguez, but your mother passed about 30 minutes ago."

Bo's eyes began to tear. "What do you mean? I thought y'all were monitoring her frequently! What the hell happened? And what about my cousin, J'nae," he sobbed with a mouth full of saliva. "Is she okay? What about her condition?"

Dr. Green stood in front of his sturdy oak desk staring helplessly at Bo. Telling family members their loved ones passed was the worst part of being a doctor and he hated it. "Mr. Rodriguez, I know how difficult…"

Bo interrupted, "No you don't know how difficult this is! I need some answers."

"Mr. Rodriguez, I hate to make this more difficult than it has to be, but there is something I need to ask you. Did your mother use any type of drugs or narcotics?"

Bo was caught off guard by the question. As far as he was concerned his mother was trustworthy and honest and broke her back to provide for her family.

"What," he questioned raising the octave of his voice. "What kind of question is that? You think my mom was a junkie. I don't believe this shit." Bo's attitude began to change dramatically. Anybody within earshot could hear his ranting.

Dr. Green closed the door to his office so that Bo would not disturb others. "Mr. Rodriguez, please calm down. The reason I'm asking is because we found traces of various drugs in her system. The tests we ran did not pick it up until her system started to fail; it was very unusual."

85

"To answer your question, no my mother didn't use drugs. So, what are you saying? Do you think somebody could have killed her?"

The doctor paused, "right now Mr. Rodriguez, I can't say with certainty, but it looks that way. I've taken the liberty of notifying the proper authorities."

"Proper authorities?" Bo's worries intensified. He took a deep breath. "The cops are already breathing down my back Dr. Green and now this shit. Unfucking believable! And what about my cousin, J'nae? Is she okay? If somebody did this to my mother, they'll do it to her."

Bo's face curled and he started to cry. He fell to his knees in despair. Dr. Green helped Bo back to his feet. He escorted him down the hall to the elevator. As they were about to step into the elevator Bo heard a familiar voice.

"I want around the clock protection on that room. No visitors." It was Isabella Cruz. Their eyes met and Isabella cracked a slight grin. "Mr. Rodriguez, it's nice to see you again. Have you been briefed on the updates of the case?"

Bo's emotions were all over the place. "What that somebody murdered my mother? Yes, I'm fully aware," he answered sarcastically with anger in his voice. "What the hell is it now? Is it Nae? Is she alright?"

Isabella looked at the officer to her left. "Mr. Rodriguez, we believe that whoever did this to your mother may be after your cousin as well. We think it may have something to do with her business dealings. Are you aware of your mother's standings with her company."

Bo was confused. "I'm not sure what the hell you're talking about."

"I think you need to come with us."

Through the hospital doors he could see detectives and uniformed cops going in and out of ICU.

"Wait a minute," Bo demanded. "Can I see my cousin?"

Isabella looked at Dr. Green who gave a slight head nod signaling it was okay.

"Alright Mr. Rodriguez, follow me. I'll give you ten minutes then you need to come with us down to the station."

Bo waited patiently as Isabella spoke with another detective in private.

86

"Come with me, Mr. Rodriguez."

Isabella escorted Bo down the hall to J'nae's room where three uniformed cops stood outside the room talking amongst themselves. Bo entered the room. He didn't know what to expect.

He whispered in her ear. *I'm sorry lil' cuz. I didn't mean anything I said to you. I'll always be here for you. I love you.* Bo gave his cousin a kiss on the forehead, his platinum Jesus piece dangled over her chest. He gently squeezed her hand and glanced over her battered body. He sat beside her bedside and held her hand the entire time.

"We have to go now." Isabella said in a low tone.

On the way to the lobby Isabella questioned Bo about his mother's company.

"Bo," she started in a comforting tone. "I know you're grieving right now, but I need to ask you off the record what you know about your mother's company. I need you to be very honest if you want me to help you. Right now, you're the only suspect and it's not looking good. They want to bring you in on murder charges."

Bo paused before speaking. He wanted to help Isabella find his mother's killer. He trusted her to keep any information he told her confidential. "Shit. I don't really know anything. You have to believe me Izzy," he paused. "She got a loan for $250,000 from a bank and she was always in and out of town meeting with people. I didn't ask her too much about the business and she never volunteered any information."

"What bank did she get a loan through?"

Bo looked into Isabella's gorgeous eyes that hypnotized him. "I'm not sure. I think Bank of America."

"Okay. Do you know who she went to see when she went out of town?"

"I don't know anything else. I'm sorry."

Isabella thought to herself there was more to the story, but she kept quiet. She knew when the time was right Bo would open up.

"Are you sure you don't know anything else?"

Bo stared at Isabella for a minute.

"I'm sure. Why all the questions all of a sudden?"

Isabella paused for a second. She didn't know whether or not to tell Bo about the specifics of the case. She began to explain slowly. "Bo, I need you to keep this information strictly between me and you. Because of the sensitivity of this case you can't tell anybody what I'm

87

about to tell you. I could lose my job and you could be in danger." She warned.

"Okay." Bo assured her.

"Alright," she started. "We believe your mother was caught up in some type of drug situation. At some time this afternoon somebody slipped into your mother's room and injected her IV with a large quantity of drugs. We believe a high dosage of Meperidine or Fentanyl, maybe even both."

Bo was stunned. "What? Where is all this coming from?"

Isabella continued. "I can't discuss all that right now, but I can tell you that drugs are part of the reason she moved away from Cincinnati. And were you aware your mother paid for the house in full *WITH CASH*. As the case develops I will inform you on what I find out. I promise."

He began thinking about the night everything went down with Fatz. He knew Fatz had money, but he didn't know how much. It damn sure wasn't enough to pay off their house in full. His mother warned him, "The less you know, the better." He wondered, *is there a connection?*

CHAPTER XII

"Hey baby, I've been waitin' for you," a soft voice whispered from the corner of the dark room. "What took you so long?"

Maleek eyes scanned the apple-scented living room. He spotted the silhouette of a coke bottle figure lounged across a chaise. Maleek cracked a slight smile as he walked through the dark, breathing in the delightful aroma every step of the way.

"Why you ova there in da dark?"

A giggle filled the quiet air, "I got a gift for you, daddy. Are you ready to unwrap it?"

"Of course I am," Maleek leaned over the silhouette and began to kiss the female. His hand slid up her naked leg and between her thighs while his fingers slowly penetrated her wet twat.

"Uhmmm, L baby, you know what I like," she purred with delight. She felt the warm feeling of Maleek's thick lips on her throbbing pussy while his fingers moved in and out. Her body moved with the rhythm of his fingers and her back arched with excitement. He gently sucked on her pussy lips while licking her clit. The sounds of him licking and sucking grew her anticipation. He removed his fingers and brushed them against her lips. She sucked on his fingers trying to hold her climax, but she couldn't. She burst like a damn leaving her passion in, around, and on his mouth.

He unzipped his dark denim Coogi jeans and pulled out his thick dick. He teased her, rubbing his dick against her pussy. He put the tip in and then quickly withdrew until she grabbed a hold of him and forced his dick in her. Their bodies moved together in unison. Her body began to grow with anticipation once again. She pushed his heavy body off of her and turned on her stomach. She moaned fiercely when he pushed his way into her ass. Both of them moaned as they reached their

89

climax together.

"Baby that was great! You got me again in about fifteen minutes?"

Maleek looked into the eyes of the gorgeous woman in front of him. "I got you, but Mo been blowin' my phone up so it's gotta be quick."

A look of disappointment showed on her face. "Anything's betta den nuttin', I guess. Ohhhh, I got another surprise for you. Close your eyes and hold out your hands."

Maleek wasn't big on surprises. The kidnapping made him very cautious and more paranoid than ever. He trusted nobody, not even his wife or son who was only four-years-old. Maleek closed his eyes and held out his hands as instructed. His manhood automatically stood at attention again. He felt a tingling sensation go up his spine. She placed a thick wad of cash in his hand. Money was the one thing that gave him instant gratification. His eyes almost popped out of his head.

"Oh my fucking God. I thought yo ass won't gon' come through. Where the fuck did you get this? I thought fo sho I was out back.

"Baby, you know I always got yo back. I have my ways, just like you." She replied eager to satisfy any of Maleek's requests.

"Chris baby, I love you!"

She smiled. Nothing made her feel better than those three words coming from Maleek's mouth. "Don't go sayin' things you don't mean," she demanded sternly.

Maleek leaned over and gave her a wet, passionate kiss before sliding his hard thick dick into her moist twat again. This time Chris could feel all the passion he was holding back. She wished that every moment with him could be that way. The one thing she wanted in her life was Maleek, but his wife, Monique was the only thing keeping them apart. Maleek's naked body pushed against hers. He wrapped his strong arms around her waist, holding her.

"Are you aight?" Maleek asked with compassion. "Wit everything that went down today, I thought you may be a lil fucked up."

Chris closed her eyes and a tear fell. She looked at Maleek before a stream of tears fell. Her arms stretched out to him silently asking him to embrace her.

"I can't believe this shit, L. It's so much going on. I don't know if I can handle it. I mean, I hate to see Bo this way and now---," Chris paused to swallow her mouth full of saliva. "Now, where do we go?" Maleek could tell the crushing chain of events devastated her.

"Ssshhhhh, it's okay. Everything is over now baby. I'm here for you. You gotta keep it together for me and Bo." Chris nodded in agreement, her eyes reddened from crying. Maleek continued to reassure her. "Look baby, I'ma take care of e'vry thing from here. Jus be cool, be quiet." He put on his clothes and stared into her eyes before giving her a quick kiss on the lips. "I gotta go. I'll call you lata." Maleek stuffed the cash in his money clip and hurried out the door.

Chris fell back, her naked body spread across the couch. The sounds off R. Kelly's, "Gigolo," blasted from her cell phone and startled her briefly.

"Hello?" Chris sniffled as she wiped her eyes.

"Hey," a familiar voice started. "I needa ride to the crib?"

"What's wrong Bo?" Chris asked while peering out the hotel window. She could hear the sadness and frustration in his voice.

"She's gone, Chris! My mom is gone and the cops got me down here at the station. They won't let me see Nae either. Anyway, can you pick me up from the station? I need to get some rest before I start making arrangements for my mom."

"Oh my God!" Chris cried in shock. "What in the hell happened? Bo, baby I'll be there as fast as I can. Stay put. I'll be right there." She threw on her clothes and headed out the door. *Shit, I gotta call L,* she thought to herself. She flipped her cell open and dialed Maleek's number. Rick Ross' "Everyday I'm Hustlin," played while she waited for Maleek to pick up. The ring back played over and over until Maleek's voicemail picked up.

"L, it's me! Nik's gone baby! Call me back! I'm headed to the station to pick up Bo. Call me back!" Chris prayed that Maleek would get the message and call her back before she reached the station. She hoped that she would pass him on her way. She started to think about everything that happened. She thought about the times her and Nikki shared in Cincinnati and all they went through together. She lost her best friend, her confidant and her lover.

Nikki and Chris were friends for a long time. They met on the streets after Nikki's husband threw her out and left her with nothing. She was a virgin to the street life and didn't know how to survive without a man or money. Chris befriended her and taught her the codes of the streets. They were like sisters and shared everything. Eventually, their relationship grew to another level one summer night.

Chris reminisced about the night her and Nikki first became intimate. *Nikki stepped out of the shower and dried her perfectly shaped body. She took a look at herself in the full-length mirror hanging on the back of the bathroom door. She wrapped her body in a soft Egyptian towel and walked in the living room where Chris was lying on an overstuffed couch.*

"Chris, do you mind putting some lotion on my back. I can't reach back there." Nikki dropped her towel and handed Chris a bottle of Bath & Bodyworks Japanese Blossom scented lotion.

Chris stared at Nikki's shapely body. She had never been attracted to another woman before, but something about Nikki standing there butt naked with her plump ass made her pussy throb. Nikki lay on the couch as Chris started to rub her back with the lotion. Nikki's back arched in response to the chill of the lotion. Chris didn't know how Nikki would respond to her making a move, but she figured she had nothing to lose by trying.

"Nik you got an ashy ass back and ass," she joked.

"Whateva heffa. Just make sure you get my whole back." Nikki laughed.

She continued to massage the lotion on Nikki's back. She moved down to Nikki's ass waiting for her to respond to the inappropriate touching, but Nikki was enjoying the gentle touch of Chris' hands. Her hands continued to rub and caress Nikki's ass until she found her thin fingers slipping into Nikki's inviting pussy. Somehow she knew Nikki wanted the same thing too.

When Nikki still didn't say anything she continued to stroke Nikki's pussy gently moving her fingers in and out of her pussy. Nikki began to show signs of enjoyment letting out soft moans. Chris placed her thick lips between Nikki's ass and twat sucking softly. Nikki's body jerked with joy. Chris' tongue moved in and out of Nikki's asshole, a sensation Nikki never experienced.

Chris could feel Nikki's bodybuilding with anticipation because her body reacted in the same way when she began to enjoy sex.

*Just when Nikki was about to climax Chris stopped. "Turn over baby,"
she whispered to Nikki. Even though they never experienced a moment
like this, this first time felt right and little did they know it would lead to
a more sexual relationship. Nikki rolled her body around staring into
Chris' big eyes. "Do you want me to stop?" Chris questioned hoping
Nikki would say no because she desperately wanted to continue.*

*Nikki responded in a soft voice, "No, baby. Keep going."
Nikki pulled Chris close to her and began kissing her. Chris pulled
away and began to gently lick on Nikki's hardened nipples, switching
between her two round breasts every minute. She moved slowly down
Nikki's body, kissing every inch. Her mouth was back on Nikki's softest
parts. Nikki felt the warmth of Chris tongue against her throbbing
pussy. Chris sucked on her like she was sucking an orange making sure
to apply the right amount of pressure.*

*She felt Nikki's hand on the back of her head pushing her face
deeper inside her. She felt the warmth of Nikki's tasteful juices on her
face and she loved it. She loved the fact that she made her best friend
cum harder than any man, including her ex-husband. She loved giving
Nikki the enjoyment she deserved and she didn't want anything in
return. Her satisfaction came from satisfying Nikki, but Nikki was
ready to reciprocate at any given moment.*

Chris snapped back to reality, a grin splashed on her face. She
looked at her cell phone and realized Maleek hadn't called her back yet,
which was unusual. She called him back again before walking in the
station, but his voicemail picked up after the first ring. She didn't
understand why his phone was off. He never turned his phone off
unless he was handling business.

Chris and Maleek were already acquainted before he moved to
Virginia. She used to run drugs for him and they ended up fucking with
each other. Their relationship dated back over eight years. It lasted for
three years until he knocked her up and made her get an abortion. After
she had the abortion he stopped fucking with her. She was devastated
and the two never spoke again until the night Fatz died. It was Maleek
that called her that night. She never thought to put two and two together
until they were on their way to VA. It was Maleek behind the set-up,
but she didn't know why.

Chris couldn't confirm 100% Maleek was behind the murder,
but her gut told her so. She contemplated telling Nikki about her

93

suspicions, but she kept it to herself. It was a smart move on her part because her and Maleek continued to be in contact after the move. She unwittingly told Maleek where her and Nikki were staying. It was not a big deal to her because he was in Ohio. However, she was just a pawn in Maleek's game. He was going to get the money Fatz owed him one way or another. It didn't matter to him that Fatz was dead; he knew Nikki had his money and Chris was the link to Nikki.

      Maleek continued to win Chris' heart by sweet-talking her and sending her expensive gifts in the mail. After getting close to her he knew it was time to make the move to Virginia, but made her promise to keep their relationship a secret. Maleek thought the move would be good because nobody knew him and he could bust VA wide open. He knew he had the best product there was and his business skills would take him far. One night he packed up his shit and headed to VA.

CHAPTER XIII

Now boarding flight 243 to California, an automated voice repeated over the echoing intercom. Maleek scanned the busy airport. His paranoia got the best of him. He walked up to the flight attendant and handed her his boarding pass.

"Have a nice flight, sir." The beautiful attendant smiled. She reminded Maleek of a Barbie doll. Her long blonde hair neatly pinned in a bun and her crisp, navy blue uniform a snug fit.

Maleek smiled at the young lady and proceeded to board the plane. Behind him a woman tried to stop her daughter from screaming. The lady tried to comfort her because she was afraid of flying. Maleek wished somebody were there to comfort him. He was about to leave the past behind again in hopes that it would stay that way, the past. But he knew that was not going to happen. He couldn't just walk away from his family and best friend.

Maleek was about to board the plane when he received a text. He didn't usually check them right away, but something told him to read this one, now. It read, *911-911 call me back baby!* The cell phone signature read, Dark Chocolate, so he knew the text was from Chris. Maleek didn't know whether to leave or stay. He wanted to get away from the drama, but he had done too much to turn back and fucked over too many people to go forward. He was at a standstill and needed to make a decision. Nobody knew about his past and he wanted to keep it that way. He began to think on his past as he pushed through the boarding passengers to exit the plane. California and Jungle would have to wait, his boy was in trouble and he couldn't let him fall.

He thought about his childhood and how it shaped his present and future while he pushed through the crowded airport. He was

introduc

ed to cocaine and heroin early on in his life. From the time he could walk and talk the streets were his way of life. His father was a well-respected pimp, while his mother was his bottom hoe. Not long after the two met Maleek was born. At the tender age of five Maleek learned how to cook crack. By the age of fourteen he was running his own enterprise. Maleek flashed back to his earliest childhood memories on the drive to the hospital.

"Daddy, what are you doin'?" A young Maleek asked out of curiosity as he walked into the dark kitchen with one candle burning on the sink.

His father turned to him. A thirty something year old pimp with slick hair and a clean shavin' face.

"C'mere boy," his father sat him on the wooden countertop facing the stove. "This 'ere is yon future." He slurred with a strong southern drawl.

Maleek swung his legs back and forth eager to hear more about what his father was doing.

His father glimpsed at him quickly as he measured baking soda, water and cocaine and poured it into a pan.

"Ya see boy, this all ya ever gone be in life. This 'ere. This is what's gone pay yo bills. Crack. It's the future boy."

At that time Maleek had no idea what his father was talking about or how much money crack would actually make him or where it would take him.

He also remembered the first time he walked in on his mother smoking crack. It was his eighth birthday and he was excited about the party his mother promised him.

The time was 4:30 p.m. and Maleek's friends started to arrive for his party. He walked into the kitchen to see what his mother had prepared for his party. His eyes surveyed the room in disappointment. His shining face disappeared and turned to a saddened one.

At the kitchen table was his mother half dressed, her eyes gazed over with a glass pipe and lighter in her hand. Maleek's mother looked up at him and cracked a half smile.

"Hey baby, go get mama a beer". She requested, not remembering what day or time it was.

Maleek didn't know how to react. He had never seen his mother like this before. "Mommy, what about my party? Where are yo clothes? Where's my cake?" Maleek fought back the tears as his eyes began to water.

Maleek's mother stumbled as she tried to stand up from the table. Her walk was unbalanced as she made her way to the living room where some of Maleek's friends were.

"Maleek," she called with frustration in her voice. "Maleek, who the hell are these muthafuckas in my living room?"

Maleek had never been so embarrassed in his short life. He ran into his mother's room and grabbed her robe. His short legs hurried back to the living room where he found his mother lying on the floor. He covered her bare chest while trying not to cry in front of his friends.

"Mama, get up. Get up!" All of Maleek's friends stared in amazement as he helped his mother to her feet. She pushed Maleek away from her as she stumbled through the narrow hallway to her bedroom where she collapsed on the bed.

Maleek tried to salvage what was left of his supposed-to-be birthday party. There was no food in the house and one bottle of sprite in the refrigerator. He grabbed three cups and poured equal portions into each glass. He then opened a cabinet and grabbed a small bottle of gin and added a little to the sprite.

"Hey, guys!" He shouted to gain the attention of his friends. "Who wants some gin and sprite?"

Not long after serving his friends his father arrived with two hoes on his arms. "Aye, boy what y'all doin' in here?" His father started in a deep voice. "Where yo mama at?"

Maleek thought he was in more trouble. "Mama, in the room. She forgot my party." He explained in a trembling voice.

His father looked at him in confusion. "It's yo bir'day boy. How old you is?"

"I'm eight, daddy." Maleek answered.

Maleek's father turned to the two women on his arms. "Don't just stand there bitches wish my son a happy birthday!" He demanded of the two hoes slapping their asses while they walked away.

The two tricks walked over to Maleek. One kissed him on the lips while the other one stuck her hand in his pants and played with his dick. It was the first time Maleek ever had an erection.

His father smiled while watching his son get his first taste of manhood.

"I think it's time you become a man, boy. Ladies take him to his room and make him a man." As he demanded, the tricks took Maleek by the hand and lead him to his room.

Ten minutes later Maleek re-emerged with the two tricks. His father and six of his friends were sitting in the living room in front of an Atari video game with a bow on it. On the kitchen table was a small cake with chips and hot dogs. Maleek didn't know how his father did it, but he did. Maleek and his friends were enjoying the Atari system when three masked men kicked in his front door waving guns.

"On the flo' now, muthafuckas. You bitches too". One of the men shouted at the top of his lungs. He kept the gun pointed at everyone while the other two men ran through the house slamming doors.

"Aye, Blu, in here!" Maleek overheard one of the men call to the other one as he opened the door to where his mother was laid across the bed.

"Let's get this bitch! Payback's a muafucka!" He heard the other man say.

Maleek cried silently when he heard the door slam followed by loud squeaking. He knew what the men were doing to his mother and it hurt. He looked over and saw the fear in his father's eyes. He had never seen his father look that way. Maleek jumped as he heard two loud gunshots. Not too long after the door opened.

"You find anything?" The man pointing the gun asked anxiously.

The other man hesitated, "Yeah we got it. That'll teach dat bitch to steal from TD. Finish in here and let's go!"

Maleek closed his eyes, because he knew what was coming. It was the rules of the streets. Leave no witnesses. He heard six more loud shouts and then footsteps. He could feel one of the men standing over him. He held his breath and imagined he was invisible wishing that the men would disappear. He heard the gun cock.

"Blu, bring yo ass!" One of the men shouted from the door.

Then they were gone. Maleek lay on the floor with his head down for another ten minutes scared to move. When he did finally get up he saw blood splattered on the walls and all over the floors. His father was dead along with his two tricks and one of his friends.

He ran to the room where his mother was and found her spread across the bed with no clothes on laying in a pool of blood. Maleek and the other five boys ran out the back door of the house to a neighbor's house.

A month later Maleek found himself in a new state with a new name and no family. He was in a program he never heard of, Witness Protection. Because he was able to identify one of the men by name and in a voice line up he testified in court. For his protection because he was so young, with no family he was cutoff from his former life.

He was placed in a detention home and bounced around from one abusive foster home to another. Maleek found solace on the streets. He ran drugs for a local dealer and over the years worked his way up the ranks and became the right hand man of one of the biggest kingpins in the area, Jungle. It was than that he learned the first code of the streets, no snitching.

Jungle became like a father to Maleek. He showed him how to handle business, keep his hands clean, and decipher crooked cops from straight ones. Maleek didn't worry about being hungry or homeless anymore. Jungle not only provided him with food and shelter, but the best clothes, cars and access to beautiful girls, woman and unlimited cash flow.

Maleek managed to rebuild his life with a young college girl he met one night at a nightclub, Monique who later became his wife. A year later his son Maleek Jr. was born. Monique knew about some of Maleek's past and current dealings, but not all. She loved the nice things Maleek afforded her, but didn't always like where the money came from although Maleek owned several legit businesses. She knew the bulk of the money was dirty and begged him to stop all together for the sake of their son, but Maleek didn't want to hear it. The conversation always ended up in an argument and usually a black eye or bruised body for Monique.

Chris was the complete opposite of Monique and never complained about Maleek's extracurricular activities. Her carefree attitude is what attracted Maleek to her. She was his ride or die chick and was down for anything. Maleek called Chris' phone repeatedly and each time it went straight to voicemail. He tried one last time before going home.

"Hello," Chris worried voice shouted through the phone. In

99

the background Maleek could hear a bunch of noise which irritated him instantly.

"Hey Chris, what's wrong. What happened with Bo?" Maleek replied trying to remain calm. Chris immediately started to ramble and Maleek couldn't make sense of what she was saying. "Slow the fuck down! I don't know what the hell you talkin' about."

Chris took a deep breath, "Nikki's dead!"

Maleek was quiet.

"Did you fucking hear me? I said…"

Maleek interrupted, "Yes, I fuckin' heard you. The BITCH is dead! Where is Bo?"

Chris was in awe by Maleek's tone and reaction. "You ain't got to be like that L," Chris stuttered. "Bo is really upset right now, but he's dealing. I think they think he had something to do with it. He didn't. What the fuck? We gotta help him. Can't you do something?" Chris was flustered and her sentences didn't make much sense to Maleek.

He took a deep breath. "Calm down, who is they? The police?"

"Yes!" Chris raised her voice in frustration.

Maleek could tell she was crying and knew she was bothered by the situation. "Shit, I'll handle it," he assured. "Just stay there until I get there."

Chris sniffled, "Okay baby, where you at?"

"I gotta stop at the house real quick and check on Mo and MJ."

Chris didn't like to hear about Monique. She did any and everything in her power to keep him away from her for as long a time as possible. In her eyes Monique was her competition and just like Maleek, Chris would do whatever was necessary to get what she wanted.

"Why you gotta go check on her?" Chris whined in a nonchalant voice.

Maleek exhaled loudly. He and Chris had been through this before. Years earlier he promised Chris he would marry her, but he didn't mean it, although Chris believed him. His words were like gold to her. Maleek would never risk losing Mo, but Chris was a chick that would do anything he wanted no matter what it was.

100

"Christine," he shouted. "I told you she is my wife. And until we get a divorce it's goin' to stay that way. So, just chill, alright! Your time will come. I'll see you in a bit." Maleek hung the phone up aggravated with Chris. He threw his luggage in the trunk of the grey Chevy Impala rental car and sped out of the airport parking lot leaving skid marks.

###

"Christine, you sure he comin'?" Bo questioned with uncertainty in his voice.

"I'm sure. You're his boy and he'd do anything for you. I'm sure just give him a little more time." Christine reassured sipping on a can of Mountain Dew while they waited in the lobby of the Suffolk Police Department.

"So, Chris," Bo began with doubt in his voice. "You and Maleek seem to be really close."

Christine stared at the snack machine in front of her. "What do you mean? With everything goin' on with your mom and cousin we felt like you were dealin' with a lot and you needed people to be there for you." Christine stood up and walked toward the snack machine.

"Ok and I appreciate that. But it just seems like you two have a little bit more going on," he commented recalling Maleek's conversation in the car. "I can't pinpoint it, but I have this nagging feeling it was you he was talking to on the phone earlier."

Christine turned around in awe. She placed her can of Mountain Dew on a white table beside her. "Wait one damn minute, Boston Rodriguez! Where in the hell do you come off taking that tone with me? What are you saying?" Christine was caught off guard by Bo's accusations. She knew Bo had suspicions about her and Maleek's relationship, but she didn't know how much he already knew.

Bo let out a sarcastic grunt, "Humph. After we left the hospital I had a funny feelin'. At first I didn't know what it was, but when I was in the car with Maleek I heard him talkin' to you. I didn't know it was you fo sho' until now. So, how long you been fuckin' my boy, Chris? And why is it a secret?"

Christine was at a loss for words. "I don't know what you're talkin' about Boston. I am not messin' with your boy," she argued defensively.

Bo shook his head. He knew Chris was lying, especially because her right eye twitched. This was her body's way of reacting when she was uncomfortable or lying, something she couldn't' control.

"That's bullshit," he started. "I know everything about you and Maleek. He already told me after we left the hospital." he continued hoping his lie would reel Chris in. "Plus, your eye is twitching. I've known you way too long."

The look on Chris' face was priceless. "Shit Bo. I don't know what to tell you. After we left Cincinnati and he moved to VA we just hooked up again."

Bo was floored. He didn't know Maleek and Chris knew each other before VA. Even more so, he wondered if his mother knew about their relationship.

Just as Bo was about to dig deeper Maleek stormed in and interrupted, "Bo, my nig, what the hell is going on?" he exclaimed excitedly, All the while cutting his eyes at Chris.

"Man, they think I got something to do with this shit! I don't know if Christine told you, but my mom passed earlier today. That's why they called me."

Maleek reached in to give Bo a hug, "Man, I'm sorry to hear that. You know I loved your mom like my own family. Mo's going to be so hurt. Bo, don't worry about anything. I'll take care of all the arrangements. Just make sure you're there for Nae. She's okay, right?" Maleek asked with fake sincerity. Chris rolled her eyes and Bo happened to see her reaction.

"Thanks, L. Nae is…she's okay, but they won't let me see her. They have cops watching her room. They think somebody killed my mom and they think Nae may be in danger. Right now, I just need to go home and get some rest. I don't think shit can get any worse."

"Bo, I'll come with you. I'm sure the house is a mess and you don't need to see that. I'll clean it up while you're resting." Chris offered.

Bo didn't want to be bothered, but he didn't want to clean up the mess left behind from the attack. "That's fine. I'll ride with L. We'll meet you at the house. Here are the keys to get in. I'ma stop and get a bite to eat so you can start cleaning. I can't handle seeing all that blood."

Chris saw the look on Bo's face and he was about to break.

102

"Don't worry about it Bo. I'll make sure I get as much of it up as possible before you get there." The three walked out of the station. Chris trailed behind.

CHAPTER XIV

Maleek and Bo pulled into the crowded parking lot of Apple Bee's, "you alright?" Maleek questioned concerned about his friend.

"I'm good. Just ready to get something to eat and get some rest." Bo responded.

Maleek pulled the keys out of the ignition, "I know what you mean, dawg. Let's get some food, toss back a couple and get you to the crib."

Bo smiled still curious about the relationship between Chris and Maleek. It was the perfect time to pry some more. Maleek was an open book after having a few drinks. "Yeah, you right. C'mon man, I'm hungrier than a hostage."

The two walked into the restaurant and waited to be seated. Trey Songz's, "Unusual," blasted through the speakers and tables of females waved their hands, snapped their fingers and sung along. A petite young woman with an untamed Afro and a nameplate that read "Michelle B." approached the hostess stand. "How many in your party?" she asked.

Maleek held up two fingers. The young woman picked up two menus off the counter. "Right this way gentlemen." She signaled for them to follow her. She seated them in a corner booth. "My name's Michelle and I'll be your waitress this evening. What can I get you gentlemen to drink?"

"Henney and Coke for me." Bo ordered.

"A shot of TQ for me." Maleek added.

She scribbled down their drinks and hurried off to place their order at the bar. Bo glanced over the menu not knowing what to order. "I'm so fuckin' hungry I don't even know what I want."

103

"I think I'ma get these ribs," Maleek said looking at the menu. He placed the menu down and peeped at his cell phone. "Look Bo, you don't have to stay at your crib. I know how hard it is for you right now. You are more than welcome to stay at the house. You can stay in the guest bedroom. You'll have all the privacy you need."

Bo was still looking over the menu, "Thanks man, but I think I'll be fine, but I'll keep your offer in mind," he remarked without looking up. He was still trying to figure out how to ask Maleek about Chris. Him and Maleek were friends for a long time so he knew Maleek would be straight with him. Bo decided to wait until Maleek had a few drinks in him before asking about the situation. "Okay, I think I'm going to have the Shrimp Scampi & Chef Cut Sirloin Steak." he finally decided.

Maleek could see that all Bo's energy was drained. He tried to ease Bo's pain a little. "Aye man, I don't know how to make you feel any better, but just know your mom is in a better place now. You gotta be strong for Nae. She still needs you."

"I know Leek, but that's my mom! I'll never see her again."

Maleek knew what it was like to lose loved ones. He lost his mother and father in the same day. "Yo dawg, I know it's tough right now, but it'll get better. I know I never talk about my peeps, but I lost them when I was young. They were killed in front of me. So, trust me I know. You just got to let go and know that she ain't sufferin' any mo'." Bo leaned back in the booth and closed his eyes.

Michelle walked up with the two drinks, "Here you are, a Henney and Coke and a shot of TQ. Are you gentleman ready to order?"

Maleek looked up at the waitress, "Yeah we're ready. I'ma have the Classic Barbecue Baby-Back ribs with fries and a baked potato."

"And for you?" the waitress asked turning towards Bo.

"Alright Michelle, give me the Shrimp Scampi and Chef Cut Sirloin with a baked potato and cole slaw." he ordered sliding his menu across the table towards the waitress. "By the way, I like that natural look on you. It fits." he added giving her a quick wink.

"Thanks," she replied grinning from ear to ear. "Okay, I'll put your orders in right now." Michelle was flattered by Bo's compliment and couldn't stop smiling. She took the menus off the table and hurried into the kitchen.

Maleek picked up his Tequila and tossed it back in one big gulp. "Ah, that's the good shit, burns when it goes down."

Bo stared at his glass. He tried to clear his head for a moment.

"Something wrong with your drink?" Maleek joked.

Bo tried to force himself to smile. He picked up his glass, took his drink to the head, and slammed the glass on the table leaving a swallow.

"Damn, slow down. You gonna get fucked up quick you keep drinkin' like that." Maleek spotted the waitress and signaled for her to come over. "Yo, can we get two more drinks, please?"

"Sure. I'll put that in for you."

Bo decided to wait until Maleek had one more drink in him before he began to probe about his relationship with Chris. Bo sat quietly in the booth while Maleek sent texts back and forth. He observed his surroundings and noticed a woman staring at Maleek. When she made eye contact with Bo she quickly turned her head.

"Yo, L," Bo whispered while nudging him on the leg. "That chick over there keeps staring at you."

Maleek took his eyes off his cell phone briefly. "Where?"

Bo shifted his head to the right trying to show Maleek the girl without drawing attention. "You see her? The girl with the short haircut at the table with the two other girls. She got on the pink Rocawear shirt and the big hoop earrings."

Maleek squinted his eyes, "oh shit! Yeah I know that broad. That's my old piece, Angel from Cinci."

"Cinci?" Bo questioned. He knew it was the perfect time to bring up Cincinnati and Chris.

Michelle walked up to the table and placed the two drinks down. An older man with a well-groomed face stood behind her with two trays full of food. "Here's your Henney and Coke and your Tequila." She turned to the man behind her and grabbed the first plate, "be careful the plates are hot." She looked at Bo with a wide smile showing all her teeth, "you had the Shrimp Scampi, right?"

Bo nodded.

"And you had the Barbecue Ribs. Here you go. You gentlemen enjoy, I'll be back to check on you."

"Thank you." Bo said politely.

105

Maleek was in his own world staring at Angel.

"L, L," Bo called to get his attention. "You alright man."

"I'm good. I wonder what that bitch doin' in VA," he snapped not once taking his eyes off her.

Bo lowered his head and silently prayed over his food. He took a couple of bites of his food before continuing his conversation. "You know her from the Cinci? You mean like Cincinnati, Ohio?"

"Yeah." Maleek responded anxiously. He picked up his Tequila and downed it like he was nervous. He closed his eyes and frowned his face as the liquor slid down his throat. He pounded his chest, a natural reaction. "I need another one, dawg." he commented.

Bo looked at Angel and turned his attention back to Maleek. "Damn L, I think you need to slow down. That bitch got you nervous and shit!"

Maleek hadn't even taken a bite out of his food. He wanted to know why Angel was still in VA and in his neck of the woods at that. Maleek was paranoid as usual. He thought Angel followed him after he met her earlier. She was one of the only people that knew about Fatz, Nikki and Chris. He knew if she wanted to she could blackmail him and cost him a lot of money plus his family.

"I'm good, man. Just bad news from the past."

Bo quickly glanced at Angel and swallowed a mouth full of Shrimp Scampi. "Yo, I didn't know you lived in the Cinci. Why you ain't neva tell me that?"

Maleek looked down at his phone while answering Bo. "Just neva came up."

Bo found it strange that Maleek never mentioned living in Cincinnati. He kept his thoughts to himself and continued to question Maleek. "How long did you live there?"

"Not long." Maleek's answers were quick and short. Bo realized getting answers from Maleek would be like pulling teeth.

Bo took a breath before asking his next question. He knew it was a good chance that Maleek would react in an aggressive way. If he did react, Bo knew he was on to something. If he didn't then either Maleek was good at hiding secrets or nothing was there. "Is that how you and Chris know each other?"

Maleek stopped texting and gave Bo an intense stare. "What the fuck are you talkin' about, Boston?"

106

Bingo! Bo hit a sensitive spot. Maleek never called him by his real name, NEVER! "No harm done L, I'm just sayin'. Chris already told me how y'all got down. It's fucked up, but that's none of my business. What *IS* my business is what went down in Cincinnati and does that shit have anything to do with us moving to VA."

"Bo, how many times have I told you to play your position? You movin' into major league territory and you ain't nothing but a minor. I'ma grown ass man and don't no other man question me about who the fuck or what the fuck I do, you dig!"

"That's cool," Bo started. "But…"

Maleek interrupted his sentence, "But nothing! I'ma tell you this one mo time," Maleek emphasized leaning towards Bo and staring him in the eye without a blink. "DON'T *EVA* question me about *MY* business Youngblood!" Maleek sank back into the booth and continued pounding away at his phone.

Bo was silent for the rest of the meal. Maleek's words were confirmation enough. He knew Chris and Maleek had some type of relationship and it must have been serious. He didn't know how serious, but he was determined to find out.

Michelle approached the table sensing the intensity. "Are you guys alright? Can I get you anything?"

Maleek didn't bother to look up.

"No, can we get some boxes please?" Bo requested. Michelle turned to walk away. "And, oh, can I get a glass of water?"

"Sure, I'll be right back."

Bo looked in the direction where Angel was seated. Angel and Bo made eye contact. She stood to walk in their direction and Bo didn't know if he should warn Maleek or not. He opted not to say anything out of curiosity.

Angel approached the booth. The click of her Guess boots grew louder as she came closer. Maleek was so engrossed in sending texts back and forth to someone that he didn't realize the she was standing in front of him.

"What the fuck? You ain't gone speak muthafucka?" she asked with a mix of irritation and anger in her voice.

Maleek slowly lifted his head. "Humph, for what," he sputtered. "I ain't got no words fo you bitch." Bo could tell by Maleek's tone the two did not end on pleasant terms.

107

"Oh, now I'm a bitch. I won't no bitch when I did that favor for you. I see how it is. I'm good enough to do yo dirty work, but I ain't good enough for words."

"Look bitch, we know what it was and what it is now. You ain't have to do me no favors. I was just tryin' to throw you a bone. But If I can remember correctly, you got what the fuck you wanted out the deal."

"Throw me a bone, nigga please. You knew damn well I was the only one that would get the shit done right. And you know damn well I didn't get what the fuck you promised me. It's all good. I see yo ass ain't changed one bit. Just remember one thing muthafucka. I hold the key to yo future and you know what the fuck 1 mean. Fuck wit me if you want to, you know where to find me, muthafucka. Now, who's the bitch?" she belted before turning to walk away.

Bo stared at Angel's plump, shapely ass as she walked away. He wanted to know more about the key that she held. He was learning a lot about Maleek in a short amount of time. Maleek was becoming somebody Bo didn't care to know. He started to wonder if Maleek was capable of murder.

CHAPTER XV

Bo began to doze off on the couch when he was awakened by a knock at the door. He opened the door and Isabella stormed in. "Is anybody else here with you?" she questioned.

"No, just me, Christine just left but she's coming back. Why?"

"We need to talk!" Isabella sat down on the couch with her arms on her legs. She looked intensely at Bo as he sat on the chair across from her.

"Okay Izzy. What's the matter? As if I don't already have a shit load of problems right now."

Isabella sighed. "Well, your shit load is about to hit the ceiling! I've been doing some investigating, off the clock, and I've found some stuff that I don't think you're going to like."

Bo's curiosity grew instantly. "What kind of stuff are you talking about?"

Isabella sat silently, not knowing how to begin to explain to Bo the information she discovered.

"ISABELLA! What the hell are you talking about?" Bo yelled growing more aggravated at her silence.

Isabella stood up and paced the floor, "Bo, this has to stay between you and me until everything is confirmed. You absolutely can not say anything or even act any different."

"Alright, alright. Just tell me damn it!"

"I think Christine and Maleek may have something to do with what happened to your mother and J'nae."

Bo had a look of astonishment on his face. Questions lingered in the back of his mind, but he didn't think Christine or Maleek could actually have anything to do with it. He questioned Maleek's intentions, but never once Christine's intentions towards his mother. He sat on the edge of the couch in a daze.

"Bo, Bo. Did you hear what I said?"

"I heard that bull shit! I know Christine has done some fucked up shit, but you can't be serious," Bo paused for minute to take in the statement Isabella made. "She was my mom's best friend and like an aunt to me and L, L's my best friend and like a brother. Where the hell are you getting this information from?"

Isabella sat on the couch beside Bo. "I know this hard for you to understand right now, but there's a lot about your mom and Chris that you don't know. And I wish that I could tell you everything right now, but I can't. I have to get more concrete information."

Bo stood up and walked as far across the room as possible from Isabella to signal his displeasure with her. "You know what, I think yo ass better do that. How the fuck are you goin' to come in here and accuse my family of doin' something like that with no fucking proof. Before you opened your mouth you should have had concrete proof! You know what, I think yo ass need to leave, NOW!"

Isabella was in shock, "But Bo---"

Bo interjected, "Get the hell out, now!"

Isabella stormed out the house without taking a second look at Bo. Her only intentions were to make him aware of what he was about to deal with. She knew it was a bad idea to work Bo's case. It was against the rules and she knew if anybody found out about the two of them she would lose her job and possibly never be allowed to work for any police department again, but this was a risk she was willing to take. Isabella started to second-guess her decision. If Bo wasn't willing to accept the truth, she wondered if she should invest any more of her time finding the truth.

After Isabella left Bo laid back on the couch. His mind was racing a mile a minute. Between the small altercation with Maleek, Chris' confession and Isabella's accusations Bo didn't know what to think or believe. His vision was now cloudy. All he knew was over a course of 24 hours his life was turned upside down. He tried to close his eyes to get a little bit of rest, but his body and soul were too restless to let him fall asleep.

He started towards the kitchen, but stopped in front of the staircase where his mother and cousin were attacked. Chris had done an excellent job of cleaning up the blood, but Bo could still see a light spot in the carpet that outlined the pool of blood. He looked up to try to keep himself from crying. He continued to the kitchen. He took the remainder of his steak and placed it the microwave for two minutes. He heard the front door shut.

"Christine, is that you?" he called over the hum of the microwave.

"Yeah, it's me," she walked in the kitchen and placed her car keys on the marble island that divided the large renovated kitchen. "What you in here doing?"

The microwave beeped and Bo removed his food, "I'm reheating the rest of my food."

"So, did you and Maleek have a nice conversation over dinner?" she inquired being nosey.

Bo sat on the barstool in front of the island. "Actually, it was the opposite."

Christine was curious to hear more. "What you mean, the opposite."

Bo figured the only way to get more information about Christine, Maleek and maybe even Angel was to tell her about the incident at Apple Bee's. "Well, some girl named Angel approached L and he went off on her. He said he knew her from Cincinnati. That's where you met him, right? Seems like everything revolves around that place. Do you know Angel too?

There was an awkward moment of silence before she spoke. "Yea, we met in Cincinnati and there's only one chick I know named Angel. And that bitch should still be in Ohio."

Bo was shocked to hear that Christine knew who Angel was. He was curious to know more about Angel and Maleek and possibly the "key" she held. "So, you know her. What else aren't you telling me Chris?" Bo asked inquisitively.

"Nothing. I mean, I know Angel, but there's not a lot to it. I used to work with her." Christine answered without wanting to answer any more questions about the past. "Bo, have you called the hospital to check on Nae?" she asked quickly changing the subject.

"No, not yet. I've been trying to rest so I can be prepared to deal with everything. Plus they got all them cops guarding her room. I'm sure she's okay for now. The hospital would have called me if there were any changes or complications."

"I think I may go back up to the hospital to sit with her if

111

they'll let me. I don't know if she will know I'm there, but she needs somebody familiar with her." Christine replied.

Bo took the last bite of his steak before speaking. "Suit yourself. I don't have enough in me right now to see her like that. I already gotta deal with my mom's funeral arrangements."

Christine was concerned with leaving Bo. "Are you sure you're going to be okay. I don't feel comfortable leaving you here alone."

"I'm fine, Chris. Please go. I'll call L to come pick me up later."

"Okay, Bo Bear," she walked around the island and gave Bo a kiss on the cheek. "Call me on my cell if you need me. I'll be back in a few."

Bo stared at Chris as she began to walk away. "Hey Chris," he called.

"Yea," she answered turning around.

"We need to finish our conversation later."

"Bo, sometimes you need to let sleeping dogs lie. You'll be opening Pandora's box and once you do that you can't close it." Christine continued to walk out the door.

Bo was now more intrigued. There was more much more to everything that happened in Ohio. He knew his mother was involved in things he knew nothing about. His life was a lie and he didn't like it.

CHAPTER XVI

"Hello," Isabella's soft voice answered.

"Hey, Izzy. Look, I want to apologize for blowing up at you earlier. I'm just stressed about everything with my mom and Nae. It was just too much coming at me too fast. I think we need to talk. Are you busy?"

"Um, just a little. Give me about an hour or so and I'll be there."

Bo hesitated. He didn't want to risk Maleek or Chris popping up and seeing her there. "Naw, not here. Can I come over to your place?"

"That's fine. I'll call you when I get home."

"Alright, talk to you in a few." Bo hung up his cell and wrecked his brain trying to figure out who he or his mother knew that still lived in Cincinnati that may know Maleek or Angel. He knew his mother had to have a phonebook with names of people she knew. He just didn't know where to look to find it.

He jogged upstairs and paused before pushing back the door to his mother's bedroom. Her bed wasn't made and the radio alarm clock beside her bed was playing Jamie Foxx's, "Blame It On the Alcohol."

Bo's eyes scanned the room searching for secret hiding places where his mother would have stored pictures, letters or any type of important documents. It would be a challenge to find anything because Nikki suffered from OCD. Her room was spotless. She was a neat freak and nothing was out of place. Her clothes were neatly hung according to color in her closet. All the hangers were even the same size and color. Her shoes were hidden behind a door that opened up into a small shoe room.

Bo started looking in boxes that aligned the shelves above the clothes. The boxes contained jewelry, gold coins and little knick-knacks Nikki collected over the years. One of the boxes contained a

handma

de ashtray he made when he was in the second grade. A small handprint adorned one side and "Happy Mother's Day" was painted on the other side. "Wow, she kept this ugly thing," he said to himself in a low voice. He smiled and placed the ashtray back in the black box

He continued to look around the room for other possible hiding spots. He opened the marble chest at the end of her bed and looked through the folded pajamas. Under the pajamas was an envelope with Nikki's name on it. Bo opened the envelope and pulled out a folded piece of paper. It was a letter from Christine. Bo skimmed the letter and was taken back by what he read.

Nik, I know the other night took you by surprise, but I didn't plan it. It was just something about your naked body that turned me on. I just wanted to please you and I could feel that you wanted it to. I'm sorry if I crossed the line, but I want this to be more than a one-time thing. I think you do too. Lemme know.

I love you, possibly in love,

Chris

P.S.
I can't get the smell of your sweet pussy off of my fingers. I lick them every day! LOL!

Bo read the letter over and over. He was floored. It never crossed his mind that his mom and Chris were lovers. That explained why they were so close, he thought to himself. Nikki and Christine did things that seemed odd to Bo, but he wrote it off as a girl thing. The kisses on the lips, the touching on the ass and the sleeping in the same bed when Christine stayed over, it all made sense.

The deeper he dug the more he found. He couldn't wait until Christine came back to the house so that he could confront her about the romantic relationship she had with his mother, not to mention Maleek. The fact that Christine was playing both sides of the fence didn't sit well with Bo. He knew it was more to Christine's character than he could ever guess and he was going to find out just what kind of person she was, if it killed him.

He stuck the letter in his pocket and continued to rummage through the chest. He found a couple of Valentine's Day cards from his father, Chris and somebody named Clasik. Phone numbers were

114

scribbled on the bottom of the cards with a plea for Nikki to call. Bo placed the cards in his pocket along with the letter. He closed the chest and looked around the room thinking of more places to search.

He looked under the bed, but the only things under the bed were a couple of blankets. He opened her dresser drawers hesitantly and shuffled through her lace bras and panties. He did not feel comfortable touching his mother's underwear. Nothing was there.

Bo was about to give up when something told him to look in his mother's closet again. He walked into the small shoe room in the back of the walk-in closet. Her shoes were arranged according to the type; pumps, heels, flats, sandals and boots. A couple of shoeboxes were on the floor. Bo opened them and was quickly disappointed when nothing was in them, but some old receipts. He turned and saw a pair of boots that looked out of place. He took the boots off the self and underneath was a hidden drawer that opened.

He prepared himself before opening the drawer. "Pandora's Box," he mumbled under his breath. He opened the drawer and found more evidence of his mother's relationship with Christine and other people he had never seen in his life. The drawer was filled with naked pictures of Christine and other unidentified men and women. Some pictures showed his mother in compromising positions he would have never imagined his mother in. Other pictures reflected memories of a good time in Nikki's life. Mixed in with the pictures was a bank statement with his mother's name on it. Bo almost passed out when he read the balance: $1, 543, 981.53. He knew her business was doing well, but not that well.

They lived in a nice size house and drove nice cars, but for the most part Nikki was a modest woman. She dressed nice and possessed nice things, but she wasn't flashy. To make matters more suspicious, the account was with a bank unfamiliar to Bo. He knew his mother was hiding a lot of things about herself. Before closing the drawer he saw a little black book. In the book were names and addresses from Ohio, Virginia, Miami, and other out of country places. Bo hoped that between the pictures and book he discovered he would be able to get to the bottom of what led to his mother's death.

He completely understood what Christine meant by let sleeping dogs lie and Pandora's box. He grabbed everything and ran to his room. He pulled a Nike shoebox off the top shelf of his closet and

115

placed all the pictures and bank statement in it. His phone started to vibrate. It was Christine.

"How's Nae?" Bo inquired before Christine could say hello.

"Bo, it doesn't look good. They said that her pressure is low and she's not responding."

"Oh my God! Have you seen her yet?"

"Not yet. They have to call somebody to get clearance for me to go in the room."

Bo was getting upset and Christine could hear it in his voice. "What the fuck? Shit!" Bo knocked down the lamp sitting on his nightstand.

"Bo are you alright? Calm down. It's going to be okay."

"Fuck you Christine!" he yelled into the phone still disturbed by his discovery. He was already on edge. His mother was murdered, his cousin was on the verge of death and everybody around him was hiding something, especially her.

Christine held the phone away from her ear because he was so loud. "Wait a minute Boston. I know you're going through a hell of a lot right now, but you need to watch your damn mouth." she fired back.

Bo took a deep breath. "My mom's dead, my cousin's about to die and yo ass fuckin' tellin' me it's gon be okay! No, it's not goin' to be okay. I don't know who to fuckin trust. I can't even trust yo bitch ass anymore." Bo hung up the phone in frustration without letting Christine get a word out. His phone started vibrating again. "What the fuck you want Chris?"

"Bo, it's Izzy. You okay?" she responded to his temperament.

"Yeah, yeah. You home?" he answered in an aggravating voice.

"I'll be there in about 15 minutes. I'm finishing up at the station, but you can leave now and meet me there."

"That's fine. I'll see you when you get there." he hung up the phone and stuffed it back into his front pocket. Bo grabbed the shoebox and ran downstairs. He opened the front door and jumped back startled. Maleek was standing in the doorway.

"Baby boy, where you goin' in such a hurry?" he inquired in a nosey nature.

"Not now. L. I gotta meet a friend."

Maleek moved to the side to let Bo walk pass. "Oh, okay. My

116

bad, baby boy." Maleek acted as if he had not snapped at Bo a couple of hours earlier. "I just came by to make sure you were, aiight."

Bo glanced at Maleek briefly, "why wouldn't I be? Besides the fact that my mom's dead and Nae's laid up in the hospital surrounded by cops. I mean, I'm good," he remarked in a sarcastic manner. "Look, I'll talk to you later." Bo jumped in his black and grey Jeep Cherokee Laredo and speed off.

Maleek wondered where Bo was off to in such a hurry. His paranoia began to kick in. Maleek was naturally curious and his conscience was telling him that Bo was up to something. Bo never hid anything from him, so he wanted to know what he was hiding now.

He ran to his car and pulled off almost as fast as Bo did. He spotted Bo's jeep stopped at a red light. He slowed down and was careful not to let Bo see him. He stayed two cars behind Bo and trailed him for twenty minutes until Bo turned into a condo development.

Maleek parked his car on a side street beside the tan colored condos. They were a newer development built two years earlier. The neighborhood was upscale and Maleek new they cost a grip to own. His curiosity grew even more. Who did Bo know that could afford to live in the condos? Maleek waited patiently making sure not to take an eye off Bo.

Ten minutes passed and Maleek hadn't seen any cars pull into the parking lot. He was about to drive off when a silver Toyota Camry pulled up. The woman driving the car looked familiar to Maleek. He stared hard waiting for the woman to park and get out of the car.

Bo saw Isabella's car pull up from his rearview mirror. He jumped out the car with the shoebox in his hand and waited for her to put her car in park. He looked around nervously sensing that somebody may be watching him. He was right. Bo had an intuition like a woman and most of the time it kept him out of trouble. He ran to open the door for Isabella. He was so amped about the information he found he could hardly wait to show her.

"Bo, what is it?" she asked as he shoved the shoebox into her hands.

Bo continued to observe his surroundings, "Izzy, I think you're right. I don't know what kind of shit is going on, but something is definitely going on. I hate to say this but I don't even know what kind of person my mother really was."

117

Isabella opened the shoebox and quickly shuffled through the pictures. She glanced at the bank statement and looked up at Bo. "We need to talk." She placed her hand on Bo's back and guided him towards her apartment.

From his car, Maleek watched as Bo and Isabella exchanged words before walking to a second floor condo. Isabella was dressed in form fitting khaki pants and a blue ruffled BeBe chiffon blouse. Her hair was pinned in a neat bun and her blue and tan earrings dangled from her ears. Even out of uniform Maleek recognized her. He hardly ever forgot a face, especially that of a cop and Isabella was the most gorgeous cop he ever saw. A couple months back she pinched him on a misdemeanor drug charge. He remembered hitting on her while she read him his Miranda's. Maleek wanted to know what Bo was doing with her and what in the hell was in the shoebox.

CHAPTER XVII

Bo's cell phone vibrated across the table. He pushed ignore and continued his conversation with Isabella. "I found this stuff hidden in my mom's room. I started thinking about what you said and there are a lot of things I don't know about."

Isabella examined the photos. She stared at one particular photo of a man dressed in a green collared polo shirt, some wheat Tims and decked out in jewelry. The man's arm was around Nikki's waist and was a man familiar to Bo. She turned the picture over checking to see if there was any writing on the back. "Do you know this man?" she asked curiously.

"Yeah, why? You think he may have something to do with all of this?"

Isabella stared at Bo like she was looking through him. "Who is he to you?"

"That was my mom's friend. They were getting pretty serious before he was murdered." Bo explained.

"Was his name Maurice Johnson?"

That name sounded familiar to Bo. He was silent for a minute. "Shit. To tell you the truth I never knew his government. All I knew him as was Fatz. My mom didn't talk about him much to me, but they were together all the time. Chris probably knows more about him than me."

Isabella continued to find out how much information Bo knew. "How was he murdered?"

"He was out with my mom one night when some dudes bum rushed our crib. They made Christine call my mom and tell her to come back home. When she came back and he walked in after her they jumped him. They shot him."

"How did they know about your mom and Fatz?"

"Damn it Izzy! I don't know."

"So, you don't know what he was in to?"

119

"I didn't get into the man's business like that. It wasn't none of mine and as long as he treated my mom right, I didn't give a shit what he did. I told you my mom didn't talk about him!" Bo remarked with a hint of sarcasm in his voice.

Isabella didn't want to stick her foot in her mouth like she did earlier so she kept quiet until she had all the facts. She continued to flip through the pictures. She raised her eyebrows as she reviewed the explicit pictures of Nikki and her Johns. "Bo," she paused setting the pictures down on the table. "I need to tell you something that you may find hard to believe."

Bo sat straight up waiting to hear the news. His phone started to vibrate again and he ignored it. "I'm listening," he said nonchalantly.

She took a deep breath and braced herself for Bo's reaction to what she was about to tell him. "Bo, don't take this the wrong way," she began. "But, there are some things, like you said, that you don't know about your mother." She continued to look Bo in the eyes even though she found it hard.

"Okay, I'm waiting." he said with a slight hint of anger in his undertone.

"Uh, how do I put this?"

The suspense was killing Bo. "Damn it, Izzy! What is it? Just say it!"

"Your mother used to be a prostitute when you lived in Cincinnati and she was into some crazy shit with Kaew Records."

Bo's eyes were filled with fire and pain. He didn't know how to respond. "How the fuck are you goin' to say some shit like that about my mom." Bo belted angrily. He stood up and grabbed his phone off the table.

Isabella tried to get him to sit down. She pulled his arm trying to pull him back on the couch, but he yanked his body away. "I told you Bo. There is a lot that you don't know."

"Do you fuckin' know this for sure or is this some partial ass information that you're still confirming?"

Isabella walked into to the kitchen and took some documents off the large marble table that was decorated with white lace doilies. She handed the documents to Bo. His eyes quickly scanned over the papers. The documents were a copy of an arrest warrant and surveillance pictures of his mom talking to a well-dressed man wearing

120

Bvulgari shades.

"So, what's this?" Bo continued.

"What does it look like Bo?" she snapped. "It's a copy of an arrest warrant from Cincinnati and undercover pictures taken of your mom and a well-known mafia hit man from Miami. I know you just lost your mom, but it's time to face reality. And the reality is, your mother was a "working woman" possibly turned hit woman and transporter."

Bo looked at Isabella ready to snap. "Yo, for real, I'm not in the mood for this shit."

"You're not in the mood," she snapped back sucking her teeth and rolling her eyes. "You're the one that said you needed to talk to me. Now, that I'm giving you the real, you don't have time for it. You know what, Boston. I'll just finish this investigation myself and once I'm done I'll turn over all the information to one of the other officers assigned to the case. I don't have time for your ego or your bullshit ass attitude." Isabella snatched the documents out of his hands. Bo's temperament was starting to piss her off and it took a lot to make Isabella mad. She was trying to do her job, but Bo was making it extremely hard.

Bo never saw Isabella so mad before. He knew she was right and he tried to regain his composure. "Izzy, I'm sorry. You're right. You're 100% right. It's really hard for me to believe, but the facts are slapping me in the face and I refuse to believe the truth. But you have to understand, this is my mother we're talking about and I don't know if I can handle all of this."

Isabella sighed, "Boston, I know it's hard for you to handle all of this and I'm sorry for your loss, but if you want to know who killed your mother and cousin, you have to suck it up and deal with it."

Bo interjected, "J'nae's not dead."

Isabella looked Bo in the eyes. She wondered to herself if she should tell Bo the truth. "Bo," she continued. "You need to sit back down."

"I'm fine Isabella. Are you telling me Nae's dead too?"

Isabella stared at Bo. Her big eyes soft like a puppy. "I'm sorry."

The wells of Bo's eyes started filling with tears. "Shit! I can't believe this! When did this happen? I mean, Chris was just at the

121

hospital before I came over here."

"Chris? Did she say she saw her?" Isabella asked sounding concerned.

Bo was inquisitive about Isabella's tone. "No, she didn't see her. Why?"

"There's something funny about Christine. I can't place my finger on it right now, but I'll figure it out." she paused. "There's a lot you don't know, and it's going to hurt like hell when you find out some things. But, I'll be here for you." She gave Bo a comforting hug. "What else did you find?"

Bo tried to refocus. He wanted to know who killed his family and why. He wiped the tears from his eyes and sat back on the couch. He went through the shoebox and held up the black book he found. "You may need this," he said holding up the book to show Isabella.

She walked over and grabbed the small address book and inspected it. She flipped through the pages and dissected all the names and addresses listed. "Bo, this will help us out a lot. I need to know that you're really down to find out what happened, no matter what or who we run into." Bo nodded his head. Isabella continued to flip through the address book when Bo interrupted her.

"And there's this," he handed her the bank statement again.

Isabella eyes grew wide in amazement as she thoroughly examined the statement. "Oh my God!" She looked up at Bo. "Did you know about this account?" Bo shook his head. "Shit Bo, your mom was into more than what I thought." Isabella started pacing in front of the 42" Panasonic television. "This is what we're going to do," she started after thinking for a couple of minutes. "Continue to tell everybody that we're investigating you. That should give me sometime to look into everything. After your mother's funeral you're going to tell everybody you need to get away and we are going to take a trip to Cincinnati. I believe that's the best place to start."

Bo's cell phone started to vibrate again. "It's Chris. Should I answer?"

"Yeah, see if she's still at the hospital." Isabella replied curiously.

Bo picked up the phone trying to sound as normal as possible. "Hey AC. How's J'nae? Did they let you see her?"

"Hey Bo Bear. I saw Nae, but only for a couple of minutes.

She's trying to hold on."

Bo knew Chris was lying because Isabella already told him that J'nae was dead. But, why would Chris lie about seeing J'nae. "So, what did the doctor say?" he played along.

"I didn't see the doctor. I just waited outside her room until they let me see her." Chris continued. "I just wanted to let you know. I'll talk to you later. I have to finalize some business and I'll check on you later." Chris hung up the phone sounding like she was in a hurry.

"So, what did she say?" she asked anxiously speaking with her hands.

Bo looked at Isabella with confusion. "She said Nae was trying to hold on. That doesn't make since if you're saying she's dead. Are you sure Nae is dead?"

Isabella was appalled. "I can't believe you're asking me that Boston. I would never lie to you about something like that. J'nae was taken out of the room earlier today. She stopped breathing and the hospital tried to get a hold of you, but we could not get an answer. I'm sorry you had to find out this way. I really am."

"I know you wouldn't lie about something like that, but why in the hell would she? Maybe she didn't think I would be able to handle it with the news about my mother. Maybe she's trying to protect me."

Isabella tried to reassure Bo. She sat on the couch and gently placed her hand on his leg. "I'm sure she has a good reason for not telling you the truth. I know this is really hard for you to handle and I think you need to go home now and relax. You're more than welcome to stay here if you want."

"Thanks Izzy. I appreciate it, but I think I'll go home. I need to clear my head and figure some things out. I'll leave this stuff here with you and you can do whatever you need to. I'll call you later." He gave Isabella a long hug. It made him feel good. He could sense that Isabella was genuinely concerned about everything going on with him. Even though he had not known her for a long period of time he knew she was a good person with a good heart. She was one of the only people he could trust.

CHAPTER XVIII

A few days passed by and Bo didn't hear from Isabella. He wondered if she made any progress in the case. He called her cell phone a couple of times, but got her answering machine. He decided to try one more time before he left for the funeral.

He walked into the dining room and closed the sliding doors that separated the dining room and living room. He dug his cell phone out of his pocket and dialed her number. The phone rang once before going to her voicemail. He left a message, "hey, Izzy it's me. Haven't heard from you in a couple of days and I just wanted to know what was up. Call me back, ASAP." He was starting to worry because this was out of her character, but he would have to put Isabella on hold until after the funeral. He walked back into the hallway and refocused his energy on the day's events.

Bo stood in the doorway fixing his tie. He was not ready to bury his mother six feet under. Up until this point he handled her death relatively well. All the things he found out about her could not be further from his mind. Bo could only think about how somber this day would be. He didn't even care that Christine may have something to do with his mother's death.

He jumped when he felt a hand on his shoulder, "are you okay, Bo Bear?" Christine's gentle voice inquired.

Bo nodded and stared into Christine's watery eyes. "Are *you* okay?"

Christine started to cry even harder. "Oh my God, Bo. What have I done? It's all my fault."

"What? What are you talking about AC?" Bo demanded thinking Christine was about to confess to something awful.

"If I would have been here with you guys, with her, none of this would have happened. I could have protected her."

Bo took a deep breath relieved and disappointed at the same time. "AC, none of this is your fault. I know you loved my mom. I'm just glad that you're here with me now." Christine collapsed into Bo's chest

124

quietly sobbing. Bo wrapped his strong arms around Christine's tiny body comforting her. "We need to finish getting ready. Maleek and Monique will be here any minute to pick us up."

Christine wiped her tears with her hands, "Alright. I just need to finish putting on my makeup and I'll be ready." She walked slowly through the hallway and disappeared into the corridor. Bo stood still in the doorway keeping watch for Maleek's car. He wished he could turn back time and change everything that happened that week. He told himself he would do things differently. He would have ignored Maleek's call that night. He wouldn't have drunk too much. Hell, he wouldn't have left the house if he knew what was going to go down. But, he knew the past was the past and he couldn't change it. He could, however, get justice for his mom and J'nae, and that's what he planned on doing.

"AC, you almost done in there? Maleek is pulling up." he called.

Christine was in the bathroom applying the finishing touches on her Mac lip-gloss. "Yeah. I'm comin'." she yelled back. She blotted her lips with a piece of tissue and kissed herself in the mirror. "Here we go," she whispered to herself. "Alright, I'm ready," she said walking through the hallway. She reached for her purse that was hanging on the wall.

Bo opened the door and moved to the side letting Christine through first. He closed the door and proceeded to walk towards Maleek's car. He stopped midway through the driveway.

Maleek rolled down the car window, "what's wrong B?"

"I think I forgot something." Bo stood in the driveway trying to remember what he had forgotten, but decided it wasn't important and ran to the car.

Monique turned the radio down and turned to face Christine and Bo. "You two look very nice," she complimented in a sincere voice. Christine rolled her eyes and looked out the window.

"Thanks, Mo. You do too." Bo said returning the compliment. He looked at Chris and hit her on the leg, nudging her to say thanks.

Christine continued to look out the window. "Thank you for the compliment, *Monique*." she snarled never once turning her head.

Monique swung her body back around and turned the radio up. She looked at Maleek out the corner of her eye. She knew something happened between Maleek and Chris long before she came into the picture. She didn't if know anything else was going on, but her intuition told her yes.

The ride to the church was quiet, which made the drive seem longer than it was. Maleek backed into the spot that was reserved for them directly behind the family car. Bo observed all the people walking into the church. He never knew his mother had so many friends because she never talked about them or brought them to the house. And Bo found it odd that none of them came to the hospital to visit her, not even a phone call or card from one of them.

Bo stepped out of the car dreading the next few moments. He was not ready to tell his mother goodbye, especially since he would have to turn around and do it all over again with J'nae even though he had not confirmed her death with Christine or the hospital.

All eyes were on him when he walked down the church aisle. He sat down in the front row and waited for the service to begin. The church was packed and none of the people were familiar to Bo except for one. He noticed the Italian man from the surveillance photo Isabella showed him. He was seated in the back of the church. Bo could hear the chatter and whispers of the people around him. All the noise stopped instantly when the pastor walked up to the podium. He was a short bald man of brown complexion. Bo only attended this particular church twice before, but his mother was a member along with Monique.

"Good morning church," the pastor began. "We are gathered here today, not to mourn, but to celebrate the life of Ms. Nikki Rodriguez," he said in a deep voice that didn't fit his appearance. He went on to preach about the sanctity of life and the terrible fate that was thrust upon Nikki, but Bo blocked out most of the sermon until the pastor called Christine up to the stage to speak. Bo was eager to hear what she had to say about his mother.

Christine walked on stage pretending to almost fall back. Two men of solid build ran over and grabbed her arms to make sure she didn't fall. Bo knew it was an act and couldn't believe her dramatics. The gentlemen helped her over to the podium to make sure she was okay.

She lowered her head and slowly moved it side to side before she began to speak. She peered over her Chanel sunglasses looking into

126

the crowded church. "Lord, one of your angels is coming to join you." The church began to roar and shout, "Amen." "Yes, Jesus! She was one of your children and you were ready for her to come home. We may be sad, but Nikki's happy. She's going home!" The roar of the church grew louder as people began to clap and shout, "Take your time". All the applause egged Christine on so she continued to speak. "Nobody knew Nikki like I knew Nikki. She was my girl, my best friend and my lover." The church fell quiet. Everybody listened intently while she continued. "Many of you may not have known this, but I am deeply saddened by her death and this senseless act of violence. Bo, I'm sorry that you had to find out this way, but know that I am here for you." She pushed up her sunglasses and exited the stage. The whole church was stunned that she would pull a stunt like that at a funeral.

Christine walked over to Bo and tried to hug him, but he rejected her. Bo stared at Christine with a look she never saw before. He was hurt and embarrassed by what she did. Words could not describe what he wanted to do to her, but he remained silent until the viewing of the body.

Bo's knees were so weak he could barely stand. Maleek rushed over to help him stand and guided him to his mother's casket. Maleek kept his word. He paid for everything, top dollar. Two-dozen pink and white roses decorated the top of Nikki's casket. Her casket was rose colored, outlined in pink diamonds and lined with light pink silk. It was the prettiest casket Bo ever saw.

He stared at his mother's lifeless body. He ran his fingers across the scar on her face, much like he did the night he found her at the bottom of the stairs. Her face was made up perfectly and she looked like she was sleeping peacefully. She was dressed in a red Armani dress with a diamond necklace draped around her neck with matching earrings. Bo did not expect for Maleek to go to such extremes. He kissed his mother's cheek and whispered *I love you* into her ear.

Bo could feel the tug of Christine's arm pulling him away. His body did not budge and he snatched his arms out of her grip. He wanted to shake his mother and tell her wake up. His mind was telling him to let go, but his heart was telling him to hold on. His eyes remained fixed on his mother's face while Christine continuously tried to pull him in the opposite direction.

The unknown man walked up to Nikki's casket. He stood

127

silently beside Bo for a moment before he spoke. "Your mother was a beautiful woman. I'm happy to see she could afford such luxury even at death."

Bo didn't acknowledge him. He couldn't make since of what the man was saying and if it meant anything. He finally sat back down and stared blankly at the flowers in front of him.

"Bo, sweetie, are you okay?" Monique asked concerned about him. Bo didn't answer. Monique shoved Bo gently to awake him from his daydream. "Bo, sweetie, are you okay?" Bo turned his head slightly, but didn't speak. Monique's attention quickly turned to Christine briefly.

"Oh Lord, why Nikki, Jesus? Take me Lord." Christine was deep into drama-land now and Monique didn't appreciate all the commotion she was causing, especially after the stunt she pulled on stage. She turned her head when she saw Christine about to throw herself on the casket.

"She is just ridiculous, Bo, I'm so sorry you have to deal with this at your mother's funeral," Monique commented. Bo didn't respond. He wished he could close his eyes and disappear. Christine crossed the line and he couldn't forgive her for what she had done. Bo couldn't wait for the day to be over, but he told himself it couldn't get much worse than it already was.

Bo left the church and waited in the family car for the service to be over. Christine opened the door and tried to sit down. "What the fuck do you think you're doing?" Bo barked angrily.

Christine's jaw dropped. "What do you mean? I'm riding to the cemetery with you."

Bo couldn't believe the nerve of Christine. "No the fuck you're not! You have the nerve to think you're going to get in this car after that shit you just did! Fuck you Chris!" Bo yelled and slammed the door almost catching Christine's fingers.

Maleek tapped on the window signaling for Bo to roll the window down. "Yo B, you aight? I know that's some fucked up shit ole girl did in there, but somebody need to ride with you. You want Mo to ride with you."

Bo's face was bright red and his head was starting to pound. "I don't care," he said nonchalantly before rolling the window back up. He closed his eyes and tried to ease his headache. He kept telling

128

himself the day was almost over and than he could be in peace by himself.

The car door opened and Monique peeked her tiny head in. "Are you okay, Boston? Maleek said you didn't want Christine to ride with you, so he told me to."

"Yeah. I can't be around her ignorant ass right now. I mean, how the fuck does she think it's okay to do some shit like that? I already knew about them anyway because I found her letters to my mom." Bo whined. Monique didn't know what to say so she listened while Bo vented. "Couldn't she have told me that shit in private? Everybody didn't need to know that shit. That was my mom's business. I mean, if she wanted everybody to know then she wouldn't of kept it a secret. I feel like I'm on an episode of Jerry Springer." Bo looked at Monique for some answers, but she didn't respond. He tapped his foot and frowned his face all the way to the cemetery.

"Bo, please keep your cool out here," Monique requested of him before they stepped out of the car, but Bo just looked at her.

At the gravesite Maleek and Monique sat on each side of Bo, keeping the distance between him and Christine. Christine leaned forward a couple of times trying to get Bo's attention, but Maleek pushed her back into the chair. "Not now Chris. This is not the time or the place," he commented with authority.

Bo's eyes were fixated on the rose colored casket while the pastor said his last few words. The large crowd started to disperse and return to their cars. Bo remained seated in front of the casket not wanting to let go of his mother.

"Bo," Monique said softly. "It's time to go, baby."

"Just give me a couple more minutes alone, okay?" he responded without looking at her.

"Okay, take as much time as you need. I'll be waiting in the car." Monique walked over to Maleek and Christine who were engaged in a heated conversation. "Hey you two, what in the hell is going on? If you haven't noticed we're in the middle of a cemetery." Monique argued in the softest voice possible.

Christine rolled her eyes and walked away. Maleek started to walk away too, but Monique grabbed the back of his two hundred dollar Versace shirt. Maleek turned abruptly and swatted Monique's hand off of his shirt. "What in the hell is your problem?" he asked

129

sternly as he stepped into Monique's personal space.

Maleek was so close to her face that she could smell traces of the orange juice he drank for breakfast. Monique's tone changed quickly. The look on his face and tone in his voice petrified her. She didn't consider Maleek abusive, even though a few altercations landed her in the hospital with broken bones and concussions and she did not want to try him. "I was just saying y'all were getting a little loud. What were y'all fussing about?" she whimpered.

"Mind your business Monique." Maleek spoke in an aggressive tone before walking off.

Monique knew something was going on with Maleek and Christine by the way he reacted. Otherwise he would have just answered her question. Monique looked over her shoulder to make sure Bo was okay. He was staring at her like he heard everything that went down. Monique walked towards the car and Bo quickly ran up behind her.

Bo opened the car door for Monique. She slid across the leather seat and looked out the window at Maleek and Christine who were continuing their conversation in the car. Bo saw Monique staring at the two and knew what was on her mind. "Mo, don't worry about Maleek. He loves you, and he wouldn't do anything to hurt you." Bo comforted her

Monique smiled and wiped away a single tear from the corner of her eye. She rubbed Bo's knee, "I know baby, but anyway how are you? Are you doing okay?"

"I'm good. Just not ready to let go, ya know. Everything just happened so fast. One minute she's in my room the next she's in the hospital fighting for her life. Damn!"

"Bo, we're here for you. I loved your mom like a sister and you're family to us, so anything you need just ask."

Bo smiled. He loved Monique and it broke his heart that Maleek did her so dirty. Monique was there for Maleek through thick and thin, but Bo couldn't tell her what was going on with Maleek and Christine. It was something she would have to find out on her own.

CHAPTER XIX

The funeral was over and Bo was ready to move on. It was time to find out who killed his mother and cousin. Before he could go any further though he needed to confirm that his cousin was dead. He dialed the number to the hospital, "may I speak with Dr. Green, please?" The nurse placed Bo on a brief hold before returning to the phone.

"Sir, may I take a message? Dr. Green is unable to come to the phone," the nurse replied with a slight twang in her voice.

Bo couldn't wait to receive a call back. "Ma'am this is urgent. I am unable to wait. I need to know if my cousin, J'nae Strong is still in ICU."

The nurse paused, "give me one moment and I'll check for you." A few minutes went by before the nurse came back to the phone. "Sir, I'm sorry, but you need to come in to the hospital. It looks like we have been trying to contact you, but we have not received a call back. We have left several messages."

Bo was confused. He did not receive any messages from the hospital regarding his cousin and the last time he was there they did not want him to visit her. "Ms. that can't be right. I haven't received any messages about the status of my cousin. Could I *please* speak to Dr. Green?" Bo begged of the nurse.

"I'm sorry, sir. He is on his rounds and you need to come in to speak with him in person. We're unable to release sensitive information over the phone. He'll be here until 8pm tonight." The nurse hung up the phone before Bo could speak another word.

Bo was on a mission to find out the truth about everybody and everything that was going on. He put on his dark rinse denim Levi jeans and a white button down with light yellow stripes. He threw on a yellow Polo sweater and some wheat colored Timberlands. He took a small bottle of D&G oil off his dresser and rubbed it against the inside of his wrists and neck. Bo always made sure he dressed well and smelled good when he left the house, no matter where he was going.

Somethi

131

ng his mother taught him.

He sprinted down the stairs and ran out the door. Christine pulled up behind his truck in a maroon Honda Coupe. She stepped out the car wearing a light blue long sleeve shirt, a pair of light denim Guess skinny jeans, a pair of white and blue strappy peep toe Guess heels and the same sunglasses she wore to the funeral.

"Hey Bo, where you goin'?"

"Out." he replied sharply.

"O-K, you don't have to be smart about It." she snapped still walking towards the house.

Bo stood in front of the driver's side door of his truck waiting for Christine to return to her car. "What is it Chris? I don't have time to deal with yo shit today."

Christine leaned against the trunk of Bo's truck. "We need to talk about what happened at the funeral. I--,"

Bo interrupted her, "no we don't need to talk. There's nothing to say. Now, if you could move out of my way I have somewhere to be."

Christine stood up and walked back to her car. "Well, I just wanted to apologize. You needed to know the truth. There's so much I need to tell you."

"Yeah, well I don't have time right now. Maybe later." Bo jumped in his truck and waited for Christine to back out. Chris Brown's "Kiss, Kiss" sounded from his cell phone. "Izzy, where've you been?" he asked excitedly. The voice on the other end of the phone didn't sound like the Isabella he knew.

"Hey Bo." she answered in a groggy voice.

"What's wrong? Why do you sound like that?" Bo could tell something wasn't right with Isabella by the way she sounded. There was a long pause. "Hello? Izzy, Are you there?"

"I'm here. Bo we really need to talk. I'm in the hospital."

"What? Why are you in the hospital? What the hell happened to you?"

"Boston, I was attacked. The night after you left somebody broke in and tried to rape me." Isabella's voice was filled with pain.

Bo did not understand how things kept happening to people around him. "Oh my God, Izzy. I'm so sorry this happened to you. You never should have been involved in this. What hospital are you at?"

132

"I'm in Norfolk General, but before you come you have to make sure nobody is following you." Isabella was almost certain that somebody close to Bo was setting him up. "Bo, it looks like somebody is trying to set you up."

Bo didn't think anybody close to him would do something so deceitful. "Set me up? Why do you think that?"

"Look at the facts Boston. You are the only suspect in your mother and cousin's murder. Now, I'm in the hospital and you were the last person to see or speak to me. Luckily, I'm alive and I can prove that you weren't my attacker."

"Shit. I don't know what the hell is going on. So, I guess you're not going to Cincinnati with me. I called you to see if you found out anything else." Bo was disappointed. He was glad that Isabella was still alive, but he wanted to get to the bottom of his mother's murder and needed her help.

"I am a little battered and bruised, but we can still go. They're releasing me from the hospital in a couple of days. We can talk more when you come up here."

"Okay Izzy, I have to make a quick stop first. I'll see you when I get there." Bo threw the phone on the passenger seat and backed his truck out of the driveway at full speed. The tires squealed when he stepped on the gas and cut the steering wheel hard. He sped down the street leaving a trail of white smoke behind him. Bo did ninety-five miles per hour down I-464 until he got to the exit for the hospital.

He pulled into the parking lot and swung is car into the first parking space he saw. He did not care that it was a handicapped parking space. He would pay the fine later. His long legs leaped across the parking lot at lightening speed. He hurried into the hospital and pressed the elevator button impatiently. Bo's body moved nervously while he waited for one of the four elevator doors to open.

The ride to the 6th floor seemed like an eternity. The elevator stopped on every floor before Bo reached his floor. His eyes scanned the area for thirty seconds before he made eye contact with the same young lady that flirted with Maleek a week earlier. Bo approached the nurse's station flustered.

"Hey, how are you?" she smiled showing all of her teeth. She remembered Bo from the week before.

Bo read her nametag, Aleighsha Wilson. "Hi, Ms. Wilson. I'm

looking for Dr. Green. I need to talk to him ASAP. It's a matter of life and death," he pleaded.

Aleighsha could sense the urgency in Bo's voice. "Sure, I'll page him right away." She picked up the phone dialed a number that was taped on the desk in front of her. "Dr. Green should be calling back shortly." she assured. She scribbled some notes on a calendar and took a sip of her coke. She was about to get up from her chair when the phone rang. "Hello Dr. Green, there's a young man that would like to speak with you." She looked at Bo for a quick second. "I'm sorry, what's your name?"

"Boston Rodriguez." he replied anxiously.

"A gentleman by the name of Boston. Yes, Mr. Rodriguez." she restated to Dr. Green over the phone. "Okay Mr. Rodriguez, you can go to his office." Aleighsha pointed Bo in the direction of Dr Green's office. She leaned over the desk and pressed her breast against the counter showing off her DD breasts. "Go down this hall, turn left at the elevators, go pass another nurse's station and his office is on the left. His name is on his door."

Bo's mind was on finding out what happened to J'nae so he didn't pay any attention to Aleighsha's flirtatiousness. He walked swiftly through the hallway almost knocking over two elderly women in his path. Bo pounded on Dr. Green's door.

"Come in." Dr. Green called through the thick wood door. Bo pushed the door open wildly causing the door to hit the grey rubber stopper affixed to the wall. "Hello, Mr. Rodriguez," Dr. Green greeted. He extended his arm signaling for Bo to take a seat. "We've been trying to contact you," he continued closing the door to his office.

"How is J'nae? Is she still in ICU?" Bo asked eager to confirm Isabella's statement.

Dr. Green sat down in a plush leather chair behind his large desk. He flipped through a chart with J'nae Strong across the top. "Mr. Rodriguez, Ms. Strong passed away due to complications caused by the head injuries she sustained. I'm sorry."

Bo was speechless. He hadn't received any messages from the hospital about his cousin although the hospital staff said otherwise. "Dr. Green, I haven't received any communication about J'nae. What is the phone number you have for me?"

"Let me see here. We have your number as 757-555-8767."

757-555-8767.

Dr. Green confirmed.

"Yes, that's correct, but I never received any messages." Bo was confused. The more questions he asked the more things became weirder. "Doctor, did anybody visit J'nae before she died?"

Dr. Green reviewed the visitation log for J'nae. "No. Wait a minute, a young lady did come to visit, but she did not enter the room. A Ms. Christine Anderson."

"Thank you, Dr. Green." Bo leaned across the desk and shook Dr. Green's hand. He exited the room with more questions than when he arrived. Nothing made sense anymore. He hoped Isabella would be able to help him make sense of everything.

Bo saw enough of the inside of a hospital to last him a lifetime. He wanted to visit Isabella, but didn't have the energy. The smell of the hospital was starting to make him sick. He sat in his truck and contemplated what he was going to do. He pulled out his cell phone and dialed the number to Isabella's hospital room.

"Hello," she answered.

Bo could hear her speaking to other people in the background. "Are you busy?"

"Hey Bo, you're okay, I'm not busy. Are you on your way?"

Bo hesitated before he answered, "uh, I don't think I'm coming. I'll wait until you get home in a couple of days."

Isabella was disappointed. Although she was working on his mother's case, she still liked him regardless and wanted to see him. Even though she would never admit it, she got butterflies in her stomach whenever he was around. "Why? I wanted to see you. I need to talk to you."

"Izzy, I can't stand the smell of hospitals right now. I'm on the phone, talk."

"Never mind. I'll see you when they release me. Do you mind picking me up?" she said with irritation in her voice.

"Sure. Just call me to let me know. In the meantime, I'll continue looking for some more information."

"Okay. I'll call you."

Bo hung up the phone and sat in the truck for a minute before pulling off. He remembered the two death certificates hidden in the basement and the man from the funeral. He raced back home to find the death certificates. Isabella would be able to tell him who Maurice

135

Johnson was and give him more information about the unknown Italian man. Bo ran down to the basement and grabbed the manila envelope with the death certificates and the key. He placed the envelope under his mattress until it was time to pick Isabella up.

Two days went by quickly and Bo was not able to get any rest because of constant nightmares about his mother, J'nae and even Isabella. His sub-conscience was giving him all the answers, but his conscious refused to accept them.

CHAPTER XX

Isabella was just as ready as Bo to get answers. She rolled her Nautica luggage to the door and did last minute checks to make sure she didn't forget anything. She peeked through the tiny peephole in the door when she heard three knocks. Bo was standing on the opposite side of the door twirling his key ring. "Who is it?" Izzy called to be cautious.

"It's me, Izzy. Bo."

She opened the door with the chain still on the door. After her attack she couldn't be too careful. Isabella peeked out the door to make sure Bo was alone. Bo shrugged his shoulders at her while she checked out the surroundings. She closed the door and removed the chain.

Bo opened the door and locked it behind him. "What's up? You ready?"

"Almost, I just need to do a final check to make sure everything is locked."

"You want me to take your bags downstairs while you're checking everything?"

"Yes, please," Isabella yelled from the back room. "And lock the door behind you."

Bo grabbed all the bags and dragged them down the stairs. He popped the trunk of the Chevy Malibu rental car and tossed the bags in it. He sat in the car waiting for Isabella to come downstairs. Bo adjusted the rearview mirror and saw a car that looked familiar. He did a double take and the car pulled off. He looked up and saw Isabella walking towards the car.

"Alright, I'm ready to get this over with," she huffed.

Bo looked behind him once again to make sure his eyes weren't playing tricks on him. "Izzy, I think I just saw Maleek's car."

"What? Are you serious?" Isabella turned her head to look out the back window. "Where, when?"

"A few minutes ago. I looked out the rearview mirror and

137

could swear I saw his car. I'm not for sure though."

"Bo, let's get the hell out of here. I really think he had something to do with my attack."

"Really, how does he even know you?"

"A few months ago I pinched him on a misdemeanor drug charge and he made a pass at me."

"Why didn't you tell me?"

"I was going to, but I needed to get more information."

"Do you really think he remembers you from that," Bo asked in a confused voice.

Isabella shrugged her shoulders. "Anything's possible, but we need to hurry up and get this case closed. The sooner the better, it's too much happening."

Bo pulled out of the complex. Him and Isabella continuously monitored their surroundings. They both had the feeling they were being followed, but neither saw any sign of Maleek.

"For some reason, I feel like somebody is following us Izzy."

"I know. I do too. That's so weird."

"Once we get on the plane we'll be fine, but I need to tell you something." Bo hesitated for a moment.

"What is it?" Isabella looked at Bo. She wanted the drama to end for her and Bo. She looked up at the planes in the sky. She knew the airport was close because of the numerous planes she saw in the sky. She just wanted to be in the sky with them.

"The guy from the surveillance pic you showed me…"

"Yeah, what about him?" she inquired curiously.

"He was at the funeral. He made a weird comment about my mom having nice things even at death. I mean, what the fuck does that mean?"

"Wow, are you serious? I don't think this good. Him showing up at your mother's funeral." Isabella paused.

"What's wrong?"

"Bo, the only time the mafia travels, especially to a funeral outside of their family, is for unfinished business. Believe me, it wasn't to pay his respects."

Bo shook his head. "I don't know what to say. I'm starting to fear for my life."

"Well, we have to deal with that bridge when we get to it. For

138

now I think you're fine."

Bo was silent. The parking lot gate arm opened as Bo pulled the ticket from the meter. He pulled into the parking lot and swung the car into a tight space almost hitting a red Blazer.

"Bo, be careful. Why are you in a rush?" Isabella screamed.

Bo ignored her ranting and threw the car in park. He popped the trunk and walked around to the back of the car. He sat Isabella bags on the ground, opened the back door and pulled his bags from the back seat. "Can you take all of your bags Izzy or do you need some help?"

"I think I can manage. What's crawled up your ass and died?"

"Nothing. I'm just ready to get this trip over with. So, c'mon."

Isabella rolled her eyes and grabbed her luggage from the trunk. She threw her carry-on bag across her shoulder and pulled her other two bags behind her. The airport was crowded and crowds irritated Bo. He pushed his way through the crowd of people and found an empty seat at his gate. Isabella followed closely behind him. They sat on a bench outside the gate in silence. An hour and a half later a woman's voice echoed over the loud speaker, "now boarding flight 215 at gate 23."

They boarded the plane and found their seats. Bo tossed the carry-on bags in the overhead bin above the seats. He starred at Isabella who was looking out the window at the tarmac. "You alright, girl?"

She turned and smiled at Bo. "Yeah, I'm okay. Just thinking about everything that's going on, especially what you told me about Moronelli."

"Me too. Well, we'll be in Cinci soon and hopefully we'll piece this whole thing together."

Bo sat back in his seat and buckled his seatbelt. He closed his eyes and minutes later the plane was in the air. When Bo reopened his eyes the plane was about to land in Cinci. He nudged Isabella who was also sleep. The plane landed ten minutes later and they de-boarded the plane. Bo and Izzy looked for the exit. Bo stood dead in his tracks when he thought he saw Maleek.

Isabella turned around when she noticed Bo wasn't behind her. "Bo, you alright?"

Bo was silent. He looked at Isabella like he saw a ghost.

Isabella walked back and shook his arm. "Bo, are you okay?"

"I could swear I just saw Maleek."

139

Isabella looked in the direction Bo was looking. "Bo, I think your mind is playing tricks on you. Let's get to the hotel." They hurried through the airport and haled a taxi. Bo reminisced about his mother as he observed the scenery on the way to the hotel. When they reached the hotel Bo checked in at the desk and they hurried to the room to get some rest.

CHAPTER XXI

Isabella sat on the edge of the king size hotel bed thumbing through Nikki's address book. She marked through names of people she was unable to contact.

"Any luck yet, Izzy?" Bo asked curiously.

"Not yet. All of the numbers are either disconnected or wrong." she said holding the telephone receiver to her ear.

"Well, keep trying." Bo encouraged. "We-"

Isabella shushed Bo. She held up her index finger signaling him to hold on one minute. "Hello, Clasik?"

"Who the fuck is this?" Bo heard a deep voice cough from the other end.

"Hi, I…" Isabella couldn't finish her sentence.

Bo snatched the phone. He could tell by Clasik's tone that he was not to be fucked with. "Wassup, Clasik?" Bo grunted in a thug like manner.

"Who the fuck is this?" Clasik asked again while inhaling smoke from a blunt.

"My man, you use to fuck wit my moms." Bo continued getting more into his thug character. Bo could hear Clasik puffing on his blunt before he responded.

"Nigga, who the fuck is yo moms. I'own fuck no old pussy. I like bitches young, hot and wet not old, cold and dry," he laughed commenting to some guys in the background.

Bo stayed in character, "her name was Nikki."

"Boy, I'own no no Nikki."

"My nig, you know my moms. I found yo numba in her phonebook." Bo confirmed waiting for a response. There was a pause. Bo thought Clasik hung up the phone, but waited another moment before he said anything.

"Nikki? You mean Nik. Dat's yo mom dukes. Yo, she a bad bitch. Last time I saw her was a couple years ago."

Bo was glad Clasik finally remembered his mother, but he needed to get information out of Clasik and he knew he couldn't do that over the

141

phone. Bo also knew it would take more than a conversation to get Clasik to talk about anything. He needed to get Clasik fucked up. "A couple years ago? We talkin' bout the same Nikki?" Clasik described Nikki to a tee. This added more fuel to the fire.

"I ain't know she came back."

"Yea, I handled some biz for her. Wassup?"

"She dead." It hurt Bo to talk about his mother in such a cold way, but he had to continue the charade.

"What? Nik is dead!" Clasik was stunned. "Dat was my numba one hoe. Thanks fo' lettin' me know." Clasik was about to hang up the phone, but Bo got a few last words in.

"Clasik, I need to holla at you 'bout my moms. Can you meet me somewhere?" Bo knew it was a long shot, but he needed some answers.

"Yea, yea. Nik was my girl. She hooked me up. Since you her son, I know you good peeps. Meet me at Passage nightclub on Main St. around midnight. I'm working there tonight. Just ask for me."

Bo was happy he was starting to make some progress. "Aight, I'll see you tonight," he confirmed. Bo placed the phone on the receiver and smiled at Isabella. "That's how you handle business," he smirked. "I'm meeting him tonight at a nightclub, Passage. Hopefully, he can give me some insight into the kind of lifestyle my mother lived."

Isabella was silent for a moment. "Bo, now remember, be prepared to accept any and everything. We about to get into some serious stuff. I know she was your mother, but there is a side of her lifestyle that you never knew about." she cautioned him again.

"I know Izzy. I'm willing to accept whatever I find out. I'm just ready to get to the bottom of this shit."

Isabella wanted to believe that Bo was ready to deal with whatever he was faced with, but she wasn't sure. Bo was in denial about everything surrounding J'nae and his mother. "Okay, I have to believe you, but for right now I'm tired. It's starting to get late and I've already called over twenty-five numbers and have only had one success. I didn't get any sleep last night and that flight drained me. So, I'm ready to pass out." Isabella fell back on the bed and closed her eyes. She could feel Bo staring at her so she kept her eyes closed to avoid making eye contact.

Bo couldn't help but notice how sexy Isabella looked in her

142

low-cut, form-fitting sweater and skinny jeans. Her make-up was perfect and her silky hair was pinned up in a bun. He approached the bed and stood in front of her. Isabella still did not open her eyes. Bo was an expert at giving women multiple orgasms and he wanted desperately to give her one.

He unbuttoned her jeans and slowly pulled them down. He gently kissed her inner thigh while he pulled down her black, red and white zebra striped underwear. Her body smelled of Bath & Body Works *P.S. I Love You* fragrance.

His tongue lightly brushed the tip of her clit making her tremble. He pushed her sweater up with his head kissing every inch of her stomach. He removed her sweater and unhooked her bra. Her nipples hardened at the touch of his thumbs. He pressed his lips against hers and their tongues intertwined passionately. His lips moved down her body replacing the touch of his thumbs with the touch of his lips and tongue. He sucked on her breasts like a baby, giving each one equal enjoyment. Isabella arched her back in pleasure as Bo made his way downtown.

 He kissed her inner thigh tenderly before burying his head into her gentleness. He sucked on her clit like a lollipop until he felt her body trembling with ecstasy. Isabella pushed his head deeper into her saturated pussy. Isabella eyes rolled into the back of her head and her legs started shaking uncontrollably.

"Sustantivo, te deseo, papi!" she whimpered. She moaned fiercely as her dam burst and flooded Bo's face. He accomplished his goal. He was about to lay down next her when she pulled him closer to her body. She reached for the crotch of his jeans trying to unzip them. Bo knew what she wanted.

He loosened his belt and dropped his jeans and boxers simultaneously. He mounted her and his thick dick penetrated her throbbing pussy leaving Isabella breathless. Her hands cupped his ass and pushed him deeper inside of her. She wrapped her long, bronze legs around his back and moved her body to his rhythm.

The moans of sweet surrender coming from Isabella grew Bo's excitement. He fought to contain himself, but it was inevitable. Isabella's warmth overpowered him. She let out a lioness like roar as Bo's strokes became harder and deeper, but gentle at the same time. She drew her knees up and pushed his chest fighting his deep plunge.

143

He stared in her eyes searching for signs that she wanted him to stop, but her eyes told the truth—she wanted all of him. She was in love.

In one long stroke he plunged all the way inside of her. Their moans were harmonious as they both reached instant gratification. They stared into each other's eyes and Bo leaned in and tongue wrestled with her. "Bo," she said softly. "You know we shouldn't have just done that. We're supposed to be here on business not pleasure."

Bo rolled over and lay beside her, both of their naked bodies covered with beads of sweat. He peered into her big brown eyes. "I know, but it's not like we haven't done this before. I just couldn't help myself. I really think we should--"

"Shh," She placed her index finger against his lips and gave him a peck on the lips. Isabella knew what he was about to say, but wanted him to remain as focused as possible on the task at hand. She rolled over on her right side and closed her eyes. Bo sat on the edge of the bed for a moment before walking into the bathroom. He stood in front of the vanity mirror flexing his naked muscles. "Okay Boston Rodriguez, game time," he said to himself before stepping in the shower.

Time was ticking by slowly. Bo was anxious to meet with Clasik. He looked at his watch and it was 11:23 p.m. Isabella was sleeping peacefully and Bo didn't want to wake her. He kissed her on the forehead and covered her bare shoulders with the blanket. He tiptoed pass the bed and closed the sturdy hotel door quietly.

A yellow cab was parked in front of the hotel. Bo tapped on the window. The driver was smoking a Camel cigarette and singing along to an old B.B. King song. He rolled down the window, "Where to?" the cabbie asked.

"Passage on Main St."

The cabbie gestured for Bo to get into the back of the cab. Bo slid across the leather seats and leaned on the door of the cab.

The cabbie adjusted the rearview mirror so that he could monitor Bo in the back seat. "Not from round 'ere, aye."

Bo looked up and saw the cabbie peeking at him. "I grew up in Cinci. I left about five or six years ago. I'm here handling some business."

The cabbie gave a quick head nod and focused his attention on the road. He turned up the music and continued to sing along to his

144

jazz.

CHAPTER XXII

The line to Passage was wrapped around the building. Bo could hear the thumping bass of the music outside the club. He approached a big white man with a low haircut wearing a black jacket with SECURITY etched in white. "What's up, man?" Bo asked.

The bouncer gave Bo an unwelcoming stare. He turned his head and took an ID from a young lady standing in line. She was 5'7" with brownish red hair. She tugged on her short dress that kept riding up her ass. The bouncer examined the ID like he was trying to pick someone out of a line up. He handed the ID back and the girl walked into the club. He still didn't acknowledge Bo.

Bo cleared his throat, "yo, I'm lookin' for Clasik." he said in an authoritative tone.

"Bena, tell Clas some dude out here askin' for 'im," the bouncer told a stocky black female wearing the same jacket.

Bo waited in front of the club braving the frigid air. He peered at his watch and ten minutes had gone by since the female went inside the club to deliver the message. Just as Bo was about to approach the bouncer again a large black man resembling a linebacker emerged from the dark entrance. "You Nikki's son?" his voice roared like thunder.

"Yea," Bo confirmed. He was intimidated by Clasik's large build. His muscles bulged and he looked like he could put a hurting on a nigga.

Clasik turned and disappeared back into the darkness of the club. Bo walked briskly to catch up to him. Clasik walked over to a petite woman behind the bar and whispered in her ear. She stared at Bo while he was whispering in her ear.

He led Bo into a small office cluttered with paper and boxes. He sat behind an outdated desk and waited for Bo to take a seat in the wobbly, steel grey chair in front of him. "What can I do for you?" Clasik began.

Bo was nervous. He didn't know the kind of person Clasik

145

was and he intimidated Bo. He broke the ice by asking a general question that would give him more than enough information. "How did you know my mom?"

Clasik leaned back in his chair that sounded like it was going to break every time he made a move. "Well, young blood, I met yo moms on the stroll years ago." he recalled.

Bo was confused, "the stroll?"

Clasik laughed so hard tears came to his eyes, but Bo didn't find anything amusing about his question. "I'm sorry, young blood. How old are you? You know what, it don't even matter." Clasik couldn't contain himself. He finally regained his composure. Bo gave him a blank stare still wondering what the hell was so funny. "Nigga, you don't know shit 'bout dese streets, do you?" Clasik laughed. "Yo motha was a hoe," he smirked. "And a damn good one. I offered my services, but she said she ain't need no pimp to protect her, but hell I liked her as more den a dolla hoe. It was something different 'bout her spirit. She won't like dese otha hoes. Even doe she was trickin' I respected her game. I'm sorry to hear she's dead. What happened anyway?" Clasik's curiosity started to kick in gear.

It hurt Bo to talk about his mother so soon after her death, but he braved his emotions. "She was murdered. First she was attacked in our house and then somebody drugged her in the hospital. I'm just tryin' to figure out what the fuck happened and who would want to do this. I'm findin' out I don't know my mother at all!"

Clasik's eyes widened. "What the fuck? I see the life finally caught up wit her ass. Shit!" He shook his head, "damn Nik! So what you want me to tell you? Nik was my baby. I'll tell you what I know 'bout her." he offered.

Bo was surprised at how cooperative Clasik was being. "Thanks man. I appreciate anything you can tell me about the last time you talk to or saw her."

Clasik thought for a moment. "It's funny, Nik called me out the blue a few years ago and wanted me to do her a favor. A week later she was in Cinci asking me to flip some caine. She laced me lovely for doin' it too. After I finished doin' what she wanted I gave her the bread and I ain't neva hear from her again."

"One more question, did you know a man named Fatz?" he inquired.

146

Clasik rocked in his chair. "Oh yeah, hell yeah I knew that nigga. He was my competition back in the day. Nik and her girl Chris used to fuck wit dat nigga hard. From what I remember Nik was dealin' wit dat nigga on some other shit. I tried to get her to come work for me, but Nik was all on that nigga dick."

"Yeah, I was kind of young, but I remember them dating. I was there the night dem niggas killed him." Bo reminisced.

Bo peeked Clasik's interest even more. "Word! I heard dem niggas went in like Scarface, flipped that nigga wig back and then dey chopped dat nigga up and left his shit in pieces, Jamaican style."

Bo chuckled, "Naw, they fucked that nigga up, but nuttin' like that. Don't get it twisted, that nigga didn't go out without a fight." Bo confirmed.

"Shoulda known dat bitch Angel ain't know what the fuck she was talkin' 'bout."

"Who?" Bo questioned to make sure he heard the name right. "Who told you that?"

"Dis bitch named Angel dat used to fuck wit dat nigga back in the day. She was runnin' her shit 'bout how her new nigga had him fucked up for rippin' him off. She one of dem uptown hoes dat only fuck wit big paper niggas." Clasik exclaimed.

Bo was getting excited, so excited his dick started to get hard. He remembered the girl that confronted Maleek at the restaurant the night they were out. He knew it couldn't be a coincidence. "Yo, do you know where I can find her?"

"Last I heard that scheming ass trick was managing some hoes at a spot on Old State Route 74. Some upscale escort shit. No matter how much dough dat bitch got she still finds a way to stay trickin'."

Bo stood up from the chair anxious to get back to the hotel. He couldn't wait to tell Isabella what he found out. "Thanks Clasik. I appreciate it man, for real."

Clasik gave Bo a head nod. Bo turned and disappeared through the dark hallway. When he stepped outside the line was still wrapped around the building. He could feel the females in the line eyeballing him. He was a fine ass brother and he knew it. Women of all races tried to get at him, but he was not worried about women right now.

Bo realized he didn't get the number of the cab company

before he got out and he needed a ride to the hotel. Just as he was about to dial information to get the number a black and silver Maxima pulled up in front of him. The windows were mirror tinted and sat on 22" rims. The window dropped down slowly. The driver was an extremely beautiful exotic looking female with flowing jet-black wavy tresses like his mom's. Her passenger was not nearly as stunning as her.

"Hey handsome, why you standing out here by yourself. You should be inside surrounded by women." The beauty joked with a Brazilian accent.

Bo smiled showing all his pretty white teeth. "Actually, I'm leaving. Do you know the number to any cab places around here."

"Baby, you don't need to call a cab. I'll give you a ride."

Bo didn't feel like waiting for a cab so he accepted the woman's offer. She unlocked the car door and Bo made himself comfortable in the back seat. The inside of the car was immaculate and every thirty seconds Bo felt a light aroma mist sprinkle on his face. He could tell that she was well polished and accepted nothing but the best in her life.

"So, what's your name cutie?" the beauty asked.

"Boston, but everybody knows me as Bo. What's y'all names?"

"I'm Gabriel and this is Ana." the driver introduced.

"Nice to meet you ladies."

"Okay, now that we're formally introduced," Gabriel smiled. "What are you doin' tonight, Boston?"

Bo wanted to get back to the hotel, but he knew Isabella was still sleep so he couldn't tell her anything until the morning. He decided to hang out with his new friends for the night. "Nothin'. Tryin' to see what you ladies gettin' into."

Gabriel and Ana looked at each other and shared a laugh. "Wanna have some real fun?" Gabriel smirked.

Bo didn't know what he was about to get himself into, but since he was in Cinci he thought he might as well have some much needed relaxation too. "Sure, what you ladies have in mind?"

Ana turned around and looked at Bo, "just relax baby, we're going to take good care of you tonight."

Bo didn't know what the ladies had planned, but he trusted it wasn't anything he couldn't handle. They pulled in front of a two-story

148

brick house with a perfectly manicured lawn. A 2009 pewter Solara coupe, 2002 money green Jaguar and a vintage Alpha Romero lined the driveway.

"C'mon Boston! You want to have a good time, we're going to show you a good time." Gabriel yelled.

Bo opened the car door and sprinted to the front door. Gabriel and Ana vanished into the maze of rooms and hallways in the house. Bo stood in the foyer and watched as a pretty girl with short black hair walked pass him dressed in a pair of green lace boy shorts and a matching bra. Bo could not help but to stare at her brown round ass that spilled out the bottom of the boy shorts that were two sizes too small.

"Hey Boston," he heard a faint voice call from the back of the house. "Boston, back here."

Bo followed the sound of the voice through the long hallway. He peeked in a room that was occupied by a tall woman wearing nothing but a pair of peach leopard thong underwear. She was standing over a man with his face buried in between her breasts.

"Bo," Gabriel called as she popped her head out of a door further down the hall. Bo continued towards Gabriel observing the sex sounds coming from the rooms around him. He began to wonder what he had gotten himself into for the night. Bo knew he was attractive and he damn sure didn't intend on paying for pussy. That was something he could get for free all day long.

Gabriel was dressed in a short see-through baby doll gown with nothing underneath. Ana was sprawled across the bed wearing a matching black and white polka dot bra and panty set. Bo liked what he was seeing, but he refused to pay for anything, especially since he wasn't forewarned.

"Gabriel, I hope you don't think…" Gabriel walked up to Bo and forced her tongue down his throat before he could finish his sentence. She cupped his balls through his jeans and massaged them at the same time. Gabriel walked Bo over to the bed and Ana pulled him down beside her. She spread his lips with hers and sucked his tongue into her mouth. Her tongue moved rapidly intertwining his in a seductive call of passion. Gabriel pulled Ana away and the women embraced in a lip lock forgetting for a moment that Bo was lying between them.

Ana lifted Gabriel's slender arms and slipped her baby doll

149

gown over her flowing, wavy locks. Ana kissed Gabriel's supple C breast. The tip of her tongue grazed Gabriel's erect nipple growing her arousal. Ana's mouth overflowed with the fullness of Gabriel's breasts. The sight of the women engaging each other also grew Bo's arousal and curiosity. He never had a threesome although he had offers, but he knew how to get women off and this time he wanted to test his skills with two women.

Bo sat up on the bed and unhooked Ana's Bra. He kissed her breasts the way she was kissing Gabriel's. Ana forced Gabriel on the bed and straddled her. She engaged Gabriel in a receptive kiss. Their moans grew loud as both of their bodies awakened. Ana filled her mouth with Gabriel's right breast while Bo pleasured the left. The feeling of two mouths on her body sent spine tingling chills through her body. Her body started to squirm with excitement.

Ana ravaged Gabriel's body with quick gentle kisses. Gabriel gasped as Ana's index finger slipped into her warm pussy. Her pleasure was compounded when she felt the warmth of Ana's breath on her twat. She pressed her thick lips against Gabriel's pussy lips and began sucking like it was a juicy plum. Ana could feel the sweet juices on her chin. Gabriel's fingers outlined the creases in Ana's tiny back while she and Bo engaged in a slow deep kiss.

"Hmm Gabby, let it out baby. I want to taste all of you." Ana murmured. Her tongue went deeper inside Gabriel when she felt the softness of Bo's lips on her pussy. Ana's lips pressed firmly against Gabriel's moistness. Gabriel clenched the satin sheets anticipating her orgasmic delight. Gabriel's passion covered Ana's face, but that didn't deter her. The closer Ana came to climaxing, the more she continued to plunge her tongue into Gabriel's soaking wet pussy. Gabriel could take no more, neither could Ana.

Bo dropped his jeans and boxers and entered Ana making her sing like a canary. He stoked her deep pussy while Gabriel wrapped her lips around Ana's chocolate Hershey Kiss breasts. Gabriel's tongue wrestled with Ana's small nipples giving her joy she had rarely experienced before and arousing her deepest inner desires. Ana caressed her breasts cupping them in enjoyment. Bo's thrusts grew harder and deeper. Ana pulled away. She turned around and placed her full lips on his thick dick. Her head bobbed back and forth bringing him to ecstasy. She stopped abruptly switching places with Gabriel.

150

Gabriel licked around the tip of Bo's dick teasing him. She slowly closed her mouth taking in all of him. She moved his dick in and out of her mouth rotating her motions, slow then fast, fast then slow. Her actions gave Bo a pleasure he only dreamt of. He grabbed the back of her head and shoved his entire dick in her mouth almost gagging her. Bo gave two more deep thrusts and let out a high-pitched groan indicating his bliss. Gabriel continued sucking until the fire in Bo died, not leaving one drop.

The three lay across the bed, Gabriel fingers circled the rings of Ana's breasts. "Did you enjoy yourself, Boston?" Ana giggled turning her head to look at him.

Bo stared at the ceiling glowing in aftermath. "Yes, I did!"

Gabriel leaned over Ana's naked body, "I'm glad. Usually, that kinda action would have cost you about fifteen hundred, ya know."

"So, why no charge?" Bo was curious. He didn't mind what had just went down, but it didn't make sense to him. He had just met these chicks and they solicited him not the other way around. He could tell they were high-class material.

Gabriel laughed. "Don't worry 'bout that, baby. Plus you fine as hell, so that didn't bother me or Ana."

"Okay, no argument here. I need to get back to my hotel. I have a long day tomorrow." Bo told the ladies. He swung his legs over the edge of the bed and picked his jeans off the floor. He could feel the vibration of his cell phone through his pocket. He peeked at his cell phone and saw two missed calls from Isabella.

He hurried and threw his clothes on, but noticed Gabriel and Ana were still lying on the bed playing with each other. Bo cleared his throat to get their attention. Gabriel looked at Bo. "Oh, I'm sorry baby. We're comin'."

Gabriel and Ana went into the bathroom together. Bo heard the sound of the shower water blasting. He was eager to get back to the hotel, but again his curiosity got the better of him. He walked over and put his ear to the bathroom door listening intently. He heard the girls giggling and laughing. Bo pushed the door open and saw them grinding in the shower.

Gabriel's perky breast glistened as the beads of water rolled off her body. Ana's chocolate body bumped up against Gabriel's plump ass and her hands playfully rubbed soap over her flat stomach. "Want to join us?" Ana chuckled kissing on Gabriel's back.

Bo wanted to continue their escapade, but he knew he had to get back to the hotel. Isabella had already called him twice and he knew she would ask him a million and one questions about where he'd been and what he found out. "Hell yeah I want to, but I gotta get going."

Gabriel looked over her shoulder at Ana. "Well baby, that's it for our fun tonight." She turned the shower off, snatched a red Nautica towel of the towel rack and wrapped it around her body. Ana followed suit. Bo sat on the bed while the women dressed. "You ready?" Gabriel asked twisting her long, wet locks into a bun.

Bo nodded his head and closed the bedroom door behind him.

CHAPTER XXIII

Bo opened the hotel door as quietly as he possibly could. He did not want to disturb Isabella, but she was sitting in a chair reading a book when he walked in. "Hey Izzy, what you doin' up?" Bo asked coyly. He knew she had a slight attitude. After living with his mother, Christine, and J'nae he knew when a woman had an attitude and an argument was sure to follow. Isabella was silent. She ignored Bo's question and continued to read her book. "Izzy?" Bo called again.

Isabella placed her book down on the wooden table beside her. She tilted her head to the side and her long black hair fell over her left shoulder. "What?" she replied in a cold tone.

"What's wrong? Why you up so late?" Bo asked in a mellow voice trying to balance their moods.

"I should be asking you the same thing." She countered.

"Hold up Izzy," he began. "We're suppose to be here on business, so why the hell do you have an attitude because I'm coming in at 3:30 a.m. if I'm out handlin' business."

Isabella huffed brashly. She knew Bo was right, but she couldn't deny her emotional and physical attachment to him. She let her feelings mix with business and that was a recipe for disaster, but she needed to set the record straight with him. "You know what Boston, you're a 100% correct. We are here on business, but at the same time, you're the one that pushed up on me. You're the one that decided to eat my pussy, fuck the shit out of me then bounce without even saying a word. You can't just do that to me and think that everything is all good. Yes, I realize what we're here for, but if that's the case, let it be that-just business! Now that that's said and done tell me

Boston, who did you go see and what did you find out since you were out *handlin'* business."

Bo was speechless. Isabella said a mouthful and he didn't know how to respond to what she said, but he wanted to take care of business. He didn't have time for foolishness. "I met with Clasik."

Isabella was interested in what Bo found out. "Really? What did he say?"

"He told me about my mom being a, uh," Bo was reluctant to say the word.

"Prostitute, a hoe." Isabella uttered coldly.

Bo was not thrilled with her choice of words or her brashness, but it was what it was. "Yeah, that. He also told me about the chick named Angel that was bragging about her man fuckin' Fatz up."

Isabella scrunched her face in confusion, "Fatz? What does he have to do with this?"

"Okay," Bo took a deep breath before telling the story about Fatz. "To make a long story short he was a big time drug dealer in Ohio and him and my mother were dating when he was killed in our apartment. After his death we moved to VA. All my mother said was that it was for our own good. Didn't I tell you this already?"

"I think you did, I'm sorry. I think Fatz is Maurice Johnson," Isabella proclaimed.

Bo tilted his head like a dog in thought. "Possibly. Told you didn't know anything about him. I never knew his name. Wait a minute, on second thought, the night he died one of the guys did say his name." Bo wrecked his brain trying to remember years back to the night Fatz died. It was definitely a night he would never forget, but some details were a little fuzzy. "Shit!" Bo continued to think, than it hit him. He remembered the two death certificates he found in the basement, Maurice Johnson. At the time he found the death certificates the name did not ring a bell, but everything was coming together. "Maurice 'Fatz' Johnson, that's his name!"

She knew Fatz was at the bottom of all the drama surrounding Nikki. "Okay, and what was the girl's name again? The one that was bragging."

"Angel. I think it's the same girl that confronted Maleek when we were at Apple Bee's the other night. I'm not sure though." Bo recalled.

154

"Hold on," Isabella was getting excited about the information Bo was giving her. "You've met this girl, Angel?"

"Not exactly. Her and Maleek had a few words at Apple Bee's. He didn't introduce us and he didn't seem like he cared to."

Isabella's interrogation skills began to kick in. "What were they arguing about?"

"I don't remember to tell you the truth, but Clasik did tell me she works at some upscale escort place on Old State Route 74."

"Is there anything else you can remember? Anything at all?" Isabella pressed.

"Yeah, she was saying something about doing his dirty work. She told him she held the key. Whatever that meant. That's it."

"Alright, this is good. In the morning we will start to track down these leads, follow-up on this bank statement and check on Moronelli.

Bo sat on the bed and began to take his clothes off preparing for bed. He threw his shirt and jeans on the chair beside Isabella. He lay on the bed with nothing but his Calvin Klein boxer shorts. Isabella could not stop staring at his half naked body.

"Boston, what do you think you're doin'?" Isabella inquired.

Bo was a little puzzled by her question. "What are you talking about?"

She pointed to the floor with her head.

"Oh hell naw, Izzy! You jokin', right?" Bo knew what she was referring to. Since they were intimate hours before and just had a falling out over mixing business and pleasure, Isabella didn't want to confuse things anymore by sleeping in the same bed.

"Bo, we just discussed this. We're here on *business*. I do not think it's appropriate for us to sleep in the same bed; therefore, you need to sleep on the floor for the rest of the trip. This way we know nothing will happen," she proclaimed sarcastically.

"This bitch crazy. Boston it's only for a couple of days." he muttered under his breath.

"Excuse me, do you have something to say?" she asked with a hint of an attitude.

"You good. Fucked up, but good." Bo grabbed one of the pillows off the bed and tossed it on the floor. He walked over to the small closet and snatched a sheet and blanket. Isabella watched while

155

Bo made a makeshift bed on the floor. She desperately wanted Bo to sleep with her. She longed for a man to hold her while she slept, something she hadn't felt in a long time, but she could not compromise her feelings any further.

Isabella settled into bed and turned on her side facing away from Bo. She lay awake in bed staring at the wall and thinking about how Bo made her feel. She knew her thoughts should be on the case, but she was having a hard time separating business from pleasure after their intimate moment. She wondered what Bo was thinking at that moment.

Bo was awake also, but he was not thinking about Isabella or sex for that matter. Bo was consumed with thoughts about Angel, Maleek and Fatz. He was anxious to know how all three tied in with the death of his mother. There wasn't much night left and Bo got no rest. Between the hard floor and his mind racing a thousand miles a minute he couldn't sleep. It was going to be a full day and he was ready to tackle it.

CHAPTER XXIV

Isabella leaned over the bed and grabbed her brown leather suitcase. She pulled out a thick stack of papers and shuffled through them. She sat up in the bed and studied the overseas bank statement. The deposits and high number of transfers to and from the account were consistent up until the day of Nikki's attack, which struck Isabella as odd. "Bo, the activity on this overseas account was active up until the day of the attack. Actually, there was one last transfer the day after."

Bo slid on his black and red Rocawear shorts and sat beside Isabella studying the statement with her. "Do you think the transfers had anything to do with that guy she was talking to in the surveillance pictures?"

"Possibly, I don't know. Can't really say at this point, but there's no way their going to give us any information on this account without either a warrant or your mother's consent."

"Well, you're gonna have to imitate her."

Isabella whipped her head around to stare at Bo. "Are you out of your mind? I'm an officer of the law. Do you know what could happen to me for doing that?"

"Okay, do you have any suggestions because getting a warrant could take a minute?"

"I don't know, Bo. But we need to find out where this money came from and what she was doing to get this money."

"Here's the deal, you think of how to get information and I'll follow-up with Angel."

Isabella agreed and continued to study the documents in front of her.

157

Bo decided to order room service as a peace offering. He ordered Isabella's favorite foods, scrambled eggs with American cheese, grits with cheese, pancakes with blueberry syrup and fresh fruits with orange juice. Bo needed a good breakfast and hot shower to jumpstart the long day ahead of him. He relaxed on the bed watching Isabella put together the pieces of his mother's murder. He appreciated everything that she was doing because the other detectives assigned to the case did not seem to do as much as she did. Isabella was so consumed with her work that she didn't hear her cell phone ring.

"Izzy," Bo called, but Isabella didn't pay him any attention. "Izzy," he called again this time shaking her leg gently.

"Hmm."

"Your cell is ringing. You gone answer it?"

Isabella reached into her purse and answered her phone. "Hello."

"Hey Isabella. It's Jack. I haven't heard from you in a while. What's goin' on with the Rodriguez case?" Jack was one of the other officers assigned to the case.

Isabella stopped shuffling through the papers to discuss the case with Jack. Bo was also curious to hear if the other detectives had any further leads. "Oh, hey Jack. I was just going over some information now. I've been following up on some potential leads. Have you found anything?" Isabella wanted to keep her location a secret. She didn't want anyone to find out about her relationship with Bo.

"Actually, I have. Are you able to meet me for lunch? We haven't seen you around the station." Jack said with a little worry.

Isabella hesitated before answering. "Uh, I don't think I can Jack. I've been so busy following up on leads and dealing with family stuff. Maybe next week, okay."

"Sure, no problem. I thought you might want to know I've been looking into some things and I came across something very interesting."

Isabella's interest peaked immediately. "Okay, what?"

"Ms. Rodriguez had quite a bit of money invested in some company in Miami. Apparently, it's a really small company with about four employees that cater to very high-powered and well-connected people. Ms. Rodriguez was on payroll for about three years and according to their records she made a lot of money. And get this it was

158

run by Nestrago Moronelli and Ramon Vicente of the mafia family."

"Really? What was she into? Did you find out anything else?"

Jack paused, "I don't know, but a whole lot from what I'm gathering. Five years ago she was involved in a domestic dispute with her ex-husband."

"What's so crazy about that?"

"She killed him."

"What?" Isabella shouted. Bo was caught off guard by Isabella's loud holler.

"She shot him at close range. She claimed self-defense. The reports say she didn't have any bruises or marks on her, but the two did have a long history of domestic violence. Over the course of a six year marriage she was admitted to the hospital for various broken bones a total of 13 times."

"Damn, this is a twist of events."

"That's not all. She collected a hefty insurance settlement because he didn't change the beneficiary on his policy."

"That's not that unusual. People forget to do those things."

"That may be true Isabella, but he was scheduled to meet with his attorney to discuss the changes two days before she killed him. Coincidence? I don't think so, but no charges were ever filed due to the volatile history between the two. She also made several trips to Miami, Columbia, Italy and Cuba. And the timeline we came up with shows that while she was in all of these places major crime bosses ended up dead. I think she was a hit woman."

"Whoa. I never expected that. Thanks for the information Jack. I'll definitely call you when I get things squared away with my family." Isabella hung up the phone and sat on the bed in a daze.

"Izzy, is everything okay?" Bo inquired anxious to know who Isabella was talking to and what she was talking about.

Isabella sighed, "Bo, why didn't you tell me about your mom and dad?"

"What do you mean?"

"About their relationship."

"Izzy, I was too young to remember anything that happened between them. After we left I only saw my dad once or twice and my mom never talked about him."

Isabella was silent. She didn't know whether or not to tell Bo

159

about his mother killing his father, but she knew the money in the offshore account came from the insurance money and payments from Moronelli. "Bo I need to tell you something."

"What?"

"That was one of the detectives assigned to the case. He said your mother killed your father in self-defense a few years ago and that she collected on his insurance policy."

"She said my dad was murdered in a robbery. I knew about the insurance policy only because that's what we survived off for a few years, but I didn't think I needed to mention that."

"Well," she continued. "Your mother had investments tied up in a business run by the Mafia. The one I showed you the picture of."

"Wait, that I don't believe. My mother was one of the most connected women in the industry around here. She didn't need to be involved in anything illegal," he blurted frustrated by the accusations.

"Bo, people do stupid things for a lot of reasons, especially greed. I think your mom became addicted to the money and the lifestyle she lived. I mean, she was spoiled by the life your father and Fatz gave her. Working with Fatz I'm sure she met a lot of well-respected men in the game. She may have gotten involved in any kind of craziness. And that's a game you don't want to play."

"I don't know. That's for you to figure out. I'm going to meet this chick Angel." Bo said with an attitude. He stormed into the bathroom and slammed the door. Isabella dove back into the pile of paperwork lying on the bed. Minutes later Bo reappeared with a towel wrapped around his waist. Isabella couldn't help but notice his chiseled chest and muscular legs.

"Could you put some clothes on please?" she griped knowing she enjoyed the eye candy.

"I need to get some clothes out of my suitcase, if you don't mind and if you do mind then close your damn eyes." Bo bent over and dug through his clothes. Isabella could see the knot in the side of the towel slipping. She bit her lip as the towel fell to the floor exposing Bo's tight ass. Bo picked up the towel and rewrapped it around his waist. He gathered his clothes and ran into the bathroom.

Isabella heard Bo's cell phone going off. She usually wouldn't look at the caller id, but something told her to. She walked over to the desk and peeked at the phone. It was Maleek. She was curious to know

160

what Maleek had to say. Bo gave Isabella the run down on Maleek and Christine after the attacks. She knew everything about them, especially Maleek.

One thing continuously nagged at Isabella. The arrest of Maleek years earlier was too much of a coincidence for Isabella. She believed that Maleek had something to do with her attempted rape, even though there was no direct evidence linking him. Isabella also had a feeling that Maleek and possibly Christine were involved in the murder of Nikki and J'nae.

Isabella could hear Bo about to come out the bathroom and scurried back to the bed like a roach when lights come on. She hopped on the bed and pretended she was there the whole time.

"Did my phone ring?"

"Umm, I think so. Wasn't paying attention."

Bo walked over to the desk and looked at his phone. He was surprised to see a missed call from Maleek, but he decided not to return the call yet. His head was spinning from all the information he gathered. He didn't know what to think of Maleek anymore. After he blew up at the restaurant Bo didn't know what Maleek was capable of.

"I'm about to go see if I can track down this chick, Angel."

"Ok, I'm going to check into this offshore account and see if I can find anybody that may have known your mother and father."

Bo walked out the room without saying a word. It was extremely difficult for Bo to piece together his mother's former life. He didn't understand the choices his mother made, but he knew she was a survivor and everything she did she did for him.

He glanced up at the lit floor number above the elevator. He stood impatiently in front of the door waiting for it to open. He stepped in the elevator and pulled out a piece of paper with an address scribbled on it. He walked through the lobby and sat down on a short plush red and gold couch. He dialed 411 and requested the number of a local taxi company. After calling a taxi Bo decided to return Maleek's call.

Maleek answered the phone on the first ring, "Bo, where the fuck you been, man? I was trying to get in touch with you! Mo is dead!"

Bo was speechless. It was too much for him to handle. He tried to speak, but no words came out.

"Bo! Did you hear me?" Maleek screamed into the phone.

161

"I heard you L. What do you mean she's dead? How'd she die?"

"She was in a car accident. Her brakes were cut and she ran off the road and struck a tree. She didn't have on her seat belt and she went through the windshield. Bo, I need you to be here. Where are you?"

"Damn, I'm sorry about Mo. Is MJ okay? He wasn't with her, was he?"

"Naw, she was on the way to pick him up. Thank God he wasn't in the car! But where are you man? Nobody has seen you in a few days."

"Shit! I'm out of town with a friend, but I'll be back early. I know you and MJ need support right now. L, I'm really sorry."

"Bo, I don't know what to do. Mo was my life. Fuck!" Maleek punched a giant hole through the wall.

"L, calm down. I know you're in a lot of pain right now, but calm down." Bo could sense the pain and anger in Maleek's voice and knew he could be erratic when he wasn't thinking clearly.

"Yo B, I need you to be here, now!" Maleek demanded.

"Maleek, I'm out of town man. I'll be there as soon as I can."

"Alright B. I see how you are." Maleek hung up the phone in fury.

Bo knew that L needed his support. Even though he was trying to find out what happened to his mother, L was there for him while he grieved and it was only right for him to be there for Maleek especially MJ. Bo walked over to the elevator that was already open. He pressed the 5th floor button several times before the door finally closed. On his ride up, Bo contemplated his decision to leave early. He decided to let Isabella know that their trip would be cut short due to everything going on at home. Isabella was generally an understanding person and Bo knew she would be okay with leaving.

"What are you doing back?" Isabella asked while pulling her yellow BeBe sweater over her head.

"Change of plans. We need to leave early. Maleek's wife died in a car crash and I need to be there for him."

"Oh my God. I'm so sorry to hear that. Okay, well let me check for flights and I'll make arrangements to leave on the next flight out." In the back of her mind she felt something wasn't quite right, but

162

she kept all her suspicions to herself. Being a homicide detective made Isabella suspicious of everyone and everything. She knew she needed to keep her eyes and ears open because she was the only one with Bo's best interest in mind. It was too much of a coincidence that people connected to Bo were dropping like flies. Now Maleek's wife. She knew it was too much of a coincidence and Maleek was up to something.

Bo made sure all of his clothes and belongings were neatly tucked away in his suitcase. He wanted to be prepared to leave in a moments notice just in case Isabella was able to secure a flight within the next couple of hours. He heard Isabella on the phone with a flight attendant negotiating the costs for changing the flight dates. He flopped on the bed and waited for Isabella to hang up the phone with the airline.

"Just to confirm, the two flights have been changed to leave tomorrow morning at 10 am and arrive in Virginia at 1 pm and you're also going to waive the fee for changing the flights due to the emergency. Okay, great! Thank you so much, good bye."

"All set?"

"Yes, we'll be leaving in the morning." she confirmed.

"Great, so I still have enough time to go meet Angel. Shit, I forgot my taxi is probably downstairs waiting. I'll be back shortly."

"Wait, Bo. Give me the address just in case."

"Yo, I'm good. Ain't nothin' gonna happen. Just chill and see what you can find."

Isabella didn't like the idea of him going to see Angel alone. It didn't sit well with her.

Bo rushed out the door and bypassed the elevator. He took the stairs down to the lobby where his taxi was waiting outside.

"Where to," an Arabic man wearing a Bengals cap asked.

Bo pulled the paper from his pocket again, "Old State Route 74."

"Sure, that's a nice drive from here."

"Okay." Bo stared out the window during the whole twenty-minute trip not saying a word to the driver until he reached his destination.

"That'll be $42.25," the cabby uttered. He pulled out a log and jotted down the mileage from his odometer. He turned around and grabbed the $45 Bo was waving through the wire gate that separated

163

the front and back seat.

"Keep the change." Bo declared before exiting the cab.

CHAPTER XXV

Bo pushed the buzzer outside of the tall iron gate that surrounded a mini mansion type house. The lawn was flawless and outlined with trimmed bushes. A young woman's voice echoed thru the buzzer.

"Hello, who is it?"

"Hi, I'm here to see Angel."

"I'm sorry, how did you get this address. This is a private residence."

"A mutual friend named Clasik told me I could find her here."

There was a long period of silence. Bo thought the young woman decided not to open the gate so he pressed the buzzer again.

"Who the hell is this?" a different woman belted. Bo could hear the attitude in her voice.

"My name is Boston, and I'm here to see Angel. I have some personal business to handle with her."

"Boston? I don't know any Boston." Angel belted.

"Maybe you know my mother Nikki or my boy Maleek."

Bo heard the gate click and pushed it open. He walked pass the trimmed bushes and water fountain until he reached the front door. A pretty woman resembling Vivica Fox greeted him at the door. She was wearing a pair of Gucci "Genius Jeans," a white Gucci shirt and a pair of studded Gucci heels. Her make-up, hair and nails were impeccable. Bo never met a woman so well put together. Even the women from the night before couldn't match her look.

"Come in. Boston, you said it was?" she reconfirmed.

"Yeah, just call me Bo."

She led Bo into a large office and directed him to have a seat in a

164

leather swivel chair. "So, Bo you said you have some personal business to handle with me.

"I don't look familiar to you?" he questioned trying to get Angel to recall the encounter with Maleek a couple of weeks earlier.

"No, not really. Am I supposed to remember you?"

"A couple of weeks ago you were in VA at an Apple Bee's and you got into a small altercation with Maleek."

Angel was quiet for a moment. She nodded her head slightly. "I remember vaguely. Why?"

"I guess you were too heated to notice, but I was sitting there when you came over."

"Okay. Sorry, I still don't remember you, but what do you want and why are you here? I have a lot of work to do.

A woman's silhouette appeared in the doorway of the office. "Knock, knock. Angel can I come in?"

"What is it, Gabby?"

"I just want to ask you—oh hey, Bo. What are you doin' here?"

Angel exchanged glances between Bo and Gabriel. "You two know each other?"

"You can say that." Gabriel replied.

"So you work for her?" Bo asked Gabriel.

Angel responded before Gabriel had the opportunity to, "Gabby, give me a few minutes please. Close the door behind you and let the other girls know I'm in a meeting. Thanks." Gabriel winked at Bo before closing the office door behind her.

"Boston, how do you know Gabby?"

"We met last night at Passage."

"Humph, okay. Is that it?" Angel was suspicious of Bo and his intentions, but she still went on with giving him the information he wanted.

"No, that's not it. I see you're not one for chitchat so I'll get to the point. What do you know about a nigga named Fatz?"

Angel leaned back in her chair and rocked a little. She tapped her manicured nails on the glossy desk and laughed under her breath. "Fatz. Now that's a name I haven't heard in a long time. Yeah, I knew Fatz and ya boy Maleek. Needless to say, neitha one of dem muthafuckas was shit."

165

"My question is how? And what did you know about Fatz death? And you told Maleek you had something on him. What were you talkin' 'bout?"

Angel chuckled, "damn Boo, you ask a lot of fuckin' questions. You workin' for the Feds or something? Do I need a lawyer?"

"Nothing like that. Like I said, I just need to know what you know 'bout that nigga Fatz. This has nothing to do with you. So anything you tell me is for my use only. Strictly confidential."

"I'ma be real wit you, Boston. I've done some things in my past I'm not proud of and I think it's about time I cleared my soul and got this shit out in the open. First off, I don't know how much of Maleek's background you know about, but he had a brother. His brother happened to be Maurice 'Fatz' Johnson." By the look on Bo's face Angel knew Bo didn't know. "I take it you didn't know."

"Shit no. L never talked about his past or his present for that matter."

"And for good reason," Angel added. "I used to fuck wit Fatz and we got into it because he found out I was messin' with Maleek behind his back. Me and Maleek started kickin' it and I ended up workin' wit him."

"Workin' wit him, doin' what?"

"Runnin' errands and lil shit like that, but anyway. Maleek thought Fatz ripped him off because he was missin' some money and a couple of packages. He accused Fatz because he said me and Fatz were the only two people that knew where he kept his stash and I had no reason to rip him off, or so he thought. I needed a come up, so I took his shit, but Fatz was his competition. They were always goin' at it, so he was an easy target. I was Maleek's eyes. Fatz had a shop and I convinced him to let me work for him and keep an eye on the other chicks."

Bo interjected, "Hold up. Fatz let you work for him even though you were fuckin' his brother who was also his rival?"

"Wasn't that easy, but good pussy and head are a motherfucker. Niggas go crazy over that shit. Plus, I dropped a dime on L. Meanwhile, me and L were still kickin' it, but we stayed away from each other while I was workin' wit Fatz. Nobody knew I was still talkin' to L. In the meantime, L started fuckin' with this bitch named

166

Christine. And she was like his puppet. He had that effect on bitches. Christine and this other high saditty chick named Nikki met Fatz one night when he was strolling for hoes."

Bo kept quiet because if it was one thing Maleek taught him it was to keep your mouth closed and ears open. He always told him if you let somebody talk enough they will tell you everything you want to know without you asking.

"That's how I knew dem broads. But, the chick Nikki looked familiar. We all use to work the same corners. Cinci is small. Fatz needed some girls to work for him that's when he went out lookin' and met those bitches. They started workin' in the shop and the chick Nikki became Fatz's main hoe. I was a lil salty at first, but I got over it. It comes with the territory. After a while I realized how I knew that chick Nikki. I used to fuck wit her old man. He was a guard for the Celtics. I didn't mind playin' the side bitch because I got what I needed from him, but that dumb ass broad was blind to the facts. Anyway…"

"Damn," Bo thought out loud.

Angel laughed. "You have no idea. At the time nobody knew Fatz and Maleek were brothers, except me. Since they were beefin' they never talked 'bout each other so nobody would have known."

It took every fiber in Bo's body for to keep him from blurting that Nikki and Christine were his peoples, but he kept quiet and let Angel finish talking.

She continued, "I kept Maleek informed about everything that was goin' on with them. See, Maleek knew his brother and he knew he was a sucker for a big ass and a pretty face. That was his weakness and downfall. The night Fatz was murdered I followed them."

"So you set them up?" he asked in an accusing tone.

"I told you, I did some things I wasn't proud of, but I didn't know exactly what L was goin' to do until it was done. Anyway, after I called L and told him they had left the house I don't know what happened from that point. All I know is Fatz ended up dead."

"Clasik told me you were going around tellin' everybody your nigga had Fatz fucked up."

"Clasik? What the fuck? That bitch was just jealous I wasn't trickin' wit him. But, who knows? I probably did. I've matured over the years. A lot of things have changed as you can see. I run an upscale escort service and I make major dough, not that chump change I used to

167

make back in the day. I'm on some other shit now. But, yes Maleek did have Fatz killed, but he didn't do it himself. L never does his own dirty work, he has other people for that."

"Do you know anything about Christine?" Bo fished for more information.

Angel sighed, "All I know is that bitch is connivin'. I don't put anything pass that hoe and neither should you. Same goes for Maleek. He's a cold-hearted bastard and if you cross him or if he even thinks you are capable of crossin' him he will kill you. Matter of fact, he's the reason I was in Virginia. He asked me to finish a job for him that his bitch Christine couldn't finish. All I had to do was stick a needle he gave me in some chick's IV that was laid up in the hospital. I didn't recognize who it was because her face was fucked up, but even still the shit didn't matter to me. Hell, I didn't even know what was in the needle he gave me. I needed the dough. I asked him later who it was and he told me that bitch Nikki. All I could do was laugh. Guess that bitch got what was comin' to her."

Bo stood up abruptly and lunged toward Angel. His light complexion face turned to red with rage. Angel pressed a button under her desk triggering a silent alarm. Two cock diesel guys dressed in jeans and plain white tees busted through the office door. Bo's hands were wrapped around Angel's tiny neck. Angel's life slowly began to slip out of her body. The two gentlemen pulled Bo off of Angel just in time.

"A baby, get up." One of the men called shaking her gently while the other man penned Bo up against the wall.

Angel moaned as she came to. She gradually stood up and balanced herself against the desk. Her security helped her into the leather chair. She stared at Bo, rubbing her neck. Her bracelets dangled from her tiny arm clanking against the desk.

"Nigga, what the fuck is your problem," she gritted. "Do you know who the fuck I am? I'm muthafuckin' A-Star. You came in here askin' me questions and then you fuckin' think you can attack me and nothin' was gonna happen to yo ass, no bitch! Before I have my men thrash yo ass tell me, what the fuck is the matter wit you?"

Bo breathed heavily as he tried to recompose himself. "That chick you killed in the hospital was my mother!"

" Oh shit!" Angel walked around the desk and stepped in Bo's

168

face. She sucked her teeth before she began to speak again. "Humph, yo momma. I didn't even know the chick like that and I didn't care. Maleek told me he would give me fifteen stacks and I knew he had that cheddar. I figured it must be an important job for that kind of dough. You know what, *BOSTON,* I'ma let you walk outta of here alive because you actually had the balls to try me and because that punk bitch bucked on me. So, fuck 'im. I'm 'bout my paper. If you don't make good on your word and keep the fuck quiet, I'm sho' gone find a way to get ya ass back."

The buff man released Bo. He fell to the ground and didn't move for a minute. Before he could stand Angel stood over him her platinum necklace dangling over his head.

"One more thing, Bo. You gone help me set Maleek up and get my money back. Got it?"

Bo nodded his head. "What you want me to do?"

"We can discuss that later. Here's my number. Call me and we can talk." She handed Bo a card. "Now, if you excuse me I have business of my own to tend to." Angel turned then walked out of the office. The two men picked Bo off the floor and escorted him to the front door.

Bo couldn't believe what Angel told him. He arrived back at the hotel with plenty to pass on to Isabella. When he walked through the lobby he saw Isabella sitting in the dining room of the hotel about to eat lunch. He pulled out a chair and joined her at the table.

"What did you find out?" she asked with curiosity. Isabella could tell Bo was shaken. He sat at the table in a daze and didn't speak a word. "Bo," she called before snapping her finger to bring him from his daze. "Bo, what's wrong? What happened?"

"Oh my God, Izzy you will never believe all the shit she told me. Maleek had my mother and Nae killed! And he got Christine and Angel to do the job. I can't believe this shit!"

"What!" Isabella yelled. The restaurant instantly fell silent. "Are you serious?" she whispered. Bo didn't know he confirmed Isabella's suspicions. "But, why would he want your mother and cousin dead?"

Bo was still steaming from the sudden shock. "I don't fuckin' know, but I need to find out. And that's not it."

"What else is there?"

169

"She wants me to help her set Maleek up."

"Why?"

"He was suppose to pay her for killing my mom and he didn't give her the money. So, now she wants her money and revenge."

"Bo, I know you're not seriously considering this?" Isabella inquired cautiously.

Bo stared at the painting on the restaurant wall and then faced Isabella, "I don't know. I need to hear it from him. I need to know why, Izzy."

"I know, but what about Christine?"

"Don't worry about that scandalous bitch. I know I can get information from her."

Isabella took a bite of her toast before speaking again. "I guess we have some questions to ask when we get back to Virginia tomorrow."

"No, *I* have some questions to ask. I need to do this on my own. They're not gonna talk to you because you're 5-0, but they're like my family so I may be able to get a little more information. Plus, we don't have anything concrete yet, except Angel's word. And if it's one thing I know it's believe none of what you hear and half of what you see."

"Whatever you want to do Bo, but be careful. By the way, I've been investigating this overseas bank account while you were gone. It seems that the bulk of the money came from the Moronelli's. It was confirmed that your mother transported and laundered millions of dollars in drugs for them. And unfortunately she did a couple of hits for them too. She was an unlikely suspect, that's why she was on payroll. She also collected on Fatz's insurance policy."

"Are you fuckin' kiddin' me?" Bo sat at the table with his hands on his legs.

"I'm not jokin'. Your mom dropped at least ten mob bosses and she was getting paid well, but she got greedy. Nestrago's partner Raymon Vincente found out she was skimming from the top and they ordered a hit on her."

"What the fuck? Do you think they had anything to do with killing my mom?"

"I don't know. There are no direct links between Maleek, Chris or the Moronelli's. On the other hand Fatz's death is looking

170

more suspicious. The insurance policy was for half a mil and your mom was the sole beneficiary."

"Fatz was cool, but I didn't know him and my mom were tight like that. I overheard her talking to Chris a couple of times about him, but I don't think she even knew he had an insurance policy and she was the beneficiary."

"I don't know about that Bo. She had to know because when he was murdered she knew where to find the papers. I don't know if she had anything to do with it."

"Of course not!"

"Well, that's not all. After your mother was admitted to the hospital somebody withdrew money from the account. I've ordered the surveillance tapes from the bank where the money was withdrawn. No surprise whoever withdrew the money was in Suffolk."

"How long will it take to get the tapes from the bank?" he inquired.

Isabella took the last bite of her toast and wiped the crumbs off of her hand before wiping her mouth. "The bank said about 4-6 weeks. At least that's something we'll be able to use when we finally arrest them."

"I guess. I'm goin' up to the room to lie down. All of this shit is making my head pound. I need some time to unwind and be at peace. I'll see you when you come upstairs." Bo pushed in the chair and headed to the elevator. He heard his cell ringing and pulled it out of his pocket. It was Maleek again. After talking to Angel Bo didn't know how to react towards Maleek. It was going to be hard for him not to say anything, but he knew if he said anything Maleek would either leave town or worse.

"Hey L, what up?"

"Yo B, when you comin' back?"

"I'll be back tomorrow afternoon."

"Dude, you can't come back any sooner?" Maleek asked frustratingly.

Bo tried to be patient with Maleek, "L, that's the soonest I can be back, but if you need to talk then I'm here."

"I do need to talk, but not on the phone. I'll see you when you get here."

Bo could hear the attitude in Maleek's voice, but he didn't

171

know what Maleek wanted to talk to him about that he couldn't talk about over the phone. He heard the phone click and shoved his cell back in his pocket. After talking to Maleek he was even more upset over the news Angel told him. Now was not the time to deal with Maleek's tantrums, especially since he was the reason his mother and cousin were dead, supposedly. Bo was having a hard time believing everything Angel told him, but he thought to himself why would she lie. She didn't know Nikki was his mother; so telling him about the murder didn't matter.

Bo was ready to rid his life of all the drama and bullshit. He was tired of being surrounded by people that had their own agendas and didn't care about him as a person. Enough was enough and he just wanted to move on with his life. Bo opened the room door and collapsed on the bed in exhaustion. His head was throbbing and he wanted to forget his problems if only for one minute. He closed his eyes and drifted to sleep.

CHAPTER XXVI

Bo awoke to find a hot meal at the bedside. He took a bite of the hot buttered roll on the silver tray. He pulled the glossy black card out of his back pocket and stared at the engraved white writing. He thought to himself about setting L up while swallowing the remainder of the soft roll. He went over in his head the consequences of going along with Angel's plan, but he wanted to find out the truth from Maleek. Bo knew when Maleek felt trapped his nerves got the best of him and he would start to break.

"Hello, is this A-Star?"

"Hi Boston. I see you decided to take me up on my offer. Smart man."

"Look, what do you want me to do?"

"Like I told you, I want my money. I never discuss business over the phone. Can you meet me in an hour?"

Bo looked down at his watch. He had slept most of the day away. "Yeah, where? I'm not too familiar with the area, though."

"That's fine. I'll send *Gabby* to pick you up. She'll be there in about 30 minutes so meet her outside."

A big Kool Aid smile splashed across Bo's face. "Oh, you got jokes."

"No jokes. I know you two feelin' each other. Consider this my gift to you for helping me. Just make sure you're at Bella Luna's in an hour on the dot. My time is valuable."

"Okay. I'll see you in an hour." Bo couldn't stop smiling. He devoured the rest of the steak and mashed potatoes that were on the platter even though he was about to go out to dinner. He didn't trust eating at

173

a restaurant he'd never been to. He was a picky eater and wanted to eat his food while it was hot. Isabella walked in the room as Bo was stripping.

"Dang, you ate that quick." Isabella observed.

"Yeah, thanks."

"Where are you headed to?"

Bo was so preoccupied with thoughts of seeing Gabriel again that he didn't hear anything Isabella was saying. Bo's naked sculptured body danced around the room in excitement. Isabella laughed inside, but she wanted to know who the woman was that made Bo so happy. The jealousy was killing her. "Bo," she yelled. He swirled around. Isabella couldn't take her eyes off Bo's hard dick.

"Huh?"

"I said, where are you going?"

"To meet with Angel again."

Isabella was confused. She didn't understand why he would want to meet with Angel after what happened earlier. She could see the hurt and Anger in Bo's eyes when he returned from meeting Angel the first time. "But, why? Didn't she tell you what you needed to know already?"

Bo grabbed his towel off the bed and ran into the bathroom. "Yeah, but we need to talk about some other stuff."

Isabella heard the shower running and knew he wasn't just going to meet Angel. She sat on the bed with her lips poked out trying to figure out how to tell Bo how she felt. She shuffled through the channels and tried not to think about Bo in an intimate way, but the attraction she felt towards him was undeniable. She sipped on half of a Co-Co Cola Bo left on the silver tray. She could hear Bo in the bathroom singing to himself. He walked out of the bathroom wearing only grey-stripped silk boxers. The sight of his body mesmerized Isabella. Bo threw on a pair of Nautica jeans, a tan Nautica shirt and a pair of wheat Timberlands. He dabbed himself with Polo oil and brushed his low wavy hair.

"Alright Izzy, I'll be back soon."

"Whateva." Isabella's tone spoke volumes.

"You got an attitude?" Bo smirked. Isabella stared at the television blankly. "Oh shit! You're jealous. This is unfuckin' believable. First you say strictly business, now you mad because I'm about to go to a meeting wit a chick that could help me settle the score with Maleek's bitch ass."

Isabella focused all her attention on Bo. "Bo, first off all you don't know if this chick is tellin' the truth. You just met her, what five maybe six hours ago. Second, I don't trust her ass and I think she setting you up, but your nose so wide open right now you can't see that. And third, I love you!"

Bo was caught off guard. He didn't know Isabella's feelings were that strong because she never showed her emotions. Bo liked Isabella, but his feelings were not as strong and it was not the best time to have this discussion with her.

"Wait!"

Bo turned to see what Isabella wanted.

"Where are you going in case I need to find you? Again, I don't trust the situation. Especially after what happened earlier."

Without saying a word, Bo turned and walked out the door. Before he could reach the elevator his cell rang. It was Isabella. Bo hit the ignore button on his phone and stepped in the elevator. His phone rang again; it was Isabella. The third time the phone rang Bo automatically hit the ignore button, but it was Gabriel. He walked into the lobby and saw Gabriel waiting on the short red and gold couch.

"Gabriel," Bo called

Her face lit up like a light when she saw him. "Hey baby, I'm so glad to see you." She jumped on Bo and almost knocked him down. She kissed his face half a dozen times before their lips locked in a short passionate kiss. On the way out of the lobby Bo smacked Gabriel's ass making it jiggle. He loved the way her ass was shaped and couldn't take his eyes off it. Gabriel's car was parked behind a taxi in front of the lobby door. Bo walked around to the driver's side and opened it for her. Gabriel kissed him again and dropped the car keys in his hand.

"You drive, baby." she giggled and palmed his ass.

"But I don't know where we're goin'"

"Don't worry. I'll get you there. I'll let you know when to get off." she smiled and pulled her seat belt over her shoulder and placed her hand on Bo's crotch. The car squealed as Bo sped off. As soon as the car was far enough away from the hotel Gabriel took off her seat belt and unzipped Bo's jeans.

Gabriel pulled Bo's thick dick out of his silk boxers. She

175

buried her head between his lap and bobbed her head up and down. Her tongue whirled around the circumference of his dick tasting every inch. She shoved the shaft of his dick down her throat and sucked on it like a straw. Bo stopped at a light and guided her motions with his hand. His foot began to slip off the brake and the car slowly drifted through the intersection. A loud horn sounded snapping Bo back to reality. Gabriel started laughing and continued her job.

"Are you ready to get off yet?" she chuckled.

"Do you." he laughed back.

Gabriel dropped her head back in his lap. The Maxima swerved across the road before Bo pulled on a dim side street. He slammed the gear into park. His head fell back on the headrest and his eyes rolled to the back of his head.

"Damn girl, yo throat's like velvet."

Gabriel's lips wrapped around his dick like a blanket. She pressed her lips against him as her tongue swirled around his dick in a sea of saliva. The pleasure was too much for Bo to stand. Bo erupted like a volcano in Gabriel's mouth. She continued to slide her mouth up and down his softening dick drinking every bit. He pushed her head away after he couldn't take anymore. She climbed back into the passenger seat and pulled down the sun visor. She reapplied her Viva La Glam Mac lip-gloss and kissed herself in the compact mirror.

"Was that good for you?" she inquired noticing the glow on his face.

The same Kool Aid smile that was on his face earlier reappeared. "You damn straight! I gotta tell Angel good lookin'." Gabriel leaned in and planted a wet, juicy kiss on Bo's plump lips. "Um girl, give me anotha one of dem." She gave Bo another kiss and then buckled her seatbelt.

"Okay, Angel said to meet her at Bella Luna on Eastern Avenue. That's about twenty minutes from here, so we better get going. She spasses out when people are late," Gabriel claimed.

Gabriel opened her glove box and pulled out her GPS. She programmed the address into the system and set the GPS on her dash. She turned up the radio and started singing along to Keyshia Cole and Missy's "Let It Go." Bo laughed. He liked how carefree Gabriel was, but he knew she was not a woman he could have a relationship with which made him think about what Isabella said before he left. Bo was silent for the rest of the ride. He tuned out Gabriel's singing and almost ignored the directions the GPS was giving.

"Baby, you okay?" Gabriel asked. "You've been quiet most of the drive."

Bo rubbed her leg, "I'm good. We should be pulling up in front of the restaurant soon."

"Yeah, actually there it is on the left."

Bo parked the car and the two walked into the restaurant. A neatly groomed waitress approached them as they entered the restaurant. "Good evening. Welcome to Bella Luna, will it only be you two dining this evening?"

"No, we're meeting somebody." Bo spoke up.

"Oh you must be speaking of the young lady and…"

The waitress was abruptly cutoff by Angel waving and calling their names. "Gabby, Bo over here," Angel waved. She was sipping on a glass of Pinot Grigio. "'Bout time. I was starting to think y'all won't gone make it."

"Well, we're here." Bo replied.

The waitress approached the table with a smile. "Hi, what will you two have to drink?"

"I'll have a water," Gabriel ordered.

"And I'll have a sprite." Bo chimed.

"Would you like another glass of wine?" she observed looking at Angel's almost empty glass.

"Yes, please."

"What's the deal?" Bo started ready to get down to business.

Angel smirked. "You don't waste no time do you? Okay, I like that." She turned her attention to Gabriel briefly, "Gabby could you excuse us for a couple of minutes?"

"Sure. I'll go freshen up and I'll be over here at the bar." Bo pulled Gabriel's chair out. "Thanks Bo," she smiled.

Angel watched as Bo watched Gabriel walk to the restroom. "You like her don't you?"

"She okay, why?"

"Pullin' chairs out and shit. Don't no nigga do that unless he like a bitch."

"Like I said, she okay."

"Just askin'. Want you to know that's my platinum hoe. She

go for $1500 for half a night, $3000 for a sleepover. So the treatment you been gettin', I'ma take a hit, but that's cool. Anyway, let's get down to business."

Bo's mood changed to serious fast. "Okay, that's what we here for."

"How close are you and that bitch Maleek?"

"That's my boy. We like brothers."

Angel paused before continuing. She saw the waitress returning to the table with the drinks. "Here's your Grigio ma'am, your Sprite and the Ms.' water. Are you ready to order?"

"Yes. I'll have the Italian Wedge and the Sweet Potato Gnocchi." Angel ordered in a demanding tone. "And for the other young lady, she'll have the Fiorentino."

The waitress turned to Bo, "And you sir?" Bo waved his hand and shook his head simultaneously to signal he didn't want anything. "Okay, I'll place your order and I'll be back to check on you shortly."

"You ain't want nothing?" Angel groaned.

"Naw, I ate before I left."

"Less money outta my pocket. Back to what I was saying, since y'all so close it'll be no problem getting him somewhere to meet you, but we gotta have the perfect place out of sight and sound proof, if you know what I mean?" she hinted.

"I got you." Bo remarked. "There's plenty of empty lots and warehouses round my way. The question is how am I going to get him there?"

"We have a little time to figure that out. Plain and simple it's got to be quick and you got to make sure he got money and or some merchandise wit him. Something worth more than $15,000. That nigga owes me interest. I need to know I can count on you to see this thing out."

Bo leaned on the table with his arms folded. "Don't fuckin' worry 'bout me. If that nigga did what you say he did then I'm down, no doubt. Yo ass betta not be on no shit. I may seem soft, but don't let that fool you." All the while Bo was plotting against Angel.

Angel finished off the rest of her wine, "I like yo style Boston. A nigga wit heart, I knew that when you tested me earlier. When you leavin' for VA?"

"In the morning."

178

"Good. The sooner the better. We need to flip this shit in gear," she chimed.

"God damn right. I'm ready. Dat nigga played me. All along he been actin' like we boys and he was so hurt by my moms death, but I see it was an act. Did he tell you why he wanted her knocked off?"

"You know better than that. He never tell why and he don't like when you ask questions." Bo continued to listen while Angel told him what to do when he touched down in VA. After giving him detailed instructions she told Bo to go get Gabriel from the bar.

"Did you order for me baby?" Gabriel asked.

"No." Bo replied not knowing Gabriel was talking to Angel.

"She was talkin' to me, but that's okay. Yea, I ordered for you." Just as she said that the waitress came out with a tray of food.

Gabriel and Angel began to eat their food and engaged in small talk, but most of evening was silent. The waitress checked on them periodically and Angel continued to fill up with white wine. Bo couldn't help but notice that Angel constantly looked at her watch. An uneasy feeling started to creep over him, but he tried to shake it off. Something told Bo to turn around and when he did he was speechless.

179

CHAPTER XXVII

"Hey Bo, what's goin' on? You look like you seen a ghost."
Maleek blurted with a devilish smile etched on his face.

Bo stared at Angel in disgust and astonishment. "What the
fuck is goin' on Angel?"

Angel slouched down in the cushioned Booth and sucked her
teeth. Bo could feel the chill in the air coming from Angel's coldness.
"Bo, Bo, Bo. Naïve, country boy Bo, did you really think I would set
up my boy? Yeah, he pissed me off with the whole fuckin' wit
Christine back in the day and yeah, he dicked me wit my money, but he
compensated well for this setup."

Maleek and Angel gazed at each other. "I did compensate you
well, didn't I baby?" He chuckled before leaning over the table and
kissing Angel. "You see Bo, I was in this game long before you. The
streets raised me and I've been running the streets of Cinci since I was
a youngin'. I got eyes and ears everywhere. So for your ass to think that
you can come up here and start askin' questions 'bout me without me
findin' out is crazy. Me and A-Star here conversed before you even
showed up." Bo was confused about how Maleek knew he was in
Ohio. The only person that knew was Isabella and he knew there was
no way she would of told anybody.

"You look confused Bo?" Angel laughed.

"Let me run it down for you Bo," Maleek started. "That night
you ran out of the house because you had to meet *somebody*, I followed
you. You went to meet that detective that arrested me months ago. I
don't know what you and that bitch talked about, but I couldn't take a
chance on gettin' caught up, so I kept track on you wit the help of that

180

stupid bitch Christine. She told me you booked two tickets to Cinci. That's when I called my girl and we started talkin'. I knew it wouldn't be long before you found out about her and lucky for me she owns one of the hottest escort services in the area and I used that to my advantage." Maleek grinned and looked over at Gabriel.

"Gabriel, your ass was in on this?" Bo cried.

Gabriel was speechless. She couldn't look Bo in the face. "Boston, believe me I didn't want to, but I had no choice. You don't know her. She---," Angel reached over and smacked Gabriel so hard her neck cracked as it turned. Gabriel held the side of her face and tears started to form in the wells of her eyes.

"What the fuck I tell you about talkin' so fuckin' much bitch. Yes, she was part of the setup. Just like you, we know people too. L was trackin' your cell phone calls and we saw that you were able to get in touch wit our old friend C-Note. Oh, you may know him as Clasik. Wit a little persuasion from L he told us he was meetin' you that night at Passage. So when you got there, they called me and told me. That's when I sent my girls to work their magic. And it worked like a charm. You think your ass would of been lucky enough to get that kind of action like that. Nigga, you fine, but not dat damn fine."

Bo was hoodwinked. He knew he was in a bad situation and odds were he was not going to make it out alive. His mind raced a mile a minute as he surveyed his surroundings to try to find an exit. His hands started to sweat and his legs started to shake under the table.

Maleek laughed silently. "What's wrong Bo? You nervous? Nothing to be nervous about baby. You think I would hurt my boy?"

Bo knew better than to answer that question. If Maleek killed his mother and cousin then he would not hesitate to kill him, but he answered Maleek's question anyway. "Naw L, I don't think you'd do anything crazy, but I am curious. Since we're putting everything out there be honest wit me, did you kill my mom and Nae?"

Maleek glanced at Angel before answering the question. "Might as well tell him everything baby," Angel commented.

"Truth be told young blood, I did. I was goin' to let the Moronelli's handle it, but I waited to long for this. Pay back is a bitch."

Bo dropped his head in hurt, "But why man? You were like family to us. So was it all an act?"

"All I wanted was what was mine. That night Fatz was killed,

181

I set it up. After Angel called me I called Christine and she told me to come through. I sent my dudes over to handle some business and when Fatz ain't have my shit that was his ass. When he died I knew yo moms would lead me to the money, but I didn't expect y'all to move way the fuck to Virginia. Christine was my personal GPS so I kept tabs on y'all."

Bo interrupted, "What does this have to do with my mom or Nae?"

"At first it really didn't. I just wanted Christine to get the money Fatz owed me and that would have been that, but your bitch of a mother was spendin' the shit like water. Shit became personal when my half a mil and coke went missin' from the house. It was only one person that could have took it and that was yo mother. I know she wasn't dumb enough to think I wouldn't know it was her. Her pussy was good, but not worth that much. Her ass got me caught up with Jungle."

"Hold up. When did she take money from you? She neva had that kind of money."

Maleek shook his head, "Nigga, dat's how naïve yo ass really is. How do you think she got the money to start that bullshit ass label of hers?"

"She got a loan from the bank." Bo said with confidence.

"Nigga please. No, she didn't. That's what she told everybody, but one of my girls worked at that bank and they said she was denied and that's when I knew she took my muthafuckin' shit. I couldn't do anything right then, I had to wait until the right moment. It took me a long ass time to talk Christine into goin' along wit the plan because she decided to grow a conscience, but she finally agreed."

"You mean to tell me Christine killed my mother and Nae for you?"

"That was the plan, but that bitch can't do nothin' right. It wasn't my intentions to hurt Nae, but she was at the wrong place at the wrong time and she had to go. Can't leave no witnesses. But Christine stupid ass didn't finish the job. So I had my baby here, do the rest." Angel just stared at Bo without saying a word. She finished off her second drink and enjoyed listening to Maleek confess to Bo.

"And what did the Moronelli's have to do with this?" Bo belted.

"Oh, I linked them up. She didn't know how to run a damn label. She needed major players involved. They gave her bread, but I knew it was a matter of time before your mom got greedy again. She got involved with shit she couldn't handle and I washed my hands of the situation. All that transporting shit and knockin' mob bosses off shit was none of my business. They wanted your mom as bad as I did."

"So what about Mo? Were you lyin' about that too?"

Bo saw the devilish grin reappear on Maleek's face. Maleek rubbed the hair on his chin. "Mo. Humph. Yeah, she's dead. She was in a bad accident or at least that's how it is goin' to play out." Maleek looked at Angel again. "Can you believe that bitch had the nerve to tell me she was leavin' me and was goin' to take my son?"

Angel shook her head.

"I couldn't let that shit happen. So my girl here offered to help me fix the problem." Maleek rubbed Angel's hand. "She cut the brake line on Mo's car, then ran her off the road. She made sure she was dead then she made an anonymous phone call to the police tellin' them there was a bad car crash. Problem solved."

Bo couldn't believe what he was hearing. He wanted to kill Maleek, but he knew Maleek always had backup some where around. "You son of a bitch! You know you're not goin' to get away wit this right?"

"Nigga, please! I'm muthafuckin' Maleek "Untouchable" Johnson. I get away wit any muthafuckin' thing I want to. As a matter of fact, nigga get yo ass up." Maleek pulled Bo out of the booth and walked behind him careful not to make a big scene. Angel pulled five one hundred dollar bills out of her purse and left them on the table to cover the check and tip. She and Gabriel walked out behind Maleek and Bo.

Maleek forced Bo into the trunk of the small rental car. Maleek jumped in the front seat and called Angel. "Yo, where you parked?'

"Two blocks over."

"Fuck dat. I'ma pick you up. Send yo hoe home and meet me on the corner." Maleek demanded.

Angel did like Maleek requested and directed Gabriel to go home. She waited on the corner for Maleek to pick her up. He pulled up in the compact car and opened the door. Angel looked in the back to

183

see if Bo where in the back.

"Where's he at?" she asked puzzled.

"In the trunk. Did you tell that bitch to go straight home?"

"Yeah. She good. You don't have to worry 'bout her. She knows how to keep her mouth shut or face the consequences."

"Glad you got yo hoes in check. Now, what are we goin' to do 'bout this nigga?"

"Whateva you do, make it quick. No time for sorrys. This is business not personal."

"You one cold bitch. That's why I love you."

Angel giggled. "Yeah, nigga. Love don't pay the bills, where's my damn money?"

"Look in the back. It's a black gym bag on the floor. All your money is in there."

Angel turned around to grab the black gym bag. Maleek pulled his silver .35 mm from his waist and struck her in the head. Her body slumped between the two seats.

"Get the fuck outta here bitch. I ain't given you no fuckin' money." he grunted looking at Angel's motionless body. He sped down the dark street and turned down a side street with no lights. He fired two rounds into the back of Angel's head before pushing her body out the passenger door.

Maleek saw two headlights in the rearview mirror. He didn't know what to do, so he tried to act like he just discovered the body on the side of the road. He was prepared to do what he had to do if necessary. The car pulled up behind the small car. Maleek noticed a female silhouette walking towards him.

"Maleek Johnson put your hands up."

Maleek squinted his eyes. He didn't know who the female was or how she knew him. He reached for his gun and pointed it at the dark figure that was still walking towards him. "Who the fuck is that?" he called in the dark.

"It doesn't matter. Drop your gun. I know you have one," the figure continued to move towards him.

Maleek fired at the woman through the dark. The woman fired back missing her target. She fired one last shot striking Maleek in the arm before he ran off and disappeared between the abandoned houses on the dark street. She ran over to Angel and checked her pulse. She

184

was dead. She could hear thumping coming from the trunk. She popped the trunk and Bo gasped for air.

"Izzy, oh my God. I'm so happy to see you! You saved my life!" Bo cried. He didn't think to ask what she was doing there. He wrapped his arms around her and held her tightly. Bo didn't realize that Isabella had been following him since he left the hotel.

"I followed you. I told you I didn't trust that bitch Angel." Isabella pointed to Angel's lifeless body on the ground. "Your boy Maleek is racking up the bodies and we're going to be next if we don't leave now." she warned.

"You're right. You were right about everything and I'm sorry I doubted you." Bo said apologetically.

"No time for apologies. Get in the taxi. We need to go!"

The two got in the taxi and sped off. Bo explained the plot that Maleek and Angel laid out. He also told her everything about her mother and Christine. Isabella listened intently and told Bo she suspected Maleek had something to do with her attack that night, especially after hearing that Maleek followed him.

They arrived at the hotel and quickly gathered all of their belongings. They rushed back to the taxi and headed towards the airport. Isabella paid the driver $1000 to not mention anything that took place that night. He agreed to keep the night's events confidential.

185

CHAPTER XXVIII

The plane touched down in Newport News, Virginia and Bo couldn't be any happier to be home. Bo and Isabella were anxious to close the case, but they knew finding Maleek would be damn near impossible. He could have been anywhere. They're next move was to close in on Christine. At least they could get some justice. They walked through the airport parking lot and found the rental car.

"What do we do now Izzy?"

"We have to get Christine to talk."

"That shouldn't be a problem. I'm sure she already feels guilty," he said.

The remainder of the drive to Bo's house was silent. Both of them were thinking deeply about what happened in Cincinnati, especially Bo. Isabella dropped Bo off at his house. He walked in the house and saw Christine sitting on the couch. His first instinct was to choke the shit out of her, but he didn't want to go to jail.

"Welcome back, Bo."

Bo dropped his bags. "Christine, don't play no games wit me bitch. I know everything!"

"What are you talkin' about?" Christine asked innocently.

"Are you fuckin' kiddin' me?" Bo walked aggressively towards Christine.

Christine became defensive, "you're fuckin' trippin' Bo. You need to calm down."

Bo raised his arm and punched the shit out of her. Christine cowered on the ground with a broken nose while Bo hovered over her. "Calm down! Do you know where the fuck I've been, what I've been through in the past twenty-four hours. No, you don't. Your boy,

Maleek

186

tried to fuckin' kill me. Not to mention the Moronelli's probably want to even the score."

"What?" Christine sobbed. She balled up on the floor crying. "I'm sorry, Boston. It wasn't supposed to turn out like this. I don't know how I got involved in this mess."

"How you got involved, really. I know about your history with dat nigga and I can't believe you would do that to my mom and Nae. If you knew what I wanna fuckin' do to you right now, you wouldn't be in the same room with me."

"Bo, that's why I couldn't kill them. I knew I hurt them pretty bad, but I couldn't kill them. I loved Nik!" Christine exclaimed. "And the Moronelli's was just a money thing."

Bo shook his head. "That wasn't love. I don't know what that shit was, but yo ass goin' to pay for this shit one way or another. If I have to drag you to the jail myself." Bo threatened.

"I can't go to prison Bo! I'll kill myself before I go to prison."

"I won't give you the satisfaction of killing yourself. I'll kill you first. The only reason I haven't fucked you up is because I don't wanna go to jail. You should of thought about that shit before you did what you did. You're going to suffer like my mom. And I hope you rot in hell muthafucka."

"Bo, please. Can you ever forgive me?" she begged.

"Hell no!" he yelled at the top of his lungs.

Christine picked up her cell phone off the dining room table.

"Who the fuck you think you callin'?" he barked smacking the phone to the floor.

"I was gonna call Ma---"

"Ma, Ma, Ma who? Bitch you don't get it. Why the fuck would you call that muthafucka? You dumber than you look. What the fuck is his bitch ass gonna do for you? You already 'bout to take the rap and be locked up for life if I can help. You know what?" Bo yanked Christine by her grey Abercrombie & Fitch shirt and threw her against the wall.

Tears streamed down her face. She was petrified. He stared in her eyes until he couldn't stand to look at her any longer. He released his grip. Her body fell to the hardwood floor. Christine lay on the floor afraid to move or look at Bo. Bo towered over her contemplating his next move. He wanted to stomp her until her face was unrecognizable,

187

but he knew he couldn't do that.

Christine didn't know what to do. She knew there was no way of escaping prison and she told herself if she ever got caught she would end her life before turning herself in, but she had to make everything right.

"Get the fuck up." Bo spoke in a baritone voice.

Christine moved slowly. When she fell to the hardwood floor she fell on her ankle and broke it.

Bo reached in his pocket and pulled out his cell. "Hey Izzy. I'm about to bring in Christine. Can you meet me at the station in about thirty minutes?" He never once took his eyes off Christine.

"Sure Bo. Meet me there."

Bo continued to grit on Christine. Violent thoughts consumed his mind, but he regained his composure before he could hurt her any further. "You know what, you're going to write your confession right here, right now."

Christine didn't move an inch and waited for Bo to return with paper and a pen.

"Sit yo ass down on the couch." He placed a notepad and pen on the marble table in front of her. "Write!" He demanded.

Christine picked up the pen and began to scribble quickly. It pained her to recall what she did to her best friend, but she knew it was necessary and she needed to face the consequences. It took only five minutes for her to right the entire confession letter. She placed the pen on the table and looked at Bo.

He picked up the pad and began to read the letter.

"...there was a struggle. J'nae fought back as I hit her over and over with the steel pipe. She ran into the hallway outside of Nikki's bathroom and I hit her one more time. She fell down the staircase and hit her head. I heard Nikki get up. She was calling for me. When she saw J'nae I came out of the dining room and stuck her with the same pipe. I blacked out. All I can remember is seeing their bodies at the bottom of the stairs. I felt like I was outside of my body..."

Bo couldn't read anymore. He fought back his tears. "Get yo ass up. We goin' to the station."

Christine was silent. What was done was done and she was ready to face whatever her punishment would be. Bo followed closely behind her as she limped to the door. He knew she wouldn't run, but he wasn't taking any chances. The ride to the station seemed long. Neither one of them spoke a word. Bo pulled in front of the station without parking his car. He jumped out and approached the first cop he saw.

"Hi, I'm looking for Isabella Cruz. I have somebody who wants to turn themselves in."

The chubby white officer peeked in the car. "Is that the individual?" he questioned confused by Christine's looks.

"Yea. Where can I find Ms. Cruz?"

"All the detectives' offices are located on the third floor, but I can take her to central booking if you would like."

Bo was hesitant. He only wanted Isabella handling the issue, but he trusted the officer. "Sure." He watched as the officer pulled Christine out the car and placed her in handcuffs. Just as Bo was about to follow behind the officer Isabella walked up.

"Hey Bo." She greeted. She saw the officer with Christine. "Officer make sure she's processed and booked immediately. This is a time sensitive case." The officer nodded in agreement.

Before Isabella could speak anymore Bo handed her Christine's confession. She quickly glanced over the confession and led Bo into the station. "This is good, but we need to have her confess in front of detectives just to make sure there was no coercion."

"That's fine. So can we do this now?"

"It'll take a couple of hours, but I'll make sure it's done as soon as possible. Until then have a seat in my office." Isabella escorted Bo to the third floor to her office. He sat in the cushioned black and grey chair. He thought about what he was going to do now that he was alone. He didn't know where or how to start his life over.

About forty-five minutes later Isabella walked into the office. "Bo, I have somebody here to see you." Isabella said softly.

Bo looked at her with tears in his eyes. He wiped the tears from his face and stared at her. "I don't want to see anybody right now."

"Okay, but she wants to see you."

Bo put his head down. "Who? That bitch Christine. I can't bare to look at her right now!"

Isabella signaled to the cop standing outside the door to let the female in.

"Boston." A weak voice cried.

Bo stood up in shock. "Oh my God!" He walked over and touched her face. He turned to Isabella. "You said she was dead. The doctor said she was dead. Why would you do that to me?"

"Bo, they had to make everybody think I was dead to protect me. After the murder of your mother they couldn't take a chance." J'nae said tearfully.

Bo hugged her with everything he had. "J'nae, I'm never letting you out of my sight!" Bo stood back and stared her. He still couldn't believe his eyes. He thought he was dreaming. He kept touching her face in amazement. "I still can't believe it's you! I love you!"

"It's me Bo," she smiled and hugged him back.

Isabella eyes swelled with tears. "I'll give you two a moment. You need some privacy," Isabella stood outside the door and waited patiently. Her cell phone rung and it was a private number. She normally didn't answer private calls, but something told her to answer this one. "Hello," she said hesitantly. Silence greeted her. "Hello, is anybody there."

"Help him and you're dead putanna!" The phone went silent and all Isabella heard was a dial tone. The phone call scared Isabella.

"Hey guys. I have something to tell you." Isabella started.

"What is it? Did you find L?" Bo inquired again.

"Not yet Bo, but you guys don't worry about that. However, we have bigger problems. I just received a disturbing phone call. I believe the Moronelli's have a hit out on you Bo. Since your mom is dead you're now the main target. Even though you didn't have anything to do with her debts they want revenge one way or another. Your mom has money some where and they want it!"

"What do you mean? We have to worry about Maleek and them. I'm as good as dead! What the fuck?"

"They're going to try to finish what they started." J'nae whined.

"Calm down. We're going to relocate you guys and put you in the Witness Protection Program, so you don't have to worry."

Bo shook his head, "The mob don't play neither does Maleek. We're not safe anywhere. All of them have the resources to locate us wherever we are."

190

"It's okay, Bo. Once J'nae testifies we'll corroborate Christine's confession and the testimony. Once we find Maleek he will be locked up for life or maybe even the death penalty."

"She's not testifying it's too dangerous! Find another way." Bo yelled.

J'nae became very emotional. "What do we do until then? I'm scared for my life. I've had nightmares ever since that day!"

Isabella was silent. Nothing she could say would reassure either of them. She knew realistically their lives would always be in danger.

Bo pulled J'nae close to him and consoled her. He knew the experience was traumatic for her and wanted to protect her. He wanted to start putting the pieces of their lives back together and so did J'nae.

Isabella knew it would be a long time before they found Maleek if they found him at all, but she didn't want Bo and J'nae to suffer anymore.

"Alright you guys, I have a van waiting in the back for you. We've arranged for you guys to be escorted to your new location."

"What about clothing and food?" J'nae inquired.

"Don't worry about all that. We've taken care of it. You'll have enough money to buy new clothes and food. Your housing is already established as well."

Bo and J'nae looked at each other helplessly. Bo turned and looked in Isabella's direction. "We're ready Izzy."

Isabella exited the room. She returned fifteen minutes later with three U.S. Marshalls with crew cuts. They were all overly muscular with square heads and slim jaw lines.

"Hey guys, these Marshalls are going to take it from here. You're in good hands."

Bo stared at Isabella. He gave her a long hug before walking out the room. J'nae and Bo followed the Marshalls outside a back door where a windowless white van was parked outside. The van resembled a van that transported dead bodies to the morgue. Bo and J'nae climbed into the back of the van with one of the Marshalls that was holding a semi-automatic gun. The other two sat in the front of the van strapped as well.

"Well, I guess this is goodbye for now guys." Isabella said sorrowfully.

"Thanks for everything, Izzy. I'll miss you." Bo climbed out the van and gave her one last long tight hug. He kissed her on the cheek and whispered in her ear, "I love you too."

Isabella smiled and gave Bo a quick peck on the lips.

He climbed back in the van and Isabella closed the van doors behind him. Bo sat in the van and held J'nae's hand as the van pulled off. They looked in each other's eyes and smiled. Neither one of them knew where they were headed or what their knew lives would be like, but J'nae would soon find out as the only sole witness to her aunt's murder it would be easy for her vision to get distorted too.

www.ingramcontent.com/pod-product-compliance
Lightning Source LLC
Chambersburg PA
CBHW071513170626
46811CB00007B/2839